Also available from Kim Fielding

Hallelujah
Love Can't series
Stars from Peril series
The Bureau series
Blyd and Pearce
The Little Library
Ante Up
Running Blind
Ennek series
Rattlesnake
Astounding!
Bones series
Motel. Pool.
Pilgrimage
The Tin Box
Venetian Masks
Brute

D0113094

TEDDY SPENSER ISN'T LOOKING FOR LOVE

KIM FIELDING

carina
press

If you purchased this book without a cover you should be aware that this book is stolen property. It was reported as "unsold and destroyed" to the publisher, and neither the author nor the publisher has received any payment for this "stripped book."

carina press®

Recycling programs
for this product may
not exist in your area.

ISBN-13: 978-1-335-97199-9

Teddy Spenser Isn't Looking for Love

Copyright © 2020 by Kim Fielding

All rights reserved. No part of this book may be used or reproduced in any manner whatsoever without written permission except in the case of brief quotations embodied in critical articles and reviews.

This is a work of fiction. Names, characters, places and incidents are either the product of the author's imagination or are used fictitiously. Any resemblance to actual persons, living or dead, businesses, companies, events or locales is entirely coincidental.

This edition published by arrangement with Harlequin Books S.A.

For questions and comments about the quality of this book, please contact us at CustomerService@Harlequin.com.

Carina Press
22 Adelaide St. West, 40th Floor
Toronto, Ontario M5H 4E3, Canada
www.CarinaPress.com

Printed in U.S.A.

TEDDY SPENSER ISN'T LOOKING FOR LOVE

Chapter One

Passersby grumbled as they detoured around Teddy Spenser and his scooter, but he remained on the sidewalk outside the cosmetics store window, silently critiquing the display.

This is all wrong. There were no winged cupids and, worse, not a single heart. Just a blue-haired mannequin in a silk bathrobe and above her, like a 3-D thought bubble, the word *LOVE* crafted with shiny silver ribbons arranged in an elaborate cursive font. The colors were wrong too: all winter whites and frosts. Even kindergartners knew that red and pink were the go-to hues for the holiday.

If the designer was trying to be avant-garde, they'd missed the mark and ended up with boring and pointless. Nothing about the display made Teddy want to buy cosmetics for himself or anyone else, and it certainly did nothing to put him in the holiday spirit. Not that he wanted to be in the mood. Valentine's Day was stupid.

It wasn't a real holiday. Nobody got the day off from work. The mail arrived just like always, full of bills and grocery-store circulars and reminders that eye appointments were overdue. And all that crap about True Love? Nothing but a marketing ploy. He knew Valentine's Day was a big moneymaker in certain industries, so he couldn't fault them for trying to make the most of it.

With a sniff of disdain, Teddy got back on his scooter and, narrowly missing a burly guy in a construction vest, continued on his way to the office. It wasn't an especially cold day, as February in Chicago went, and bits of dirty snow were the only vestiges of the last storm. The sky was a washed-out gray that seemed to begrudge any thoughts of spring, and Teddy shivered despite his parka, ski cap, and gloves. His ancestors, who'd spent possibly thousands of years surviving winters in England and Scandinavia without Gore-Tex or central heating, would probably consider him a wimp.

Soup. He was definitely going to have soup for lunch today—something thick with butter and cream and potatoes and maybe even cheese. A meal that would act like a layer of insulation for his freezing inner self. He might even have chocolate for dessert. Not Valentine's Day chocolate. He refused to eat any of that—at least until it went on clearance.

Reddyflora, *where beauty and technology meet*, occupied a suite in a nondescript building on LaSalle, just a couple of blocks from the Daley Center. Teddy dragged his scooter up the three flights of stairs since the ancient, creaking elevator always sounded as if it were ready to plummet into the pits of hell. The office was in the back of the building, where tiny windows looked down on an alley clogged with garbage bins, and dropped ceilings made everything feel claustrophobic. As far as Teddy was concerned, the building's only advantages were on the ground floor: a Mexican fast-food joint and a sandwich place.

Shortly after he was hired, Teddy had asked the founder and CEO, Lauren Wu, why she hadn't set up her HQ in the suburbs. For the same money, she could have leased a spacious suite in a modern office park, and employees would have benefited from cheaper nearby housing.

"The 'burbs?" Lauren had been incredulous, using the same tone she might use to describe something scraped off the sole of her designer shoes.

"Sure. Hinsdale, maybe, or Wilmette."

"The Loop is cutting-edge, Teddy, and that's where we want to be. Because Reddyflora is cutting-edge too, right?"

He squinted at the flickering lights in the hallway before stashing his scooter in a corner of the sizable warren of employee cubicles. Lauren had an office of her own, of course, which included a couch she sometimes slept on. The only other coworker with a private space was Romeo Blue, the company's software engineer.

"Romeo Blue," Teddy muttered as he hung his coat

and scarf on a wall-mounted hook. No way that was his real name. It sounded like a porn star or indie musician, not a guy who got paid to tap away at a keyboard all day.

"Hey, Teddy!"

Teddy waved at Imani Wallace. The job title on the nameplate for her cubicle was Fiscal Analyst Extraordinaire. Right now she was frowning and motioning him over. "I've been waiting for you forever," she said when he arrived.

"It's not even eight yet."

"I've been here since six."

He tried not to make a face. He'd known when he accepted the job that Lauren expected her employees to put in long hours, but he wanted to see at least a glimpse of sunlight. Imani wasn't likely to, at least not today. She rarely headed home until almost seven.

"Is there an emergency, Imani?"

She peered at her screen. "No. But I've been pricing out the base model, and the figures are not looking good. Unless we can cut costs, we're not going to turn a profit."

"We could raise the price."

"Uh-uh. We're maxed out already—your own reports say so."

Although he knew she was going to say that, he sighed anyway. "Send me the numbers. I'll see if I can find a way to cut some corners or sub some cheaper materials."

"Yeah, okay, fine." Her attention was back on her computer screen.

Teddy navigated to his own cubicle—his nameplate announced Design & Marketing—sat down, and booted up. He'd done as much as he could to brighten the space: reproductions of tourism posters, patterned adhesive paper on the metal drawer fronts, and vintage desk accessories he'd unearthed at a thrift shop. His chair cushion matched the drawer fronts, and the soft glow of a real lamp somewhat successfully battled the overhead fluorescents. A small rug covered the ugly floor tiles, despite it being an annoying trip hazard. He might not have a view, and the air always smelled like floor cleaner, but plenty of people toiled under far worse conditions.

He made his way through the overnight accumulation of emails, most from vendors trying to sell things Reddyflora didn't need or couldn't afford. Imani's spreadsheets had arrived, so he turned his attention to examining them. He didn't like numbers, at least not when they were arrayed in soulless columns, but cozying up to them was part of his job.

Within an hour, the suite was bustling with activity. Conversations, people walking around, printers spewing paper, phones ringing. It was like the soundtrack of an office, and it made Teddy smile. He could almost imagine himself as an actor in a musical, as if at any second he and Imani and the others might burst into song. Something with clever lyrics about how they were toiling away as they chased their dreams.

"Hey."

Teddy hadn't noticed anyone come up behind him, and he startled so violently that he almost knocked over his coffee. He spun the chair around and discovered Romeo Blue looking down at him, stone-faced.

"What?" Teddy knew he was scowling and didn't care.

"Can we speak in my office, please?" As usual, Romeo's voice was low, his words clipped. As if he refused to spare much energy to speak to Teddy.

"I'm busy right now."

"As soon as you can then." Romeo spun and marched back to his office, leaving its door slightly ajar.

Teddy could have followed him; Imani's numbers weren't so urgent that they couldn't wait awhile. But he remained stubbornly at his desk even though he could no longer focus on the computer screen. Romeo Blue. Teddy had googled him once, just for the hell of it—not at all to dispel lingering notions that his coworker was a spy working under a really stupid alias. It turned out that Lenny Kravitz used Romeo Blue as a stage name back in the eighties, and that was more than a little weird since *this* Romeo resembled a young Lenny Kravitz, albeit with a darker complexion and a different clothing aesthetic. Kravitz probably didn't wear suits from Zara. And to be honest, although Kravitz was gorgeous, Romeo was even more so, with perfect eyebrows, velvety eyes, and a mouth that—

"Nope!" Teddy stood abruptly and grabbed his coffee mug. He needed a refill.

He finished off that cup, visited the depressing bathroom he'd been fruitlessly begging Lauren to redecorate, and chatted briefly with the cute copy-machine repairman before finally knocking on Romeo's open door and stepping inside. And then, as always when he entered this room, Teddy glowered.

It was a fraction of the size of Lauren's office, with barely enough room for a desk, two chairs, and a computer stand. Despite that, it was a real office instead of a cubicle. But what truly annoyed Teddy was that Romeo hadn't even bothered to decorate the space. There wasn't a single knickknack or picture, and the mismatched office supplies—a black stapler and taupe tape dispenser—appeared to be from the discount bin at Staples. The only touches of personality were the three computer monitors—*three* of them, for God's sake—and, of course, Romeo himself.

Maybe Romeo thought himself so decorative that his mere presence sufficed. Or he didn't want any other objects to detract from his glory.

Also, he smelled like sandalwood, bergamot, and vanilla. Dammit.

"You could put a nice landscape print there." Teddy pointed at an expanse of bare white wall. "A palm-tree beach or snowy mountains. If you framed it right, it would even look a little like a window, and your office wouldn't be so claustrophobic."

Romeo squinted at him. "I have screen savers."

Teddy didn't point out that the only visible monitor displayed a massive block of tiny text that was probably programming code. He stared pointedly at Romeo instead, eyebrows raised. "You commanded my presence?"

"I asked you to come talk to me, yes."

"Here I am."

"Right." A flicker of emotion, which Teddy couldn't identify, crossed Romeo's face. It didn't seem like a particularly positive emotion, but then he'd rarely seen Romeo crack a smile. He was probably too full of himself to be caught feeling happy with the peons, ordinary-looking people who worked in cubicles and attempted to put together interesting outfits from resale stores and vintage clothing shops.

Romeo grabbed a tablet—apparently three monitors weren't enough—and came around the desk to stand beside Teddy. He didn't quite loom, but compared to Teddy's five-eight in his Bruno Magli boots with the thick heels, Romeo was closer to six feet. In loafers.

"I put something together for the midrange model." Romeo tapped at the tablet a few times before handing it over.

The mock-up was rough, but it was clear enough to make out details. There was the vase Teddy had spent so many hours designing: a simple powder-coated steel frame around a cylinder of clear glass, and, in front, a gently curved video screen. He'd worked really hard with other Reddyflora employees to make sure the screen would be durable, affordable, water-resistant, and—most important—attractive. The results were excellent, production costs weren't as challenging as with the base model, and consumers would be able to program the screen to match their mood and décor. Even when the screen was blank, the vase looked nice. Teddy had made sure of that.

But now he furrowed his brow and enlarged the image. "What the hell is *that*?" Something dark and bulky was just visible at the back of the vase, butted up against the metal frame. He swiped a few times until the tablet showed the back of the vase. "Is that your unit?" He was too upset to blush over his unintended double entendre.

"Yes."

"But it's really big!"

"It has to be. It needs to house a processor and battery and USB port, and it needs to be waterproof. Plus there's the sensor." He pointed at a plastic prong that extended from the unit into the bottom of the glass vessel.

"You didn't tell me it would be this big."

Romeo blew a puff of air. "I did my best. I can't bend the laws of physics."

"Scale it down, then. Get rid of some of the bells and whistles."

"Which bells and whistles would those be? The ones that give it power? The ones that make it think? The ones that provide input from the flowers, which is the entire raison d'être for the unit in the first place?" For once, Romeo's voice was raised.

Well, Teddy was pissed off too. "Your unit is fugly! Who's going to want to buy a vase that looks like ass? And not good ass either."

"Find a way to camouflage it."

Teddy growled. "*Find a way to camouflage it.* Do you think I have a magic wand? Good design takes time, Romeo, and you can't just throw stuff together on the fly. God, and we almost have the specs worked out on production costs. But if I start adding more pieces, Imani will eviscerate me. Slowly."

"I can't help any of that." Romeo took the tablet and

moved back toward his chair. "This is what we're going to need to make the software operate." His jaw was set and his eyes flinty.

Teddy opened his mouth to argue but couldn't think of anything convincing. He didn't know squat about programming or about the hardware needed to make gizmos run properly. He designed and marketed, making things look pretty and convincing people they couldn't live without them, all without blowing the company's budget. He had no idea how to work that now.

Through gritted teeth he managed "Send me those files," before marching out of Romeo's office and into the cubicle area. His imaginary upbeat show tune had been replaced by a wailing lament. Crap.

Time to find some lunch.

Chapter Two

"Jennifer Murray had another baby. I saw it on the Facebook. Very cute little girl."

Teddy slumped a little deeper into his couch and considered switching to speakerphone. If he did, would his grandmother hear the crinkle of waxed paper as he snacked? "That's great, Gram. I'm happy for her."

"Do you remember Jennifer Murray? You used to play with her when you came to visit. She had strawberry-blond pigtails, but now I see in the photos that she dyes it auburn."

What Teddy mostly remembered about Jennifer Murray was an altercation at the playground, during which she'd demanded that he relinquish the swing. When he'd refused, she'd punched him so hard in the stomach that he'd fallen, skinned his knees, and ended up with bark splinters embedded in the palms of his hands. For the remainder of his two-week stay at his grandmother's, she'd called him Dead Ted.

Instead of reminding his grandmother about that unpleasant summer, he used his free hand to pull another Ritz cracker out of its sleeve. He'd munched through the better part of a package during this call, and when he was done, he was going to need to vacuum away the crumbs.

"Maybe her hair has changed shades naturally," he offered.

"No, it's dyed. I can tell. It's a good dye job, though. She probably has it done at a salon. Although now with two little ones at home, I don't know if she'll have the time for that."

"Hmm." He nibbled the cracker as quietly as possible.

"I think it's a good idea to have your children as close in age as possible. I had three boys in four years, you know. It wasn't easy, but I'd rather that than have one in diapers and one learning to drive."

"Gram, if this is a subtle hint that you want grandkids, you're wasting your time with me. Talk to my brother."

She made a *pfft* sound. "I'm never subtle, sweetheart. You know that. If I wanted you to have children you'd know it." She was quiet for several beats. "But do *you*, Teddy? Want kids, I mean."

He ate another cracker, this one very fast. Now he was thirsty but lacked the courage to walk the few feet to his kitchenette for a glass of water. He might freeze along the way. He'd just have to suffer his parched throat while staying cocooned in three fleecy blankets and a cashmere scarf around his neck.

"I like children, but I doubt I'll have any."

"Lots of gay couples adopt, sweetie. Or they have surrogates."

"They do, but I'm not a couple. I'm just me. And I'm not brave enough for single parenthood." This time he ate two crackers at once, which didn't help with his thirst but did stop him from blurting out anything rude to his grandmother. She loved him. She cared about him. It wasn't her fault that he found relationship-related discussions toxic.

"Teddy dear, you're young. You have time for your life to go all kinds of unexpected places. Don't rule things out so easily."

"But I don't want unexpected. I have everything mapped out. Our vases are going to be really successful." He hoped he sounded more confident than he felt. "I'll send you one of the first ones off the production line."

"And I'll pimp them to everyone in my garden club."

His grandmother's unexpected choice of words made Teddy spray cracker crumbs across his blankets and probably halfway across the apartment. "Pimp, Gram?"

"I'm on the Facebook. I know all the hip new terms."

They chatted for a few more minutes, mostly about her upcoming trip to New York City, organized by her local senior center. She was going to see three Broadway shows while she was there, and she promised to send him the playbills.

By the time the call ended, Teddy was out of crackers and so dehydrated he worried his skin would begin to crack. His landlord would come searching when the rent wasn't paid, and find him in a desiccated heap on the couch, surrounded by crumbs and blankets. At least he'd look stylish in his Burberry scarf.

Maybe Reddyflora's next project should solve dilemmas such as his: a person alone in his apartment, wanting something fetched but too cold to get it himself. What if someone could figure out a way to give a robot vacuum arms and a smidge of artificial intelligence? That would be ideal—then Teddy could use an app to send it for a glass of water, and it could clean the floor as it went. The gadget could have a cutesy, friendly name—Bobby the Butler Bot, perhaps—and come in bright colors to match various décors.

Teddy rubbed his chin thoughtfully, wondering if Bobby could be manufactured at a viable price point and, more importantly, how feasible the software would be.

But that turned out to be a mistake. His runaway thought train went straight from software to software developers, and that meant it headed directly to Romeo Blue. Such an aggravating man, all smug in his dumb boring office with his ugly unit.

Damnit. Teddy didn't want to think about Romeo's unit.

The next morning, Imani flew at Teddy before he even had his scooter stowed away. "What the *hell* is up with those new specs, Teddy?"

Well, it wasn't as if he hadn't known this was coming.

He shot her a long-suffering look before stripping off his outerwear and hanging it up. "I need coffee before this conversation. Do we have coffee?"

"Second pot just brewed."

She hovered impatiently while he filled the humongous three-dollar clearance mug he'd found at Target. It had a cute little rainbow design, but more importantly, it held enough coffee to caffeinate a small army. Or at least enough to fortify him through a discussion with Imani.

She wheeled her chair across the floor to his cubicle and waited with crossed arms as he got himself situated. "Well?" she demanded at last.

"It's Romeo's fault." Okay, perhaps not the most mature response, but it *was* absolutely accurate. "He claims the electronics housing has to be big to fit everything, and it is capital-U ugly. I had to make some design changes to camouflage it."

"We can't afford those changes. Look what they did to the price per piece! You gobbled the profit margin right up." She waved a paper at him, which was an especially bad sign. Like everyone else at Reddyflora, Imani did the majority of her work electronically, but when she thought something was crucial or terrifying, she printed it out. Quite possibly so she could brandish the bad news theatrically, as she was doing right now.

"We can't afford not to make the changes," Teddy replied glumly. "Nobody in their right mind would buy the vase otherwise."

She heaved a heavy sigh. "I don't want to be a narc, but I'm gonna have to tell Lauren."

"Yeah. I figured."

"You sure you and Romeo can't work this out somehow?"

Teddy imagined himself trying to reason with Romeo, who'd only glower back at him and shake his head. Maybe Romeo would throw in some obscure technical jargon for good measure, or spout physics equations to support his arguments. "Not without a magic wand."

"We haven't budgeted for those."

For the next hour or two, Teddy buried himself in writing ad copy and sending emails to press representatives in hopes of enticing them to write articles about Reddyflora. Usually he enjoyed these activities, but today he kept getting distracted by activity outside his cubicle. He was all too aware when Romeo arrived and attempted to make a beeline for his office before getting waylaid by Imani. And Teddy noticed too, when Imani emerged from Romeo's office a short time later, grumbling at the papers clutched in her hand.

She skulked until Lauren click-clacked into their presence in her Jimmy Choos, at which point Imani insisted, "We need to talk, Lauren."

Teddy was staring at his desktop, but he could practically hear Lauren wince.

It was nowhere near lunchtime, so Teddy tried to fabricate another reasonable excuse to escape. It was too early in the season to hope for a tornado warning, and Chicago was generally lacking in serious seismic activity. Could he manufacture a wardrobe malfunction, perhaps? But today he wore a pair of 1940s pleated trousers that he adored far too much to damage, even in the interest of avoiding conflict.

In his upper right-hand desk drawer, behind the extra packs of staples, paperclips, and pens, Teddy had a secret weapon. It didn't look like much from the outside: just a small square box covered in a pale turquoise velvet. The kind of box you might use to present a ring, which had in fact been its original use. It had once contained a band of black titanium edged with rose gold. Not the Tiffany version, which Teddy couldn't afford, but a nice, less-expensive rendition. The engagement ring had looked so good on Gregory's finger that he'd said he might want to use it as a wedding band. Now it sat somewhere at the bottom of the Chicago River, where Gregory had thrown it when they broke up.

But Teddy still had the box. And inside was a tiny rectangle of some cheap metal—a zinc alloy, he suspected—stamped with four letters: *LOVE.* He'd found it on a curb a week after Gregory left, and he'd picked it up and saved it. He didn't know why. He could probably buy a full gross of identical tags for twenty bucks on Amazon. Yet he'd tucked it into that stupid box and taken the box to work, and every time he peeked inside, he felt better about life. It was as if the little charm was a promise that difficult times would eventually pass. Happiness, the letters implied, waited just around the corner.

Today he didn't believe that, but the tag improved his mood anyway. Even faux cheer was better than nothing.

He'd just tucked the box back into the drawer with a

sigh when his phone buzzed. A text from Lauren: Come see me.

Shit. He wondered whether it was the profit margins on the base model that had her agitated, or his blowup with Romeo. Neither would be fun. And he couldn't procrastinate with her as he had with Romeo yesterday.

Teddy cast a longing look at his desk drawer, stood, and trudged a path through the cubicles. He knocked on Lauren's closed door and waited for the invitation to enter.

Lauren, her hair pulled into a neat bun, wore a black sheath dress and a white cropped jacket with black floral embroidery. She stood next to a massive glass-topped desk with a base of reclaimed hardwood and metal train rails. Her aesthetic was definitely minimalist, and the desktop held nothing but her laptop and a small arrangement of dry-stacked round stones. A small gray couch sat unobtrusively in a corner. Elegantly framed black-and-white photos of single flowers hung on the wall—a tulip, a lily, a rose, an allium—each with a bare stem, as if they awaited the perfect vase. She'd replaced the overhead fluorescents with a modernist chrome-and-crystal chandelier, and a geometric area rug in grays and faded blues covered much of the floor. Her chair had a tall back but delicate lines.

"Have a seat." She gestured at one of the three chairs in front of her desk, low-back things that looked nice but felt uncomfortable no matter how you sat in them. Teddy nodded and obeyed, and she smiled warmly. "I tried that Indian place you mentioned, and it's amazing. Thanks for the rec."

"Glad you liked it."

"You're right about the décor there too. It's fresh enough to surprise without being jarring or distracting."

Her praise came off as genuine rather than an attempt to soften the blow of whatever was coming next. Partly because, all her aspirations of innovation aside, she was the type of person who let you know exactly what she was thinking and feeling. If she didn't like something, she said so plainly. But she was also forthcoming with compliments, which made working for her much more bearable, despite the questionable choice of office building. Plus she had vision and drive.

"Their drink menu needs more imagination," Teddy said. "I mean, it's okay, but…"

"Nothing new. Yeah. It'd be good if the chef took a quick glance beyond the food."

He scooched his butt on the seat in vain hope of a better perch. "Their dessert choices, though—" But before he could wax rhapsodic about the rose chai cheesecake, someone knocked on the door.

"Come in!" Lauren called.

Teddy's heart sank when Romeo walked into the office. He'd really been hoping for Imani. The only solace was that Romeo looked as unhappy as Teddy felt. Lauren, on the other hand, appeared entirely cheery as she waved Romeo to a seat. "We were discussing Indian food."

"I already had lunch. And I'm allergic to some curries."

She chuckled. "Not to eat now, Ro. Teddy told me

about a new restaurant, and I was just letting him know how much I liked it."

"Oh." Romeo ducked his head and stared at his hands. His tightly curled hair was always perfectly shaped. He had long, broad-tipped fingers with very neat, clean nails. He probably booked manicures and other pampering treatments at regular intervals.

Lauren crossed her arms atop her desk and her expression grew serious. "I have bad news and good news."

Teddy clamped his lips to avoid blurting out any double entendres about Romeo's unit, and Romeo simply looked bewildered. "News?"

"Mmm-hmm. As I'm sure you're both aware, we're inches away from starting production—but cash flow is tight, tight, tight."

"Imani just gave me the new numbers this morning," Teddy said, feeling a little frantic. "I'm working on it. And Romeo and I are in conversation too." That was an exaggeration, perhaps, but not quite an untruth.

She waggled her hands. "I know, I know. You're all busting your butts on this. I've noticed the long hours you've been putting in, and I super appreciate you. But you can only squeeze things so much, right? And we all want quality products. We want Reddyflora to shine. And…guys, we're in trouble here."

Teddy's throat felt too thick for words, so he was grateful when Romeo asked the obvious. "How much trouble?"

"Layoffs. I've already cut my own salary to the bone, and there's not much more I can do except shrink the payroll." Lauren stared at a spot somewhere over Romeo's shoulder.

Teddy struggled to appear stoic. He'd been unemployed before and he could survive it again. But dammit, he'd really hoped this job was going somewhere. He'd believed in Reddyflora. A quick glance showed Romeo cool as ever, but of course he knew that his job was safe. Nobody could make smart vases without a software guy.

"You mentioned good news?" Teddy asked.

And Lauren's demeanor changed instantly, her eyes sparkling and her shoulders twitching with excitement. "Yes! I'm so psyched over the newest development."

Teddy and Romeo exchanged confused glances. "What's the development?" Teddy asked, not sure he wanted the answer.

"A potential investor! She believes in us and is almost ready to pump a whole lot of money into our production. She'll get fully behind our marketing too, which is important because she has all the right connections. With her on board, everyone can keep their jobs." She tapped her fingers on her upper arms. "And you know who she is? Joyce Alexander!"

With difficulty, Teddy suppressed a squeal. "*The* Joyce Alexander? Seriously?"

"Yes!"

"That's incredible! How did you even—wow, Lauren, this is huge!"

"I know!" she sang. "I just found out less than an hour ago, and I had to take some time to calm down before I could even talk about it to anyone. I mean, it's not just a fat bank account we're dealing with here, but celebrities. Media! With her help, I can see us splashed all over the major décor mags and lifestyle blogs. Reddyflora vases could be the must-have accessory. Like those Brno chairs and furry cushions everyone was buying a few years back."

"Like ubiquitous succulents," said Teddy, who was way over that trend, especially since all of his plants had promptly died.

"Exactly! We are the succulents of the future!" Lauren and Teddy leaped to their feet and high-fived with such enthusiasm that they almost toppled the little stone cairn.

"Who's Joyce Alexander?"

Both Lauren and Teddy gaped at Romeo, but it was Teddy who spoke first. "The fashion goddess?"

Romeo shook his head. "I don't really know fashion."

That was news to Teddy, who thought Romeo always looked well put together, but Romeo seemed sincere. Teddy collapsed into his chair. "Okay. So, she first hit it big in the seventies with these floral dresses with strong Victorian influence. Lots of lace and taffeta and full skirts. She hit the right price point too—girls in the 'burbs could afford them for prom and other special occasions. Eventually she branched out into men's fashion, and she got away with selling retro looks even in the eighties and early nineties when everyone else was doing those godawful neons and boxy blazers and acid-washed jeans." He shuddered.

"The eighties were a long time ago." Romeo still looked puzzled.

"Right. But she evolved. Managed to keep her brand strong right through grunge and then hit it even bigger with goth. She was doing jewelry and cosmetics and fabrics and furniture. She became a lifestyle brand."

"She had a resort in Vermont," Lauren chimed in. "And a line of interior paint colors."

Romeo didn't look impressed. "You're using a lot of past tense here."

Teddy slumped melodramatically. "She's...moved on to another plane."

"She's dead?" Those delicate eyebrows shot upward.

"If she were dead she couldn't really offer to back us, could she? Unless Lauren's been negotiating via Ouija board."

Lauren shook her head emphatically. "Nope. I never do business with the deceased. You can't trust 'em."

Repositioning himself in his seat, Teddy suspected this might be the strangest workplace conversation he'd engaged in. This year, anyway. "She's stepped away from most of what she used to do. Sort of retired. In fact, she's a bit of a recluse nowadays. But she remains a grande dame of fashion, a doyenne, and she pops up every now and then to put her seal of approval on something she especially likes. And when she does, everybody suddenly has to have it. Last year it was brightly colored vegan snakeskin boots with kitten heels."

"Kittens?"

Teddy groaned and was thankful that Lauren stepped in. "Don't worry about it, Ro. Take my word for it: she's still a huge big deal. And if she backs us, we'll also be a huge big deal. No layoffs. Capital for future projects."

Although Romeo didn't look nearly as excited as Teddy felt, he asked a pertinent question. "Okay. But why do you need us? Money's Imani's gig."

Teddy had become so caught up in the whole idea of Joyce Alexander, he'd forgotten that Lauren needed something from them. He cocked his head and waited.

But Lauren didn't answer right away. She sat in her tall-back chair and straightened the laptop on the desk. She adjusted a stone or two on the sculpture and then sat back, looking as if she desperately wished she had something more to fidget with. She cleared her throat. "Well. Joyce hasn't made up her mind yet. I need to make a really convincing pitch. And *that* means you two need to get your shit together."

All the Joyce Alexander giddiness fled Teddy like helium escaping from a popped balloon, and he wasn't cheered up by Romeo's expression, which resembled that of a man who'd accidentally swallowed a bug. "We're trying," Teddy ventured.

Lauren nodded. "I know. But ticktock, guys. I head to Seattle in three days, and I need an answer before then. Tell me how we're going to make this work."

Chapter Three

They were meeting in Romeo's office, which made sense due to the privacy and his bank of monitors. But it was also unfair—a home game advantage that made Teddy scowl. He decided to tilt the scales a bit more in his favor by bringing supplies. As he schlepped everything from his cubicle, however, it occurred to him that he might be overcompensating. Not only did he have his laptop—sporting a skin in a retro 70s color palette—and the rainbow mug from Target, but also a ballpoint pen with a purple barrel and floating gold foil, a memo pad with a coordinating purple cover, and a stainless water bottle. Teddy planned to stay well hydrated during their meeting, and he'd certainly add a dash of color to Romeo's bland space. But it was a lot of stuff to carry.

Luckily, the door to Romeo's office stood ajar. As Teddy pushed his way inside, Romeo grunted from behind his desk and, without looking up from his screen, asked, "You planning a hostile takeover?"

"Maybe." Teddy took longer than strictly necessary to arrange his belongings. The room felt chilly, and now he wished he'd brought a cardigan too. Maybe he should insist on running home to fetch one before they began.

But Romeo appeared perfectly comfortable in his white shirt and black suit, as if he were a moderately stylish federal agent. Jeez, what if he *was* acting undercover? What if the FBI secretly suspected Lauren of using Reddyflora as a front to launder cartel money, and Romeo's insistence on making the vase either ugly or expensive was part of his way of gathering evidence? Teddy spent a moment trying to imagine what evidence Agent Blue might believe he possessed. When he couldn't come up with anything, he decided that perhaps Romeo was not working undercover after all.

Too bad. He'd make a dashing law enforcement officer, with his tight jawline and— The pen slipped from Teddy's fingers and rolled under the desk, forcing him to crawl inelegantly to retrieve it. When he squiggled back out, dignity in tatters, Romeo was staring at him.

"What?" Teddy demanded.

Romeo gave himself a brief shake. "This Alexander lady...she's really a big deal, huh?"

"I guess not to *everybody*. I doubt she's been shortlisted for a Nobel Prize. But in some circles? Yeah. A big deal."

"Oh."

"Look. I really don't want to blow this, okay? I want our products to be a success." And Teddy most definitely didn't want to end up back in one of the jobs he'd had before.

There was nothing wrong with working retail, and he'd enjoyed some of the customer interactions, but he'd been employed at places offering few occasions for creativity. Sometimes he had recurring nightmares that he'd had to return to slaving away at a discount clothing store—the kind with endless racks of identical T-shirts and jeans—and that Gregory showed up as Teddy was trying to wrangle an enormous pile of discarded items in the dressing room. In the dream, Gregory laughed and took photos of Teddy to turn into memes.

Romeo was scratching his lip. "Can we approach the problem logically?"

"Instead of emotionally, you mean? I know Reddy-flora is a business, and Imani's numbers are about as objective as anything can get. But design *is* emotion. I mean, that's what good design does—it stirs emotions." Teddy looked around for a way to illustrate his point; his gaze fell on Romeo's cheap and incredibly boring pen. Teddy snatched it and held the pen up before Romeo could stop him.

"What do you feel when you look at this?"

"Feel?"

"Yeah. Like, what comes to mind? Or to heart."

Romeo blinked at him. "Um, I need it to write with."

"Anything else?"

"I…guess I get annoyed when they suddenly run out

of ink." He looked a little lost. "I like blue ink better than black," he added with what appeared to be a smidgen of hope.

"Right." Teddy set down Romeo's pen and held his own aloft instead. "Now what do you feel?"

"Um...it's pretty? The gold stuff is kind of cool." Romeo grabbed the pen away and tilted it this way and that, watching the flakes float. He seemed almost hypnotized by the motion, in fact, until he jerked his shoulders and put the pen back on the desk. "I have no idea what you're getting at, man."

Teddy suppressed an irritated huff. "I told you. Emotion. Both of our pens can write. Maybe yours is even better at it. Mine uses these special ink inserts that don't last very long. But yours is, like, the most ho-hum thing in the universe, whereas mine is pretty cool. If you lost your pen or someone stole it, you wouldn't care as long as you had something else to write with. If I lost mine, I'd be seriously bummed. And that's design, Mr. Blue. It makes you *feel* something."

Romeo tapped his fingers on the desk. "Fine. You're emotionally attached to your writing instrument. So?"

"So, how much did your pen cost?" When Romeo just stared at him, Teddy waved a hand. "Yeah, I know. You got it out of the supply cabinet. But I happen to know you can buy a sixty pack of them for less than ten bucks. That comes to..." He tried to do the math in his head.

"Seventeen cents each."

"Right," said Teddy, who didn't actually know if the figure was accurate. It was close enough, for his purposes. "Seventeen cents. My pen, on the other hand? Nine ninety-nine, plus tax."

Romeo pursed his lips disapprovingly. "You could've bought sixty of mine for the price and never freak out if you lost one."

"True. But mine was just a little splurge. Some people pay hundreds for Montblancs. You know—just like rich people will fork over a hundred grand for a Mercedes when a Ford Fiesta will also get them from point A to point B."

Teddy was really warming to his subject, so much that he'd stood up and was waving his arms around as if he were delivering a TED Talk. But Romeo didn't make an appreciative audience. He was squinting at Teddy. "What does this have to do with our job?"

With a sigh, Teddy sank back into the chair. "Nobody *needs* a vase. I mean, you don't even need fresh flowers, but if you do have them, you can stick them in anything. A drinking glass, an empty soup can…whatever. But our goal is for people to want to buy our vase. To see it in a magazine or on a store shelf and think, 'Jeez, I wish I owned that!' We want people to add it to their wish lists and drop hints to family members when their birthdays are coming near. And how do we do that? By making them *feel* something about our vase."

"And we do that via good design," Romeo said.

"Yes!" Teddy felt as if he'd scored a touchdown or nailed a winning free throw or achieved something else sports related. Not that he'd ever excelled at any of those things—riding his scooter being the sum of his athletic pursuits—but he could imagine the sensation.

Romeo, on the other hand, didn't look pleased at all. He was staring at a spot somewhere over Teddy's left shoulder, where Teddy knew perfectly well there was nothing to see except a blank white wall. "What if that Mercedes has no engine?" Romeo's voice was even, almost emotionless. "What if your pen leaks ink everywhere? People still might feel something about the products, but those feelings are going to be negative. And nobody's going to want to buy."

Teddy considered pointing out that even negative feelings were something. Lots of famous designs earned their fame, a least in part, due to the heated—and not always positive—reactions they engendered. Architects such as Gaudi and Gehry, fashion designers such as McQueen, cars such as the DeLorean...people talked about them. Remembered them.

But controversy wasn't what Reddyflora was going for, so Teddy kept his mouth shut about that part.

"Fine, then," he said. "We need to figure out how to make the vase both look good and work well. Without going over budget."

"And we have two days."

They exchanged bleak looks, for once in complete agreement.

When no miraculous solutions descended from the heavens—or from the personal injury lawyer with the offices above them—Teddy slumped in his chair. "So how do you want to start?"

Romeo looked slightly startled at the question. Then he grabbed his tablet and scooted his chair around the desk, placing himself next to Teddy. "Let's begin with another look at what we're dealing with." He poked at his screen for a moment before leaning in close so that Teddy could see too.

The vase was still a monstrosity. That hadn't changed overnight. The black plastic casing clung to the beautiful streamlined shape as obtrusively as possible. "It's like an alien in a really bad horror movie. It's injecting its seed, which will soon burst forth as alien larvae to infect all nearby items of home décor."

"Yeah, except this alien has all the brains. Your vase is as dumb as a rock. It's a symbiotic relationship—mutualism, not parasitism. Like ants building fungus farms. Your vase is the fungus."

Teddy turned his head to give Romeo a *look*, and it would have been a wonderfully withering look too, enough to make Romeo withdraw his stupid analogy. Except when Teddy looked at him, he suddenly realized exactly how close Romeo was. Inches away. Near enough for Teddy to see that the man had perfect pores, dammit, and his eyes were so deep and soft and warm you could fall into them and never be cold again. And looking down didn't help one bit, because then Teddy focused on those long, strong fingers hovering practically over Teddy's lap.

"Lunch!" Teddy hopped out of the chair, nearly sending the tablet flying out of Romeo's hands.

"What?"

"It's, um, eleven oh seven. Which I guess is early for lunch, but this way we'll avoid the crowds. Plus I ate breakfast at oh–dark–thirty today and I'm starved."

"We have a deadline." Romeo's scowl was mighty.

"But we have to eat. We can get right back on this afterward, and if I have to stay late, I will." But if so, he really hoped Imani was also planning to stick around, because being alone in the office with Romeo at night... Oh, that idea sent Teddy's brain in all sorts of NSFW directions.

"You're not going to settle in until you've eaten, are you?"

"Nope. We can do something quick, like the sandwich place downstairs."

Romeo jerked his chin toward the far corner of the room, where a backpack was propped. "I brought mine."

Teddy shouldn't have felt rejected. It wasn't as if he'd asked Romeo on a date, for God's sake. It wasn't as if Teddy wanted to date anyone, let alone this particular man. That bitter little twist in his heart was annoyance at Romeo's impatient expression; that was all.

"Fine. Enjoy your whatever. I'll be back in a while."

Teddy absolutely did not flounce out of Romeo's office. Nor did he have a fleeting hope that Romeo noticed the nice fit of the vintage slacks over his ass.

Teddy strongly considered going somewhere across town, maybe that Greek place with the heavenly moussaka and glacial service. But sleet had started to spit from the sky, and since he wasn't in the mood for braving the weather, he settled on the sandwich place downstairs after all. They had soup too, but it was split pea with ham, which didn't move him. He ended up with PB&J on multigrain, a side of mac and cheese, and a large serving of self-pity. All washed down with a bottle of Vitamin Water that would probably do little to flush the toxins from his system.

He couldn't quite face returning to the office once his meal was done, so he decided somewhat masochistically to visit Instagram. At the top of the feed was @gbrewes with his 47.5K followers and photos of himself and the new boyfriend in fancy restaurants and scenic locales. Teddy knew he should have unfollowed Gregory immediately after their ugly breakup two years earlier, but he hadn't been able to click the button. As if repeatedly ripping the scab off his broken heart was a better idea.

But if Teddy and Gregory had been still dating, then Teddy could text him right now and bitch about how impossible his coworker was. Teddy would give lots of examples, too—Romeo's stubbornness, his air of perfection, his haughty presence in his bland kingdom of an office. And Gregory would be sympathetic, maybe, because he always enjoyed when Teddy criticized people. Hell, Gregory would often join in, even if he'd never met the people in question. He was good at criticism.

Maybe—if they were still dating—Teddy and Gregory would make plans to meet for dinner at that trendy new sushi place, where Gregory would arrange his food for perfect Instagram shots, and Teddy would do bad imitations of Romeo. And afterward they'd head to Teddy's apartment because Gregory had three roommates, and they'd have a quick romp in the sheets before Gregory went home.

Leaving Teddy alone and feeling a little used, maybe.

Which was why it was a *good* thing that Gregory was history and that Teddy had vowed to remain single for the foreseeable future.

A pair of tourists sitting at the next table were arguing about what to do now that the lookout atop the Willis Tower was closed due to weather. She wanted to do a mobster tour; he complained that it was too nasty outside and they should go to the Field Museum. Neither seemed to be enjoying themselves, and they appeared sick of each other's company. Maybe that was the fate of all relationships: eventually even vacations became a chore. Better to stay single.

By the time he gathered his wrappers, napkins, and empty bottle, the couple had descended into sullen silence. Teddy paused as he passed them on the way to the trash cans. "Would you like some advice from a local?"

They perked up and nodded eagerly. "Sure would," said the man. "I guess we weren't really prepared for this cold."

Teddy didn't mention that today's temperatures were almost balmy for early February. "The Field's nice, but d'you want to try something a little more offbeat? The Cultural Center is just a few blocks away. Really cool architecture, and it's free. There's usually a couple of exhibits going on there. And just up the street from that is the Writers Museum, which I think is worth a visit."

"Ooh, writers!" the woman said. Her husband also looked intrigued.

"Yeah. Spend a few hours in those places and then take a quick stroll through Millennium Park if it's not too bad out. Then take a Lyft to Pequod's and dig into some deep-dish. How much longer will you be here?"

"Three days," the man said.

"Great. Plenty of time. Hit the Field Museum tomorrow morning before the hordes of field-trip kids get there. Invest in a souvenir blanket and it'll keep you warm for the mobster tour and the river architecture tour. You can wing it after that. Maybe the clouds'll lift long enough for you to get to the Sears Tower."

"Is that the same thing as the Willis?"

"Yeah." Teddy gave a mental sigh. It would always be the Sears Tower in his mind, stupid corporate naming rights be damned.

The couple thanked him, and Teddy threw his trash away. Maybe he should take a day off from work and play tourist in his own city. It might help lift his mood. Ugh, but first he had to deal with Romeo and his stupid unit.

Chapter Four

Romeo must have been standing just inside his office doorway, spying through the slightly opened door and waiting for Teddy to return. As soon as Teddy stepped inside the suite, long before he reached the coat hook, Romeo accosted him with righteous indignation. "You were gone forever."

"I was gone long enough to have a sandwich, and mac and cheese. Calm down." Even Teddy winced a little at those last two words. He'd been fed that phrase repeatedly over his life, beginning when he was a toddler throwing tantrums because his cartoon-watching time was over, and continuing right through the day Gregory told him they were done. He'd never once actually calmed when somebody said that to him. Possibly nobody in the history of the world had ever calmed down when told to do so.

Pretending not to notice Romeo's glower, Teddy sailed the rest of the way across the suite and divested himself of the parka and scarf he hadn't actually needed. He patted his scooter for good measure. To be honest, it seemed a little forlorn. Then he girded his loins and followed Romeo into his office.

"How long have you used a scooter?" Romeo asked as soon as they were settled in their chairs. He was sitting close again, but this time he had three tiny breadcrumbs on his tie, which pleased Teddy very much. At least the guy hadn't yet invented lunch-proof office wear.

Which was an interesting idea, actually.

Teddy shook his head to clear it. "A couple of years. Why? You're disappointed I'm not arriving in a chauffeur-driven limo like you probably do?"

Romeo gave him an odd look and replied with a touch of acidity. "No. I was interested in whether it was a good form of transportation. I guess expecting polite conversation from you is too much to ask."

Teddy almost—*almost*—stuck out his tongue. "We're not supposed to be chitchatting, remember? Very important deadline."

That got him a grunt in return, but then Romeo turned his attention to his tablet and brought up the image of the vase. "I was thinking about this over lunch. How about if you list the most important aspects of your design, and then I list the most important aspects of the hardware. That way we have a baseline to begin with."

It was, Teddy had to admit, a good idea. He grabbed his memo pad from Romeo's desk and clicked open his purple-and-glittery-gold pen. "I'll take notes."

"We could do that on here." Romeo brandished the tablet.

"We could also do it on papyrus or basalt columns, but my notebook works fine." Teddy didn't even know why he was arguing this particular point, except that he could. And he won, too—Romeo rolled his eyes but stopped protesting.

"Okay," Romeo said. "Tell me what you need."

A simple enough request under the circumstances, yet it sent a shiver down Teddy's spine to hear Romeo say those words. "Um...okay. Price point. I think this is something we can both agree is critical, right? The vase has to be inexpensive enough that people of relatively moderate means can afford it, and the manufacturing has to be cheap enough that we make a profit."

"What are *moderate means*?"

"No champagne and caviar, no limousines. People who commute to work on scooters and eat sandwiches for lunch, and who have limited budgets for making their homes or offices look nice."

Romeo's eyes were narrowed, not in anger but in concentration, as if he were trying to parse some hidden meaning from Teddy's statement. There was no hidden meaning, however. Teddy had meant exactly what he'd said.

"Fine," Romeo said. "Write that down."

Teddy did, making sure to use his neatest handwriting. He'd been proud of his penmanship when he was a kid. In grade school he'd written his name with extra curves and squiggles for the *y* and fancy little flourishes underneath. He went for a more minimalist look now.

Affordable price point. When he was done, he looked at Romeo expectantly. "Any other common ground?"

"Well, size. We're working on the midrange vase, so…" He set the tablet on his lap and held one hand about eight inches above the other. "About yay tall, right?"

"Yep. Not just to keep the cost down, but because some of us live in a shoebox and don't want a huge honking statement piece taking up half our apartment."

"Agreed, then. No behemoths."

Teddy felt the corners of his mouth lift a little as he wrote *Eight inches* on his memo pad. And then, because he couldn't help himself, he snickered. "Bigger is not always better, you know, and eight inches is plenty."

Romeo snorted, but it was a relatively friendly snort. "What else are your dreams made of, Teddy?"

"Not vases. Okay. It has to look sleek—no blocky protuberances. Modern, because that's part of what we're selling. Unique, so it catches people's eyes. And it has to work with a lot of different decorative styles, so it can fit in almost anywhere." He wrote as he spoke, then eyed the list. "That's not asking so much. Six things."

But Romeo's mouth was scrunched up as if he wasn't too sure. "Maybe it's a short list, but those aren't easy asks."

Teddy shrugged. "You asked what I need. How about you?"

As it turned out, Romeo's list was longer and a lot more technical. His tablet contained precise measurements for all the little electronic bits and pieces, plus he had specs about temperature and moisture and airflow. "We don't want to electrocute customers," he pointed out.

"Yeah, I guess not. Hey, wouldn't it be cool if there was a device for electrocuting people? I mean, nothing fatal or even dangerous. Just, like a little zap when you want to get their attention or want them to stop doing something. Or to make them go away."

Romeo was giving him that look again. "We're not zapping anyone."

"I know," Teddy said cheerfully. He hadn't really meant it, of course—it had just seemed like the suggestion might needle Romeo a bit. And, well, mission accomplished.

"Let me see the list," Romeo demanded.

Teddy handed it over, but kept his pen. If Romeo wanted to add something, he could use his seventeen-cent Bic. But although Romeo scraped his lip with his teeth and mumbled things under his breath, he didn't write anything more. Finally he handed the pad back. "All right. How do we reconcile this?"

They played with designs on Romeo's tablet for a long time, taking turns making changes to the vase's look and schematics. Every now and then, Teddy did something ridiculous   like shrinking the sensor almost into nothingness—mostly because it was sort of fun to watch Romeo sputter. Also, Romeo sputtering was better than

Romeo serious, his head bent close enough to almost touch Teddy's, the warmth of his body making Teddy forget he'd originally felt chilly in this room.

Sometimes they took a short break to stretch their cramped muscles and rest their screen-blurry eyes, or maybe one of them would hurry to the bathroom or fetch fresh coffee. Romeo drank his out of an extremely ordinary and boring navy-blue mug. It had no rainbow designs and not even a cutesy saying. With so many fun mugs in the world, why would anyone choose one like that?

Five o'clock came and went. The hum of the rest of the Reddyflora employees, audible through Romeo's open door, ebbed away. After a while, big band music started to play, which meant Imani was the only other employee left. During the day, she wore earbuds, but she preferred using the speaker when she had the office to herself. Or, in this case, when she was sharing with just Teddy and Romeo.

Romeo handed the umpteenth iteration to Teddy, apparently noted Teddy's answering lip curl, and groaned. "This is hopeless." He stretched out his long legs and let his head loll back on the chair. But even though he must have been as exhausted and frustrated as Teddy, Romeo still looked unrumpled, as if he might stride off to a nightclub any moment and nod at paparazzi along the way.

Teddy hadn't bothered to look in a mirror since lunchtime, but he was positive his hair had escaped the restraints of product and was doing its weird little frizzy thing. His skin, pale even in the summer, must look fish-belly white under the fluorescent glare. And the suspenders that had looked so stylish this morning felt like twin boa constrictors trying to scrunch him into a ball and swallow him whole.

Also, he was hungry again. A pizza would truly hit the spot, but he didn't mention that.

Romeo sat back up and rubbed his forehead with both hands. "Don't you have plans for tonight?"

"Sure. Finish work. Vegetate in front of Netflix. Sleep."

"Really? I would have thought you'd— Never mind."

Teddy didn't want to never mind—he wanted to follow that intriguing half statement to its end. What *did* Romeo think Teddy did with his time off? And why did Teddy care?

"At this point, I just want to go home," Teddy said.

"We could quit for tonight and take this up first thing in the morning. I guess."

"Nah." Teddy shook his head. "Because when we come up with a solution—*if* we do—we still need to give Imani time to run the final numbers. And if those check out okay, the crew will have to draw up better images for Lauren to show Joyce Alexander. That takes time."

"I know."

They sat without talking for what felt like a very long time. Imani's music wafted in, and if Teddy really concentrated, he could hear the slight hum of the building's heating system. The walls were too thick for traffic noises or the rumble of the el to make their way inside.

Romeo's chair was a nice one, with a high back and leather upholstery. Comfortable, probably. But the one where Teddy sat had narrow armrests and a back that hit him in the wrong place, not quite giving the support he needed. He shifted a few times and then sighed.

"It's not like we're trying to cure cancer," Romeo said. "Or colonize Mars. This shouldn't be so hard."

"Mmm."

Count Basie's lively riffs floated into the room, making Teddy tap his toes despite his mood.

"Joyce Alexander," Teddy said quietly. "Man, if you'd have told younger me I might someday be designing something she'd see… I'd have lain down and died."

"Literally?"

"Figuratively. Did you have someone like that? An idol. Who rocked your world?"

Romeo shot him a quick look. "My parents."

Ah. Well, that was probably healthier than fixating on a fashion designer. "So…what would your parents do if they were in this office right now?"

"Mama would feed me. That's pretty much her go-to when it comes to life problems." He pitched his voice higher. "'Everything works out better with a full stomach, honey.'"

"She's got a point there."

Romeo's soft smile was almost heartbreakingly handsome. "I guess she does. My dad, though, he'd just tell me to stop moping around and get the job done. He might throw in a *lollygagging* or *dillydallying* while he was at it."

"Lollygagging?" Teddy tried really hard not to chortle

like a twelve-year-old. He mostly succeeded, thanks to a camouflaging cough.

"Yeah, I've got a whole suitcase of dadisms like that I could unpack for you. That's what happens when a guy loves language and digs retro stuff. When I was little we'd listen to Chuck Berry and Little Richard and watch all those tacky old flying saucer movies on Saturday afternoon TV."

That made Teddy slightly envious. His parents had always seemed too busy to spend much time with him. Not that they were neglectful by any means, but he was pretty much left to entertain himself. Now he closed his eyes and imagined Romeo as a child, living in a house decorated in midcentury modern, with his mother wearing a polka-dot swing dress and handing Romeo trays of food, and his father sitting nearby in a cardigan and tie, maybe with a pipe in hand. A Black June and Ward Cleaver.

Okay, that was ridiculous, but…

"Googie!" Teddy leapt from the chair, his little explosion making Romeo startle violently.

"Wh-what?"

"I think I have a solution, and it's Googie!" Teddy did an impromptu little dance around the room. He wanted to kiss himself for being so clever.

Romeo, on the other hand, had backed toward the door while wearing an expression that said he was seriously considering escape. Maybe he thought Imani would come to his rescue.

After a few more jig steps, Teddy took pity on him.

Besides, it was time to share his brilliance. "Googie is an architectural style that was popular in the fifties. You've seen it plenty of times even if you don't know what it's called. It was supposed to be very space age and modern. Think of the original McDonald's, or the famous Las Vegas sign. Pastel colors, geometric shapes, boomerangs and those atomic loopy things..."

"Yeah, okay, I know what you're talking about. Like *The Jetsons*."

"Right!" Teddy hummed a bar of the theme song.

"How are the Jetsons going to help us?"

"They're not. What we need to do— Wait. Maybe the Jetsons *can* help. Jane and, uh, what was her husband's name?"

Romeo answered without hesitation. "George. And their kids were Judy and Elroy. Rosie was the robot maid and the dog was Astro."

Despite his excitement, Teddy paused. He hadn't expected Romeo to be such an expert on the cartoon. But at least Romeo's weird knowledge was going to make this easier. "Suppose Jane and George decide to buy a new vase for their cool pad. Dig, daddy-o? What's that vase going to look like?"

"Um...not too different from ours."

"Bingo! And if we sweep the legs of the frame out a little— Gimme the tablet."

Romeo did, and then he loomed over Teddy's shoulder while Teddy used basic graphics software to alter the mock-up of the vase. Instead of running straight up and down, the new lines of the steel frame curved outward, widening at the base, a little like that spaceship-looking building at LAX.

"See?" Teddy pointed. "This way the frame hides most of the electronic casing. And if we use silver-colored plastic instead of black, it'll blend in even more."

Romeo grabbed the tablet and peered closely. "You can't cover the USB port."

"We can make sure that stays accessible."

"With that frame in the way, it's going to be impossible for anyone to get at the electronics if they need repairs."

Teddy huffed. "Do you honestly think anyone's going to bring this thing in for repairs? I don't even know where you'd take it, and if you *did* find a place, it'd be cheaper to just buy a new one."

Although he mumbled something that sounded like *wasteful*, Romeo didn't put up a fight. "And this meets all our needs?"

After a quick review of his original notes, Teddy nodded. "I think so. The vase'll have a little more personality than we intended, but that's okay. I think the design will work with a lot of different decorative styles." He took another look at the image. "Hmm. The probe's still kind of ugly."

"Maybe we can frost the glass. But how much are these changes going to increase the price?"

That was the big question, wasn't it? "Dunno. Let's ask Imani."

They bounced against each other in the doorway, trying to get through at the same time, but Teddy did a little duck and feint move that got him out first.

Imani watched apprehensively as they marched toward her cubicle. "I'm not refereeing. You're both grown men—you work it out."

"I think we already did," Teddy said proudly. "We need you to check the numbers for us."

That surprised her for sure, but she turned down her music and held her hand out for the tablet. "Show me what you got."

Although Romeo obeyed, he was frowning. "It's late. This can wait until morning."

But she stared at the screen and waved dismissively. "I got this. Go home."

Teddy felt a little guilty as he wound the scarf around his neck and zipped up his parka, but by then Chick Webb and Ella Fitzgerald were in full swing and Imani was engrossed in her screens.

Romeo and Teddy walked down the stairs together, Teddy hefting his scooter. There was an awkward little moment when they reached the building's exit, and for one or two heartbeats, Teddy thought Romeo might propose they find some dinner together.

But then Romeo sniffed and shoved a knit cap over his head. "See you tomorrow."

"Yeah. You too."

That witty bit of repartee echoed in Teddy's head for the entire journey home.

Chapter Five

Teddy's morning was more fraught than usual, in part because he'd slept poorly. He woke up crusty eyed and fuzzy headed, and the previous night's burger and fries still sat heavily in his stomach. Getting ready for work took enormous effort. For once, he didn't even enjoy surveying his closet. He would have rather remained home in sweats and fuzzy slippers.

But he got dressed in his usual February layers and braved the great outdoors, where the sky was the color of dirty washing machine water and the pedestrians seemed determined to wander directly into Teddy's path. He had a dozen near collisions before reaching the office, breathless and even more out of sorts than when he'd begun.

As he lugged the scooter up the stairs—which seemed

steeper and more numerous than usual—he tried to figure out why he was in such a crappy mood. Sure, he was
nervous to find out what Imani had to say, but at least
he and Romeo had come up with a potential solution.
That was a lot more hopeful than if they'd struck out
completely—or come to blows. Especially since Teddy
hadn't been in a physical fight since Jennifer Murray
punched him on the swing.

When Teddy reached the Reddyflora suite, the main
room was unoccupied. But Lauren's door was closed,
which probably meant she and Imani were in confer-
ence. After removing his outerwear he dithered for a
bit—starting up some coffee, booting up his computer,
straightening a few items on his desk. He was tempted
to peek inside the box at the little charm, but he resisted,
instead sitting and staring at nothing while humming
tunes from *Dear Evan Hansen*.

He greeted other employees as they arrived but didn't
engage in his usual chitchat. *You're lollygagging*, he accused
himself, but the admonition didn't help.

Finally Romeo appeared, and he and Teddy had a brief
conversation from across the room, made up entirely of
hand gestures and facial expressions. Romeo clearly got
the gist of it—meeting in progress; no news yet. He nodded and hurried into his office.

Imani emerged ten minutes later, papers clutched in
her hands. She headed straight to Teddy's cubicle. "Lauren wants to see you and Romeo."

An elastic band tightened around Teddy's chest. "Now?"

"Yep."

He couldn't read anything from her expression. She was probably an excellent poker player.

"Imani, I'm going to die right this second if you don't tell me whether it's going to work. Die. And you will be held personally responsible."

"I'll get off the hook," she said with a shrug. "My girlfriend's a lawyer." But then she smiled and gave his shoulder a quick squeeze. "It's going to work."

The elastic band evaporated, leaving Teddy almost dizzy with newfound oxygen. "Oh, thank God."

"Nah. Thank *me*. Now go talk to Lauren." She headed toward Romeo's office.

Today Lauren wore a gray suit and shell-pink camisole, and she would have looked as chic as always except her bun was uncharacteristically messy. Still, she gave Teddy a warm smile. "You guys are miracle workers," she said.

"Does this mean Joyce Alexander—"

Before he could finish the question, Romeo entered, wearing another of his federal agent outfits. At least he'd taken off the jacket. Although a white shirt/black tie/black trousers combo would have been boring on anyone else, of course he looked gorgeous. Which he undoubtedly knew. He greeted Lauren and folded himself into one of her chairs, his long legs elegantly crossed. Although he fussed a bit with the trouser pleat, which lost him a few coolness points.

Lauren took a seat, her palms flat against the glass top of her desk. "Thank you both for working so hard on this problem."

Gratitude was nice, but Teddy wanted to know about Joyce Alexander. "Imani says the numbers work out."

"They do. Production costs will go up a little due to the extra shaping and the frosted glass, but increasing the price by a dollar will cover it without pricing us out of range."

"We don't have to frost the glass," Romeo offered.

Teddy shot him a glare. "Yes, we do. Ugly probe, remember?"

Romeo opened his mouth, no doubt to argue, but Lauren cut him off with a wave of her hand. "It's fine. The glass will look nice."

"And Joyce Alexander?" Teddy tried not to bounce in his chair.

"Is still interested in hearing our pitch." But before Teddy could do an encore of the previous day's celebratory dance, Lauren shook her head. "But there's a complication."

Oh no. That was a terrible word. It was right up there with *We have to talk* and *I got the test results back*. He didn't want to know about complications. He wanted, in fact, a simple world, like in a Broadway musical, where the small problems would all be wrapped up within three hours and there would be a soaring reprise at the end.

"Complication?" Romeo asked. Teddy wanted to kick him.

Lauren gazed at them solemnly. "As you know, I was supposed to fly to Seattle to meet with Joyce."

"Was?" Teddy also didn't like the past tenseness of this.

"Was. But I've had an emergency come up." She

scowled. "It's a stupid emergency, but I need to deal with it anyway."

Romeo leaned forward with an expression of concern. "Is everything okay?"

"Ugh. My sister. It's her wedding anniversary, and she and her husband have reservations for one of those all-inclusive resorts in the Caribbean. You know—the kind where you can sit on the beach all day drinking mai tais instead of freezing your buns off or slowly losing your mind while stuck in traffic on the Stevenson Expressway."

"That sounds nice," Teddy said dreamily. He'd never visited anywhere tropical, but Gregory did so regularly, and he sure looked happy in his poolside selfies.

Lauren curled her lip. "Right. Nice. Except they have two daughters who are definitely not invited along on this trip."

Romeo grinned, looking not at all like his usual grim self. "You have nieces! How old?"

"Ten and twelve. My mother was supposed to stay with them while the parents are gone. Grandparent bonding, yadda yadda. But suddenly my mother has fallen head over heels in love with some man, and they ran off last weekend and eloped. Can you imagine? That woman is sixty-four years old and she's mooning around like a teenager."

If Teddy hadn't been opposed to romance, he would have oohed and aahed a bit. It was sweet, really, that Lauren's mother had found someone to feel so deeply about and that she and her new beau had done something impulsive. Except it was also foolish. "How long have they known each other?"

"Before they got married? A week!" Lauren threw her hands up in exasperation.

Teddy clicked his tongue. "I don't believe in insta-love."

"Neither do I!" Lauren stood and paced her office a few times. "She's old enough to know better. She used to lecture me to be careful and not step into relationships too quickly. And now she does this!" Again with the hands in the air.

"She's a grown woman," Romeo pointed out quietly.

Lauren blew a raspberry. Then she threw herself back into her chair. "Anyway. Since Mom's currently off having a honeymoon in Las Vegas, of all the ridiculous places, I'm stuck with my sister's kids for the next week." She shuddered.

Romeo seemed puzzled by something, but Teddy didn't ask him what. Instead, he sighed heavily. "So no meeting with Joyce Alexander. You can't reschedule?"

"No. Her calendar availability is very limited. It's now or never. Which is why I'm sending you two."

"I'm sorry, Lauren. Can you say that again?" Surely he must have misheard her.

"You and Romeo are going to Seattle to pitch to Joyce Alexander. I spoke to her about it this morning, and you're all set. She says she's eager to meet you."

Teddy's brain went fuzzy. "I get to meet Joyce Alexander? Oh my God, I get to meet Joyce Alexander!" He was hyperventilating and might possibly pass out, but didn't much care. He turned to face Romeo. "We get to meet Joyce Alexander!"

Romeo stared back, unimpressed.

This was really the kind of news that required a half hour of gushing, followed by a few oh-so-casual mentions on social media just in case Gregory was paying attention. And then Teddy could spend the rest of the day planning what to pack. What should he wear? An outfit that slyly referred to Joyce Alexander's classic looks? Or maybe something entirely different and original. Something that spoke to Teddy's *own* sense of style.

But even as he considered these questions, a realization set in, sending Teddy plummeting to Earth like Icarus when his wings melted.

"Why the hell does Joyce Alexander want to meet me? Meeting you, I understand completely. You're our fearless leader. Or Imani, since she knows the numbers up and down. Or Romeo, the brain behind the software. I get that. But me?" Because if he failed at this mission, not only was he going to look bad in front of Joyce fricking Alexander, but he was going to take Reddyflora down with him.

"She wants to meet you *and* Ro." Lauren spoke slowly and patiently, the way you might explain to a drunk person why they couldn't have their car keys.

"Yeah, I get that. But why me? I can send her the designs and marketing plans."

"She doesn't want *plans*, Teddy. She wants people."

That sounded alarming, and even Romeo shifted uncomfortably. He had said only a word or two since

Lauren's announcement, instead studying his fingers or scratching his lower lip.

"Wants people for what?" Teddy asked.

Lauren threw her hands up. "I don't know. Look, she's incredibly picky, right? You know that. She told me she has unerring instincts about what will work and what won't, but she needs a personal connection. She doesn't trust technology."

Finally Romeo spoke. "That's not very promising, considering we're making high-tech products."

For once, Teddy agreed with Romeo completely, and he nodded.

Lauren let loose an exasperated huff. "Just go with it, okay? This is really, really important. She's not going to torture you. And you'll get to escape the Midwest for a few days. I'll fly you guys to Seattle, you spend a few days showing her how wonderful you are, and then she's on board and Reddyflora is a huge success."

Romeo was staring at his hands again, as if this entire discussion bored him. He probably thought Teddy was ridiculous for freaking out. But Jesus, this was Joyce Alexander they were talking about. The woman whose look Teddy had tried to emulate in his bedroom when he was thirteen, much to the distress of his butch younger brother, who shared the room. The woman whose menswear older-teen Teddy had sighed over in catalogs and store windows, wishing he had both the money and justification for buying them. The woman whose signature amber-and-honey-scented candles sat, right this minute, in antique dolphin-motif holders in the center of

Teddy's Ikea-hack coffee table. In contrast to all that, he was just Teddy Spenser, who rode to work on a scooter and slaved away in a cubicle before returning to his shoebox apartment with the unreliable water pressure and inconsistent heat.

Lauren smiled. "I'll have Skyler set up your reservations."

Midway Airport was packed with disgruntled passengers, many of whom were yelling at airline employees as if they'd caused the ice storm. Teddy, however, was content in his own little world near the gate. He had a salted caramel hot chocolate, a bag with two donuts, and a Kindle stuffed with books he'd been dying to read for months. His alpaca-silk scarf—hand knit himself—felt cozy around his neck, and his carry-on bag made an excellent footrest. Plus, Romeo wasn't saying a word; slouched one seat over, he was engrossed in his phone. Perfect. Unlike Romeo, Teddy didn't even have his earbuds in; he kind of liked the chaotic rumble of hundreds of background conversations and gate announcements. Airports were fun for people-watching, and the later their flight was, the longer he had to psych himself up for interacting with Joyce Alexander.

"It's going to be really late when we get there."

Teddy looked up from his book. "Not *that* late. It's two hours earlier there."

"Late enough, by the time we get out of the airport and ride to our hotel. Sea-Tac's not especially close to downtown Seattle, you know." He waved his phone, apparently as a form of proof, but Teddy couldn't see the screen.

"Did you have plans to meet up with someone there?"

"No."

"Do you turn into a pumpkin after midnight Central time?"

"No."

"Then what difference does it make *when* we get there, as long as we get there before our meeting in the morning?" Teddy didn't travel often, but when he did, he tended to go with the flow. He couldn't control weather or flight schedules, so he might as well sit comfortably and wait instead of stressing.

"We'll be tired."

"You can sleep on the plane."

Romeo shook his head. "Not gonna happen."

"Well, unless you have a line on a private jet that can whisk us away right now, there's nothing we can do about it. Seattle is famous for coffee, right? We'll mainline some in the morning."

Ordinarily, Teddy might also have been worried about being too tired to function well. He and Romeo had remained at the office very late last night—outlasting even Imani—as they prepared materials for their presentation. But Teddy was too keyed up to feel sleepy.

Before Romeo could start complaining about anything else, Teddy pointedly turned his attention back to his Kindle. He was reading Tab Hunter's autobiography, mainly because Romeo had gotten him thinking about the fifties. Man, that must have been an interesting time—a box office star who was also gay during a time when people had to hide it. If Teddy had been in Hollywood back then, would he have found a way to cozy up with the rich and famous? Probably not. He would have probably worked in a store somewhere. Ooh, but the fashions! Those broad-shouldered suit coats and snazzy hats, the saddle shoes, the—

"Do you think it'll be much longer?"

This time Teddy didn't even look up from his book. "Dunno. Why don't you go find something to eat?"

"I'm not hungry."

"You don't have to be hungry to enjoy airport food. Or you can buy something for later."

Romeo shook his head.

Before Teddy could respond appropriately, the gate attendant gave a nearly inaudible announcement. Their plane was finally ready to go. Thank goodness. But despite all the griping, Romeo didn't look happy.

Skyler had warned them they'd be traveling on a tight budget but had ponied up the extra fifteen bucks each to get them priority boarding. Stepping into the plane after a three-hour delay, they had their pick of seats.

"So where are we supposed to sit?" Romeo looked confused as he scanned the interior. Obviously he was too high-and-mighty to be familiar with discount airlines.

"Anywhere we want. Why don't you grab that window seat?"

Oblivious to the impatient line behind them, Romeo stayed put. "I'd prefer the aisle, please. More legroom."

Teddy rolled his eyes at the subtle dig over his height

and scooted in. Fine. He liked the window better anyway. He buckled up and watched Romeo settle in. They'd scored big: the flight wasn't full, so they got to keep a vacant seat between them. Teddy looked forward to spreading out once they were in the air. He didn't even sigh too heavily when a young woman with an infant and preschooler occupied the row across the aisle. Maybe the kids would sleep.

It seemed to take everyone an inordinate amount of time to get situated. Teddy was going to complain, but then he noticed Romeo's tight jaw and bouncing knee. He was also intermittently scratching his bottom lip. When the flight attendant did his safety spiel, Romeo fixed his full attention on the guy, even going so far as to consult the safety card in the seat pocket in front of him.

Crap. Romeo hadn't just been aloof in the airport—he was nervous.

"Want a donut?" Teddy held the open bag toward him.

"No. Thanks."

"They don't feed you on this airline, you know. Just drinks and pretzels. Did you buy something to eat?"

"I'm not hungry."

Teddy put the bag away since he wasn't really hungry either, and examined his seatmate more closely. Romeo was gripping the armrests tightly enough to turn his knuckles white, and that was definitely a bead of sweat near his hairline. He looked like a man about to face a firing squad.

"I dated a flight attendant," Teddy announced.

Romeo turned his head and blinked at him. "What?"

"Flight attendant. It sounds really exciting, doesn't it? I thought so anyway. Also he was really hot—way out of my league, actually. But I was working retail at the time, and our schedules hardly ever meshed, and when Gregory *was* in town he was always jet-lagged. So it didn't work out. He told me a lot of great stories, though."

"Like what?"

Teddy launched into a few of his favorites, such as the couple who'd attempted to join the mile high club and got stuck in the lavatory, the guy who'd tried to board an alligator as his alleged support animal, and the high school choir that serenaded the entire plane for a large portion of the flight. They were good stories, and Teddy told them with all the details he could remember. Romeo didn't even seem to notice when they took off.

"Do you wish things had worked out for you two?" Romeo asked eventually.

"Eh. Not really. Sure, it was fun, but I'm not the relationship type."

"You'd rather play the field?"

"Yeah."

That was a lie. Teddy had spent almost no time in the field either before meeting Gregory or after their breakup. He'd swipe right every now and then, sure, but he worked long hours and didn't have time for complications and entanglements.

"All that true-love stuff?" Teddy continued. "I guess it works out for a few people, but they're the minority. They're like those women who dance around in tampon ads, cramp-free and wearing all white. Maybe there are some women who do that on their period, but I've never met one, and the ads create unrealistic expectations. True love is a marketing ploy."

"What about Lauren's mother?"

"Well, ask me again in six months."

Romeo looked at him for a long moment, nodded, and bent over his phone. He seemed more relaxed now. Mission accomplished, even if Teddy had expounded rather more than he'd intended. He buried his nose in his Kindle. Tab Hunter was waiting for him.

The flight attendant arrived soon afterward to take drink orders. "Um, Scotch?" Romeo said, as if he weren't sure.

"Sure," she said. "Seven dollars, credit card only."

Romeo squirmed to remove his wallet from his rear pocket. As he handed over the card, he cut his eyes in Teddy's direction. "I'm paying for him too."

Teddy hadn't expected that. "No booze for me, thanks. Just two bottles of Bloody Mary mix, please."

After the flight attendant completed the transaction and moved on, Romeo looked at Teddy. "Are there rules against drinking on a business trip?" He seemed serious, which was weird.

"I don't think so. I mean, you should probably be sober when you meet Joyce Alexander, but that won't be until tomorrow." He sighed. "It's just me. I'm the world's biggest lightweight. One drink and I'm incoherent, two and I'm out cold." A lesson he learned young and hard.

"Oh."

The baby across the aisle had been fussing sporadically

since takeoff and now erupted into wails. The mom's efforts to soothe him with a pacifier didn't appear to help. The little girl, meanwhile, was wiggling in her seat, sending crayons rolling off her tray table and into oblivion. "Mommy, I have to go potty!" she stage-whispered. Her mother looked at her, looked at the flailing baby in her arms, and seemed ready to burst into tears herself.

Romeo leaned across the aisle. "Ma'am? If you'd like, I can hold the baby while you help your daughter." His face held a gentle smile that Teddy had never seen on him before.

"Are you sure?" the woman asked. "He's throwing a fit."

"I think I'll survive. I've seen worse."

Teddy stared, openmouthed, as Romeo stood and carefully took the baby. The woman hurried toward the lavatory with the little girl, and Romeo stood there in his five-hundred-dollar suit, bouncing the baby on his shoulder. Possibly just as shocked as Teddy, the baby stopped crying. He started poking at Romeo's face instead, and when Romeo pretended to gobble the baby's fingers, the kid actually burst into giggles.

The mother returned with her daughter five minutes later. By then Romeo and the baby were besties, with Romeo making a series of ridiculous noises that made the baby laugh so hard he was hiccupping. Romeo was laughing too, and Jesus, he looked gorgeous. Teddy was pretty sure he'd never heard him laugh before, but right now it looked entirely natural on him, as if it were something he should be doing all the time. He seemed almost reluctant to hand the baby back.

"Thank you so much," said the woman.

"Hey, it was no problem. He's a great little guy." Romeo turned his charm toward the little girl. "I bet when he's a little older, you're going to show him all the ropes. Teach him how to do things right."

The girl puffed out her chest. "I'm gonna show him how to color. Right now he eats the crayons."

"Crayons taste nasty."

Argh. Romeo was even more adorable when he wrinkled up his nose like that.

The family resettled with the little girl in the aisle seat, and she and Romeo commenced a deep conversation. They consulted about sticker placement in her Disney activity book and shared some of her pretzels. With her mother's permission, Romeo let her watch a few cartoons on his phone.

The baby fell asleep, and the flight attendant gave Romeo a pack of free drink coupons. The mother gazed at Romeo as if contemplating a nomination for sainthood. And Teddy ignored his Kindle to stare at Romeo, amazed for the remainder of the flight at the transformation from antisocial pedant to kind, playful young man. Where had this version of Romeo been hiding for the past year?

The tension returned to Romeo's body as the plane prepared to land. They bounced slightly harder than usual, and he clenched his jaw so tight that it hurt to look at him.

But then they were taxiing in and pretty soon Teddy and Romeo were through the Jetway and headed toward the airport exit, their luggage rolling behind them. Romeo walked fast. Teddy could have asked him to slow down, but that was too humiliating, so he hurried instead, dodging oblivious travelers as best he could.

The rideshare pickup zone at Sea-Tac Airport was a confusing area inside the parking garage. People clustered with phones and suitcases while an endless line of cars pulled into and out of numbered bays. Waiting for their Lyft to arrive, Teddy nearly got run over three times as he spun around to watch the activity. He played a little mental game, trying to see if he could guess each person's hometown from their clothing. The ones with the heavy parkas and knit hats were probably visitors from the Midwest or East Coast, while the ones in expensive rain gear were likely locals. And that unfortunate young couple shivering nearby—the girl in yoga pants and light sweater, the guy in khaki shorts and a sweatshirt—had to be from California.

Romeo was an island of quiet among the chaos, tracking their driver on his phone.

Teddy had just survived a minor collision with a middle-aged woman's purple roller bag when Romeo finally looked up. "He's pulling into number twenty-four."

As it turned out, getting there required maneuvering through more traffic, both human and motorized. But their efforts were rewarded by a turbaned man in a silver Prius, who greeted them with a smile and helped stuff their luggage into the trunk. Romeo slid into the backseat, and Teddy sat in the front. He liked to chat with his drivers.

Ajeet was originally from Varanasi, a city in Northern India, but had lived in Montreal for eight years before relocating to Seattle two years ago. He was working on a doctorate in history with a specialty in comparative colonialisms, much to the dismay of parents who wanted him to be a physician or engineer. But his girlfriend, a law student, was very supportive. Somehow the topic of Alaska came up, which caused Ajeet some confusion—Was it a city? Was it near New York?—and Teddy had a fun time explaining it.

Their downtown hotel had a pleasant lobby, not too fancy, but with some nice modern touches that complemented the old building's classic bones. Teddy would have introduced a few more splashes of color to counteract the gray Seattle days, but at least the designers hadn't tried to make the midlevel property look fancier than it was.

"Romeo Blue," his coworker said to the blonde woman at the reception desk. She didn't bat an eye, so points for her. After clacking at her computer for a moment, she smiled. "Ah, yes, there we go. One standard room for two guests and two nights."

"One guest," Romeo corrected.

"Oh, I'm sorry! It says two. No problem, though. We have a credit card on file, so here you go." She handed him a little paper sleeve containing the room key before turning her smile to Teddy. "And your name, sir?"

"Teddy Spenser." He spelled the last name because nobody ever got the second *s* right.

The woman frowned. "I have your name, but it's showing you on the same reservation as Mr. Blue."

"Well, the same person made them and they're on the same credit card. But we have two rooms."

A long pause followed, made more ominous by her deepening frown as she worked the keyboard. "I'm sorry," she finally said. "We have a reservation for both of you in one room."

Teddy considered calling Skyler, but it was already late in Chicago. "I guess you can put my room on my credit card until tomorrow, when we can get this straightened out."

"But you don't understand, sir. We're fully booked. There are no other rooms."

Shit. "Okay. Then can you recommend another hotel in the same price range?"

She sighed. "I can try, but it won't do any good. There are three big conferences in town this week. The whole city's at capacity—and even if I found something, the rates would be sky-high."

Teddy and Romeo exchanged dismal looks. But Teddy was a professional, and he was going to meet Joyce Alexander in the morning, so he needed to act like an adult. Dammit. "Fine," he told her. "But let me know if a room opens up. Maybe you'll have a cancellation."

"Of course. I'll make a note of it." She gave him a key too, but without the little paper sleeve.

Romeo and Teddy rode the elevator to the eighth floor

in silence. *I can handle this*, Teddy coached himself silently. It was just for a couple of nights, and they'd probably be so busy that they'd spend little time at the hotel anyway. At least Romeo wasn't throwing a tantrum about being stuck with him, which was a small surprise. And it wasn't as if the guy was a chatty Cathy. Plus they each had plenty of work to do when they weren't in a meeting. They could stake out their respective spots in the room, hunker over their laptops, and ignore each other. It would give Romeo a taste of what it was like away from the rarified air of a private office.

Yes, Teddy concluded as they trundled down the eighth-floor hallway, he could handle this. It was no big deal.

Then Romeo unlocked the door. They both entered—and saw the one and only bed.

Chapter Six

They stared at that bed for a long time, as if it might magically morph from one king size into a pair of doubles. Teddy moved to a different spot in the room, but that didn't help either—still only one bed. And nothing changed when Romeo set his suit bag on a chair and scratched his lip.

Teddy used the room phone to call the front desk and was informed that no rooms with two beds were available. The clerk sounded slightly annoyed that he'd asked.

Teddy hung up with a sigh. "I could call Skyler." Even as he made the suggestion, he knew it was useless.

"Skyler won't be able to help."

"Maybe...the clerk was wrong. I bet I could find a room somewhere."

They whipped out their phones and tapped away as if in a competition. The outcome proved to be a tie: both dropped their hands in defeat at almost exactly the same time. The clerk had not been wrong. Apart from dodgy motels in the suburbs and a couple of suites with prices higher than the Space Needle, there was not a room to be found.

"Not even a manger," Teddy moaned.

For some reason, that seemed to make Romeo angry. "It won't kill you to share with me. I don't have cooties."

If someone had waved an honesty wand over Teddy's head at that moment, he would have admitted that cooties were hardly his worry. His real concern was getting up close and personal with a coworker who annoyed the hell out of him—and was distressingly hot. Who had also recently proven himself to not be an asshole, at least when it came to helping mothers on airplanes and charming small children. But no honesty wand appeared, so Teddy scowled instead.

"I'm hungry," he announced and headed toward the door.

It wasn't raining, just sort of heavily misting, which still made extended walking unpleasant. Teddy and Romeo quickly agreed on one of the first restaurants they came to. It turned out to be an upscale steakhouse with a long gleaming bar, heart-stopping prices, and dim mood lighting. It was the last of these that bothered Teddy the most, but as they sat in their plush booth with menus in hand, he focused on the numbers beside the dollar signs. "I don't know if this place is in our budget."

Romeo waved a hand dismissively. "We skipped lunch, and Lauren's springing for only one room. She can buy us some prime rib."

"They want over a hundred bucks for a four-ounce steak!"

"So don't get the Japanese beef."

The waiter came by then, stopping any further arguments. Teddy ordered a seventeen-dollar Manhattan with an absinthe wash. He'd sip it slowly so he didn't get wasted. Romeo stuck to water, which was irritating.

All around them, couples carried on hushed conversations, silverware clinked against plates, and waitstaff glided between the tables. This was the kind of restaurant to impress a date or to celebrate anniversaries and promotions. It wasn't really Teddy's type of place, and certainly he and Gregory had never eaten anywhere so upscale. Gregory always claimed to be too busy, and Teddy was always too broke.

Romeo was scratching his lip again. Next time Teddy went by a drugstore, he was going to pick up some Chap-Stick and hand it over. Or maybe Burt's Bees—that stuff was great. But then Teddy had a brief but clear mental image of smoothing that balm onto those lips and... No. Danger. That was a no-fly zone for sure.

His drink arrived and he took several large gulps.

Romeo cleared his throat, breaking the long silence. "What do you think this Joyce Alexander woman wants from us?"

Teddy had been giving this considerable thought. "I guess she wants to hear about my designs and your..."

"Coding."

"Right."

"We could have discussed it via email. Or Skype."

"Maybe she's a Luddite." Teddy crunched up his face. "No, that doesn't make sense. If she was, she'd never consider backing smart vases. I don't know what she wants."

Teddy shrugged.

Romeo looked quietly panicked, but before he could say anything more, their food arrived. Teddy had ordered a petite filet mignon—American beef, so it wasn't quite his monthly rent—and a baked potato. The steak was delicious, possibly the best he'd ever eaten, in fact. "That's weird."

"What?" Romeo glanced up, fork hovering over his New York strip.

"We're from Chicago, right? Hog-butcher to the world, yadda yadda. You'd think our famous Midwestern beef would beat Seattle's, but this is amazing. I'm definitely going to have to try seafood while we're here, and if I discover that we have superior salmon back home, then I'll know I've been transported to Opposite Land. And that would be good because it means I'm about to become rich and successful and beloved by all. And you're going to turn frumpy and—" Oops. That was more than he'd meant to say. He employed a mouthful of potato to shut himself up.

Romeo, hand still in midair, was staring at him with his head cocked. "You don't think you're successful now?"

"You've seen my cubicle. And my scooter."

"I think your cubicle looks nice." Then it was Romeo's turn to hurriedly shovel food into his mouth.

Teddy had no idea what to make of that. He was surprised that Romeo had even noticed his cubicle décor, let alone admired it. Well, he might as well take the compliment at face value. "Thank you. Your style is, um, more minimalist."

"No, I like...nice stuff. Like you have."

"But your office?"

Romeo ducked his head. "I get distracted easily. That's why Lauren stuck me in an office to begin with. So I can concentrate on my work."

Stuck him in an office. It had never occurred to Teddy that Romeo might view his private space as a punishment rather than a perk. It meant that Romeo got left out of the office banter and the spontaneous give-and-take sessions everyone else engaged in. When Skyler told a joke or Imani did a spot-on impression of a politician or celebrity, Romeo missed out. And when the rest of the crowd got restless at the end of a long Friday and decamped en masse for a bar, nobody thought to pop their head into Romeo's office and invite him along.

An unfamiliar emotion settled heavily in Teddy's stomach, and he realized it was guilt. "Maybe you could just paint the walls an interesting color and get a nice light fixture. That wouldn't be too distracting, would it?"

Romeo's answering smile—small, sweet, and tentative—took Teddy's leaden guilt, gave it wings, and sent it fluttering into his heart as something else altogether. Something he absolutely did not want. He gave the re-

mains of his steak a vicious stab with his fork, but that
didn't help.

They didn't speak much as they finished the meal, and
neither of them wanted a twenty-dollar slice of cake for
dessert, so they settled the bill and started silently back
to the hotel. The mist had intensified into a cold drizzle
that found its way down the back of Teddy's neck despite
his popped collar. He should have brought his parka, but
he'd figured it would be overkill for Seattle's moderate
temperatures. Besides, two weeks ago at a thrift shop
he'd scored a Todd Snyder tweed windowpane topcoat
that was infinitely more stylish. He wanted to look good
for Joyce Alexander.

"I'll sleep on the love seat if it bothers you that much."

Teddy blinked raindrops from his eyelashes as he
looked up at Romeo. "What?"

"You look like you're marching to your doom. But
there's a love seat in our room. If I use that little table as
an ottoman I could sleep there."

"You are way too tall to sleep on the love seat."

"You want the love seat then?"

"We can share the bed, Romeo. It's big."

Which sounded sensible enough as they were entering
the lobby. But then Teddy had to stand close to Romeo
in the elevator and smell his cologne, which was subtle
and fruity and actually might have been just his shampoo. And as they walked down the hallway, the brush
of fabric as Romeo swung his arms against the body of
his trench coat reminded Teddy of the sound of rus-
tling bedsheets. Finally, inside the room, Teddy saw the

moisture glistening like faceted gems in Romeo's close-cropped dark curls.

Maybe the love seat wasn't such a bad idea after all. But a quick glance confirmed Teddy's fears: it was far too small even for him, and the squishy cushions would kill his back. Bed it was. Luckily he was exhausted and a little tipsy and would probably fall asleep quickly in spite of everything. "I'm gonna turn in. Big day tomorrow."

"I have some work to do first. But I can take my laptop down to the lobby."

Teddy gestured at the desk. "Stay here. You won't bother me." Over the past decade, he'd shared space with roommates who liked to blast music in the wee hours, and he'd lived in apartments with so little soundproofing he'd yell *"Bless you"* when his neighbor sneezed. His current studio was fairly quiet, but light leaked in under the door to the corridor and around the curtains no matter what he tried. A little tip-tapping at a computer was no big deal.

"Thanks." Romeo gave him another of those smiles, as if Teddy had granted him a huge favor. With no meat to stab, Teddy opted to hurry into the bathroom instead.

By the time he emerged, brushed, washed, and co-cooned in a pair of corgi-print flannel pajamas, Romeo was already seated at the desk and peering at his screen. He turned around to look at Teddy but then made a weird little squeak and quickly swung away.

"Sorry," Teddy said as he hurried to the bed. "Didn't mean to interrupt. I'll be asleep in minutes, though, and I've been assured I don't snore."

Without taking his eyes off the screen, Romeo nodded.

The bed was amazing. Back home, Teddy slept on a double-bed mattress long past its prime. His bedding was cute—teal peacocks in warm months; cranberry toile flannel in cold—but inexpensive and a little threadbare. Plus he didn't have a zillion pillows. Now he arranged everything carefully, noting the acres of space between himself and what would be Romeo's spot, and snuggled under the duvet. The only light in the room came from Romeo's screen, and most of that was blocked by his body.

Perfect. Comfortable, cozy, and he'd barely even notice he was sharing the bed. He probably wouldn't even wake up when Romeo joined him.

Except Teddy couldn't fall asleep. His eyelids kept stubbornly opening, his gaze turning to the figure bent over the desk. Wide shoulders. A vulnerable-looking nape, where the skin was undoubtedly as soft as expensive suede. Long fingers that kept rising up from the keyboard to rub a spot just in front of one ear or scratch at those lips.

Oh, dear. Teddy suppressed a groan. This was going to be harder than he thought.

Chapter Seven

Thanks to the time difference, an early bedtime, and nerves, Teddy woke up unreasonably early. Instead of doing something sensible like getting out of bed, he rolled over to look at Romeo, who was still fast asleep.

Big mistake.

With his lips slightly parted and his long eyelashes fanned over his cheekbones, Romeo looked young and innocent and beautiful, a mythological god taken from a painting and brought to life. Only he was neither a god nor an art piece, but rather a living, breathing human being. A coworker. The irritating computer guy with the office. Only…it turned out he wasn't as irritating as Teddy had thought.

Teddy slid out of bed and padded over to the drawer

containing his clothing, groped in the dim light for his exercise outfit, then slipped into the bathroom to change. Romeo was still sleeping when Teddy crept out of the room in search of the fitness center.

When he returned nearly an hour later, sweaty and famished, he intended to head directly to the shower. But he stopped in his tracks when he entered the room and discovered Romeo standing by the armoire wearing nothing but a pair of green-plaid boxer shorts. His hair was damp, and he threw a quick smile in Teddy's direction. "Wondered where you'd disappeared to."

"Exercise," Teddy managed to say. What he was thinking, however, was *Lord give me strength*. He generally wasn't a huge fan of boxers; few men could rock the look. Romeo, however, was the exception. Long, strong legs, full ass, flat belly—his choice of undergarments showcased them all. Even the colors were fine complements to his skin tone.

Apparently oblivious to Teddy's condition, Romeo nodded. "I should have known you worked out pretty religiously." Then his eyes widened and he clamped his mouth shut.

Not wanting to dive any deeper into that weirdness, Teddy scurried into the bathroom. It was only after showering, shaving, and brushing that he recognized a problem with getting dressed. He considered and rejected the idea of putting his grungy exercise wear back on and finally sighed and wrapped a towel around his waist. Creeping into the main room, he had a distressing flashback to the junior high locker room, where he'd lived in terror of being judged by his peers—he'd been a late bloomer—or even worse, popping a woody. Back then, he'd found creative ways to change without exposing too much skin and often hid strategically behind locker doors and pillars. Now here he was, a grown man, clutching a length of white terry cloth for all he was worth.

Romeo had put on slim-fitting black trousers and a crisp white shirt; an unknotted navy tie hung loosely around his neck. He'd been gazing out the window, but after he turned to look at Teddy, his eyebrows rose. "Is that what you're supposed to wear when meeting a famous fashion designer?" His expression was deadpan, and he'd never joked in Teddy's presence, so it took Teddy a moment to realize that Romeo was kidding.

"Yeah," Teddy replied with a grin. "It's the latest thing. Didn't you know?"

"So I'm overdressed."

"Afraid so. But it's okay because you look so damned good in everything."

Damn. Teddy had intended that last bit to be a continuation of their banter, but even as the words escaped his mouth, he knew how awkwardly they would land. Instead of frowning or looking annoyed, however, Romeo widened his eyes and then quickly looked away. Teddy tried to steer them back to safe ground. "I think I'll buck fashion and put on clothes too. It's a little chilly for towels."

"I'm sure you have an amazing outfit all ready to go."

Romeo still wasn't meeting Teddy's gaze, and now he sounded...wistful?

"Um, yeah."

Feeling ridiculous, Teddy gathered his clothing and took it into the bathroom. Once dressed, he fussed with his thick hair for an unusually long time. It was an uninteresting light brown, and the strands twisted into weird curls unless he attacked them with a lot of product. He also hadn't had time for a haircut before the trip, so the tapered fade on the sides was longer than ideal. Eventually, however, he and his pomade managed to tame the top into reasonable spikes. He just had to hope the mist wouldn't melt them.

Romeo was sitting on the bed with phone in hand when Teddy emerged. "Oh," said Romeo, looking pained.

"What?" Teddy looked down at himself, searching for a fashion faux pas.

"How do you—? Never mind."

"What?"

"How do you find such interesting stuff to wear? You always look so...interesting." Romeo winced, apparently at the awkward wording.

"Thrift stores, mostly."

"Seriously? You mean you walk into Goodwill and come out looking like you should be strolling down a runway?"

This wasn't a conversation Teddy had expected. Not even close. He took a moment to assess his current attire. Before packing, he'd spent a lot of time trying to decide what to wear when he met Joyce Alexander. He'd eventually settled on a fairly dressy vintage look: black trousers, white shirt, gray tie, black sweater-vest, close-fitting herringbone jacket. His bloodred boots with the pointed toes added a pop of color. He hoped he appeared hip and sophisticated.

"Slightly more upscale thrift than Goodwill," he finally answered. "But I don't know why you're so agog over it. My stereotype of computer guys is Dockers and monochrome Oxford shirts, but you always look sharp."

Romeo emitted a long, noisy sigh. "My mama and my sisters."

"Huh?"

"Mama and my sisters tell me what stores to go to. I find a salesclerk and beg for help." He looked distressed over the admission. Yet as soon as he'd said those words, the final remnants of Teddy's annoyance fled. Romeo wasn't an antisocial, arrogant asshole. He was sweet and...a little insecure. Teddy blushed with shame at his past shoddy treatment of Romeo. Clearly Teddy was the asshole.

"I think your mom and sisters are steering you well."

"Yeah?" Romeo picked up the end of his tie and let it drop. "But I'm so boring."

"No, you have a consistent professional look that works well for you. Can I offer you just one tiny bit of advice?"

Romeo gave him a wary look before nodding.

"Wear more green, Romeo. You look good in it."

Had they been meeting an ordinary person, Teddy and Romeo would probably have gone to her office or, if she didn't have an office, met at a restaurant. But Joyce Alexander was no ordinary person. She sent a gleaming silver Rolls Royce to pick them up.

"Holy shit," Romeo muttered as they climbed into the back seat. Teddy agreed.

The seats were upholstered in butter-soft gray leather with piping that matched the mulberry-colored carpeting. The dashboard and door interiors boasted lots of gleaming wood. Matching fold-down wooden trays were mounted on the seat backs in front of them. And although the car was probably from the fifties or sixties— Teddy wasn't savvy enough to place it more precisely—it looked showroom new. How much did a vehicle like this cost? A hell of a lot more than his scooter, that was for sure.

Riding through downtown Seattle felt like cruising slowly on an enormous yacht. At least, that's what Teddy imagined. He'd only been on three kinds of boats: canoes at Boy Scout camp when he was ten, the flat boats that took tourists up and down the Chicago River, and the large boats that offered dinner cruises in Lake Michigan. In any case, Teddy enjoyed today's journey, including the stares from people in other cars. It was the closest he'd come to feeling like a celebrity, and it was fun. It also helped distract him from his anxiety over meeting Joyce Alexander.

Romeo, on the other hand, wasn't pacified. In fact, he was a bundle of knee-shaking, lip-scratching nerves. He didn't even gaze out the window, preferring instead to stare at his fingers or his shoes.

"She's not even your idol," Teddy pointed out. "You never heard of her until the other day."

"So?" Now Romeo was rubbing a finger along the crease in his trousers.

"So why do you look like you need to breathe into a paper bag?"

Teddy heard Romeo swallow before answering. "I don't… I'm not very good at meeting with clients."

Oh. So it wasn't Joyce Alexander per se that had him going nuts, but rather the thought of meeting *anyone*. That wasn't something Teddy related to. His jobs had always involved a lot of human interaction, both when he worked in retail and, more recently, when he'd been able to put his design and marketing skills to use. He'd always enjoyed that aspect of his employment. How else were you supposed to know what the customer wanted if you didn't chat with them? Even better if you got to know them a little bit, because then you could take a stab at fulfilling desires they couldn't voice—desires they maybe weren't even aware of.

"I can try to do most of the talking, if you want. Unless she asks coding stuff. You're going to have to answer that, but you can probably pretty much let your presentation speak for itself, and I can deal with the basics."

Emotions washed over Romeo's face. Embarrassment was one of them, but so was raw gratitude. "Thanks," he muttered, dropping his gaze away from Teddy and back to his own hands.

The driver took them over a bridge, and Teddy gazed at the water below. A lake rather than an ocean bay, he suspected, but he wasn't sure. He hadn't studied Seattle's topography, and really, they could be heading anywhere at all. Maybe Joyce Alexander lived in a secret cave in the mountains—decorated stylishly, of course—or a mansion hidden deep in the forest. Either of those would suit her somewhat reclusive personality. Teddy spent a pleasant several minutes reflecting on where he would live if he had all the money in the world. He liked Chicago, so maybe he'd find himself a grand old estate in Lincoln Park. But what would he do, rattling around by himself inside thousands of square feet? Well, he could hire servants of course. And sleep in a different bedroom every night of the week. Hmm. Maybe a penthouse on Lake Shore Drive was a better option. The interior would be modern and sleek, and there would be a wide terrace where he'd host parties overlooking Lake Michigan. Imagine Gregory's expression when he saw Teddy's Instagram photos!

Okay. None of that was ever going to happen. Plus, Gregory could go fuck himself.

"Are you okay?"

Teddy blinked at Romeo. "Huh?"

"You sort of groaned just now."

"I'm…" Teddy's face heated as he tried to think of a plausible explanation that wouldn't make him sound pathetic. Fortunately, the car turned into a driveway and paused for a gate to open, which gave Teddy an escape. "Oh look, we're here."

Joyce Alexander lived in neither a cave nor a secret place in the woods. In fact, the neighborhood was fairly ordinary, if you considered multimillion-dollar homes ordinary. Her house turned out to be a huge one with white wooden siding, broad porches, and what seemed to be acres of preternaturally green lawns. The estate resembled photos Teddy had seen of the Hamptons. Which was the wrong coast entirely, but nevertheless...

The driver took them around to the back of the property, where stately evergreens towered above pavement. He stopped the car at the bottom of a concrete stairway. A tall middle-aged man stood there in a vintage Joyce Alexander suit, every silver hair carefully in place, his sculpted face expressionless. He might have been a statue, except when the driver got out and opened the car's back doors, the man gave Teddy and Romeo a tiny nod.

"Welcome, gentlemen. Please follow me."

Romeo looked as if he'd rather take a running leap into the nearby lake, and Teddy's stomach was doing its best to tap dance its way around his kidneys. But they trudged dutifully up the long set of stairs and wiped their shoes on a big mat before entering the house through double doors.

Although this was clearly the back entrance, it opened on to a big foyer with a marble floor, gold-striped wallpaper, and a huge crystal chandelier. They had a brief peek through an archway to a kitchen as their guide led them through a side doorway into a sunken seating area. He waved imperiously at a pair of delicate framed chairs upholstered in what looked like fluffy white sheepskin. They sat. "Ms. Alexander will be with you shortly." He swept out of the room.

"It's…white," Romeo said, low voiced.

That was entirely accurate. A plush white rug covered most of the highly polished light wood floor. The white walls contained deep square niches, each brightly lit and displaying a single crystal vase. The room's other two chairs were white brocade, the ornate coffee table clear Lucite, and a baroque silver-framed mirror hung over a white marble fireplace mantel. Instead of logs, the fireplace held an arrangement of large white crystals, as if flames had been turned to ice. White porcelain swans flanked the fireplace. A rounded alcove housed a sleek piano—not surprisingly, also white. And overhead, the glass chandelier was shaped like deer antlers.

"You should like it," Teddy said. "It reminds me of your office."

"My office isn't this shiny."

They sat in silence for what felt like hours. Teddy was tempted to play with his phone but kept it tucked away. Sometimes he stared at his slim leather messenger bag, which he'd leaned against his chair, but the bag wasn't very entertaining. Romeo fidgeted.

Then Joyce Alexander arrived, and Teddy understood her decorating scheme.

She alone provided the pop of color. Today she wore a floor-length dress of deep maroon set off by white lace. A wide embroidered ribbon ran under the bodice, creating an empire waist. The dress might have looked too youthful on most women in their seventies, and it would have seemed hopelessly retro on almost anyone, but Joyce Alexander carried it off. As she should, since it was one of her own designs. Her hair, cut in short waves, was as white as the surroundings, and her makeup was understated. Although she had lines on her face, she carried herself tall and straight, and she was stunning.

Teddy and Romeo had scrambled to their feet as soon as she arrived. For a moment Teddy considered wiping his sweaty palms on his pants, but he decided that was too obvious. He hoped his smile was less shaky than Romeo's.

"Welcome." Her voice was rich and musical, as if she were singing instead of talking. "Welcome to my home."

She shook Romeo's hand first and then Teddy's, smiling over their introductions. "Please, call me Joyce. Tea should arrive in a minute. Unless you'd prefer coffee?"

What Teddy would have preferred right at that moment was for his tongue to work properly. "Tea is great," he said in what he hoped was understandable English, and Romeo nodded stiffly.

"Please, have a seat." She took her place on one of the brocade chairs and waited for them to settle. "I hope you had a pleasant journey. Did you find suitable accommodations?"

Teddy thought about the one hotel bed and waking up so close to Romeo. But he managed a smile. "We did, thank you."

"I loathe hotels. All those strangers around you. Noises in the middle of the night, beds that are either too hard or too soft, plumbing that never suffices, awful towels… and the idea of dozens or even hundreds of rooms, each with the same floor plan and furniture and linens and ugly art—it's horrible."

Although Teddy didn't think cookie-cutter hotel rooms were one of the greater faults of modern civilization, he didn't argue. She could have said that the Hilton chain was part of a Satanic conspiracy, and he would have sat there on her weird, uncomfortable chair, grinning and bobbing his head. Because this was Joyce frigging *Alexander*, for God's sake.

She pushed her hair behind an ear, revealing a large diamond earring. "Well, that's enough small talk. I'm not fond of that either. I'm old and rich and a bit powerful in my own way, which means I can be rude if it suits me. It often does." A hint of humor played in her pale blue eyes, so Teddy couldn't tell if she was entirely serious.

For what was probably two or three minutes she simply sat there, head cocked the slightest bit, staring at them. Sweat formed at Teddy's nape and tickled down his back; it took enormous effort not to wiggle. Romeo, on the other hand, apparently couldn't resist fidgeting. He smoothed his trouser seam over and over until Teddy wanted to slap his hand and make him stop.

Maybe it would be best to simply dive into the presentation. Lauren had warned them to keep it simple, but Teddy had a spiel to recite and a sheaf of colorful, clever spec sheets and brochures to show off. He'd stayed up late preparing all of that. And Romeo had a PowerPoint presentation on steroids, complete with spinning images and buttons you could click for close-ups.

But what if she thought he was presumptuous for starting the presentation without her invitation? God, he didn't want to offend her right from the start.

Just as Teddy was opening his mouth to say something—God, *anything*—the silver-haired man entered with an improbably oversized tray. He set it on the coffee table with motions so smooth and precise that Teddy concluded the guy might be a robot. No human could have such impeccable hair, such a perfectly aged face, or such impossibly blue eyes.

"Thank you, darling," Joyce said.

The robot man smiled. "Anything else, my dear?" His voice sounded real enough.

"Not now, thank you."

The man sailed away, leaving Teddy to wonder at that *dear.* He was fairly certain most employees wouldn't use that term with their bosses, so who was the guy to Joyce?

She didn't seem inclined to shed any light on the matter, rising from her seat and pouring tea from a shiny silver pot into three delicate china cups. "They're rather plain, aren't they?" she asked, indicating the cups, which were white and unadorned.

Since she seemed to want an answer and Romeo looked blank, Teddy stepped in. "I guess you wouldn't want anything to compete with the pot itself. It's gorgeous."

That seemed to please her. "Precisely. This piece was created by Pavel Sazikov in 1834. And here we are, using and admiring it nearly two centuries later. That's a hallmark of good design." She handed a cup and saucer to Romeo and another to Teddy before returning to her chair with her own tea. She spent some more time staring at them, this time over the rim of her cup. Romeo made a tiny clattering sound—his hand shaking the porcelain—and Teddy sipped the hot liquid and tried not to burn his tongue. The drink tasted like yard clippings and incense.

"So…" Joyce set her cup on a tiny table beside her. She hadn't actually drunk any of the stuff. "Tell me about your project."

Teddy and Romeo exchanged brief panicked looks. They had spent hours preparing, but now that felt like too little. They could have discussed this more, maybe during the flight or over dinner last night. Too late now. Joyce waited expectantly. Since Romeo still couldn't seem to find any words, Teddy searched for some of his own, trying to remember the speech he'd agonized over creating.

"People have been sticking cut flowers in water for at least a couple of thousand years. Styles have changed, but the basic technology hasn't—we're still doing things the way the Etruscans did. Our vase revolutionizes that by incorporating modern technology. Consumers can change its look to match their moods or the day's latest trends. This makes it a good option for people who have limited storage and so can't really buy lots of different pieces. That's a versatility nobody else can offer. The design is sleek and clever but not intrusive. But there's more. Our vase can also offer useful information such as weather reports, news headlines, or text notifications. Very handy when you don't have your phone nearby.

And finally, our vase includes a probe that checks the chemistry of the water and of the flowers themselves and gives consumers feedback on how to prolong the life of the bouquet."

There. That wasn't a bad spiel. "Do you have questions about the specs or the costs? Romeo has a video thing, and I have brochures." He started to reach for his messenger bag but stopped himself.

Joyce remained expressionless. Which was better than frowning or making a ward-evil sign, but not as good as throwing stacks of money at him. Jesus, time stretched in weird ways in this house, and every minute felt like an hour. Teddy would look far older than the silver-haired man by the time this meeting finished.

After taking more decades to smooth a bit of lace on her dress, Joyce turned her gaze to Romeo. "And how about you?"

He sat up straighter, nearly spilling the tea. "I'm on the tech end. I design—"

"Yes, I know. I want you to tell me about your project."

"Um, I have a pres—"

"In *your* words. Without the electronic bells and whistles."

"Oh." Romeo took a deep breath and looked up at the ceiling, as if inspiration—or cue cards—might be hanging there. When he let the breath out again, it sounded like a sigh.

"The main innovation here is how we're using information. I mean, images, push notifications, chemical analyses—you can find those lots of places, right? But not in this combination, and not for this particular use. The interface is totally intuitive, so there's no learning curve at all. Nobody's going to be scared off by complicated apps. It runs smoothly as an integrated whole."

That was a lot of words for Romeo. More than he usually said in Teddy's presence over an entire day, in fact. Romeo even added a few more. "If you'd like to see a detailed video, it'll explain a lot."

But Joyce didn't seem any more impressed than she had been by Teddy's speech. She stared some more. Then she stood. "I'm going to need a little time. Please make yourselves comfortable. Would you like more tea while you wait?"

If Teddy drank more tea, he'd need a bathroom-finding expedition, and he didn't quite have the courage to admit to Joyce Alexander that he had to pee. He realized this was stupid. She had to realize that he urinated; he wasn't a robot, for God's sake. But it still felt too weird to call attention to it.

"We're fine," he said with an attempt at a calm smile.

Teddy was hoping the magic time stretching would end when she left, but it didn't. The tea cooled in his cup while Romeo fidgeted. "You know, you didn't even mention flowers," Teddy pointed out at last. "Or water. You didn't even say the word *vase*. You just talked about software."

"You went on about Etruscans."

"I mentioned them once. That's not *going on*."

Romeo humphed. "And you sounded like an infomercial. 'But wait! That's not all! We'll even throw in these Ginsu knives!'"

"You're not old enough to have seen Ginsu commercials."

"I *have* seen them. There's this little thing called the internet? YouTube? You were probably too busy with your Etruscan pals to notice."

It wasn't professional to kick your coworker during a meeting at Joyce Alexander's house, unfortunately. Teddy had to settle for an evil glare, which Romeo avoided by staring at the crystals in the fireplace. Coward.

Time dragged on. Was this how product pitches usually proceeded, at least when the pitchee was a slightly eccentric celebrity? And what exactly was Joyce doing? Maybe she was deep in consultations with lawyers and accountants. Or maybe she was on the phone with Lauren, chewing her out for sending such a pair of incompetents.

He poked gently at his messenger case, in which his brochures and spec sheets huddled, unwanted and unloved. They were pretty great too, with witty wording and with color schemes and graphics that referred to Googie design concepts without pushing the theme too hard. He'd even included a couple of sly, subtle hints of Joyce Alexander's aesthetic in hopes to influence her subliminally.

Teddy couldn't sit a moment longer. Although Joyce hadn't ordered them to keep their seats, she also hadn't invited them to leave the room. So, hoping he wasn't making a terrible breach of etiquette, Teddy rose and wandered the room, pausing to visually examine the decorations. Every one of her crystal doodads was worth a fortune, and that didn't count the luxurious piano and designer furniture. Teddy had never particularly entertained dreams of wealth—he wanted comfort and relevance, not decadence—but he paused for a bit to consider what he might buy if he had piles of money at his disposal.

A bigger home, a car instead of a scooter. A huge closet filled with clothes. He'd still haunt thrift shops, because that was more fun and challenging and sustainable than buying new. Mmm, but he'd probably buy a bunch of new footwear, like those amazing boots he'd spied in a store window last week. Gorgeous things with—

"What are you doing?" Romeo hissed from his chair.

"Nothing. Just looking."

"Don't touch anything."

"I'm not six years old, Romeo. I can control my impulses, and I know how to look with my eyes and not with my fingers."

The skeptical look in response deserved a retort, but getting into an argument in Joyce's house wasn't wise. It could wait until they were back at the hotel, hopefully after Joyce's promise to back the project.

After a few more tours of the room, Teddy sat down again. He unlocked his phone and opened Instagram, wondering how Gregory would react if Teddy posted a photo from Joyce Alexander's house. Except Gregory didn't follow him on social media, so he'd never know.

He tucked the phone away and picked up his teacup and saucer instead, seeking some neutral activity for his hands.

At long last Joyce returned, holding a slim silver pen and a small notebook covered in one of her signature fabrics. Teddy couldn't read her expression as she sat down, arranged her skirt, and opened the notebook.

"I have concerns," she said. The pen point hovered over a page.

Teddy's stomach clenched into a queasy ball. *Concerns* was even worse than *complications*. He waved feebly at his messenger bag. "I can show you some of the results from our focus groups. We gathered a lot of good feedback there."

"I have all the specs," Romeo offered. He waved his phone. "And the video with mock-ups of the software."

But she gave her head a tiny shake. "My concerns aren't about the vase itself. They're about the two of you. I have no doubts you're each very talented, but together? In order for a design to work, the patterns must complement one another. I'm fearing that you simply clash."

While Joyce seemed distressed by her announcement, and Romeo was looking down at his own feet and scratching his lip, Teddy felt like he might burst into tears or throw up, or possibly both. He lurched to his feet and unsteadily set the cup and saucer on the table beside the stupid antique pot that would probably cost him six months' rent.

"I'll, uh, call for a Lyft," he mumbled and started for the door.

Joyce stood, blocking his way. "Wait! You mustn't give up so easily."

"But—"

"I said I have concerns. And I do. But that's not the same as rejecting the project altogether. I need more information." She nodded toward Romeo. "More data, yes? Then I can make my final decision."

Teddy's lungs eased enough that passing out seemed less of a possibility, although puking was definitely still an option. "Data?" he squeaked.

Joyce broke into a wide smile. "Gentlemen, I propose a test."

Chapter Eight

Teddy had always hated tests. Back when he was a student, just thinking about them made him sick to his stomach, and by the time the exams actually rolled around, he was lucky to keep his breakfast down. Worse, no matter how hard he studied and how well he knew the subject, his mind inevitably went blank as soon as he picked up a pencil. The minute the test was over, everything flooded back with complete clarity.

He'd made it through school by busting his ass on all the assignments, grabbing every bit of extra credit, and praying to whichever gods would listen. In college, one of his professors had even taken pity on Teddy and given him special dispensation to take her exams as oral interviews rather than traditional written tests. He'd taken every class she offered and aced them all.

And now, with Joyce Alexander grinning expectantly at him, Teddy was disheartened to realize he wasn't over his terror of tests.

"Test?" Romeo didn't seem put off by the idea—in fact, he appeared more eager than he had all day. "Sure, I can tell you anything you want to know."

"I'm sure you can, darling. But that wasn't the sort of test I was referring to. Think of this as more of a trial, if you will. An assessment."

"We can get a physical mock-up of the product to you within a few days if you—"

She held up a hand, her perfectly manicured nails sparkling in the light. "Not an assessment of the vase. An assessment of *you*. Both of you."

That sounded about as horrifying as an algebra quiz, but Teddy attempted to maintain a calm facade. "Do you have reservations about our credentials? I know we're both pretty new to this kind of business, but Lauren chose us out of hundreds of applicants because she's confident we have the right skills." He said this proudly; getting this job offer had been a high point of his life. Romeo perhaps felt the same way, because he nodded eagerly.

But Joyce waved her hands. "It's not your qualifications that concern me. Gentlemen, I am ancient. No, don't shake your heads politely. I could be your grandmother, and I am not ashamed of my age. I have used my years well and learned a great deal. So I can tell you with considerable experience that it takes more than good credentials to create success. It takes, well, chemistry. And perhaps even a sprinkle of magic."

If anyone else on the planet had said that, they would have sounded delusional. But this was Joyce Alexander—resplendent in her beautiful dress, inside her beautiful home—and she could get away with it. Teddy found himself agreeing with her even though he didn't exactly understand what she was planning. What she said applied perfectly to the design world. If the components of a design were merely suitable, the result would be acceptable but boring. But if those components played off one another well and if the stars aligned just right? That's when you ended up with something spectacular. Memorable.

"What do you want us to do?" Teddy asked.

She gave his shoulder a gentle squeeze. "Now, that's what I like to hear! Gentlemen, I've devised a list of three key characteristics I'm looking for. I'm going to give you tasks to demonstrate each of them. And to keep the tests a bit more neutral—and, frankly, more interesting—I'm not going to name the characteristics until the tasks are complete."

Romeo's brow was furrowed. "So...you're going to see if we can do things correctly but you're not going to give us your standards or criteria beforehand?"

"Yes."

"I don't see how we can possibly succeed if we don't know what we're trying to do."

"What you're trying to do, darling, is your best. I sincerely hope that's enough."

★ ★ ★

Neither of them spoke during the ride back to the hotel. Teddy wanted to speak—he had a *lot* to say—but kept his mouth zipped due to the driver's presence. Romeo stared out his window expressionlessly. He didn't even fidget or pick at his lip.

Wordlessly, Teddy and Romeo got into the hotel elevator and went to their room. Once inside, they simultaneously reached for their phones, but Teddy won that particular duel. Lauren's phone rang only once before she picked up.

"Calming breaths, Teddy," she said over the speaker.

"You spoke to her already." He wasn't sure whether to be alarmed or comforted by this.

"Yep. We had a good chat."

"Um…good?"

He waited for Lauren to give more specifics, but she remained silent. Romeo tried to grab the phone away, and Teddy had to do an awkward little twist-dive to avoid him. "We left the brochures and stuff with her, but I doubt she's going to look at them. They're probably already chucked into her sterling silver recycling bin."

"I told you our success was going to rely on you and Romeo and not the promo materials."

Great. "What kind of test is she giving us?" Teddy demanded, hoping there was no hint of a whine.

"I can't tell you. I promised her. It wouldn't be fair. Just follow her instructions, okay?"

He wanted to point out that it also wasn't fair to be tested when he didn't know on what or according to which rubric, but he glared at Romeo instead. Romeo glared back.

Teddy sighed. "How long is this going to take?"

"Three more days. Skyler's changed your plane and hotel reservations. Can you stay in Seattle that long, or is there something you need to get back home for right away?"

A tiny apartment with drafty windows. A job that might or might not still exist when the week was up. A social life less exciting than his eighty-year-old grandmother's. "I guess not," he admitted.

"Okay, good. What about you, Romeo?"

Romeo shrugged. "I can stay."

That was interesting. Was his life as stripped-down as Teddy's? Maybe, but that train of thought could wait for later. Much later.

"Lauren, we ended up sharing a room, and there's only one bed. The hotel people said nothing else is available."

There was a long pause before she responded, and when she spoke, her tone was careful. "I'm sorry, guys. Is this a problem?"

Well, shit. If Teddy said it *was* a problem, he was going to look like a difficult little asshole. And anyway, sharing with Romeo wasn't painful. In fact, sharing a bed with Romeo was the opposite of painful, and that was the real problem.

Teddy took the coward's way out. "I'm fine," he said. "But Romeo might not be comfortable with it."

Romeo narrowed his eyes and crossed his arms. "I'm fine too!" he said emphatically.

"Good," she said. "Remember, we've got a lot at stake here. I want—we *all* want—Reddyflora to succeed."

"Yeah. I know." The weight of responsibility made his shoulders sag.

"So roll with the punches, okay? I need you guys to do your best. It'll be worth the hassle if Joyce backs us. And you guys will get juicy bonuses." Then she ended the call, leaving Teddy and Romeo to stare at each other.

"I'm not a prima donna," Romeo said. "And I don't think you have cooties. I'm an adult." He looked hurt, as if he'd been offended by the suggestion that he was too delicate to deal with Teddy's company.

"A lot of adult men would object to sharing a bed with another man. Especially with a gay man."

A hint of a smile tugged at Romeo's lips. "That's because they think they're irresistible. Like, just because a dude's into other dudes, that means he can't stop throwing himself at *all* other men. Especially straight ones."

Slowly blinking, Teddy felt realization dawn. It wasn't that Romeo had failed to ping Teddy's gaydar, but rather that Teddy hadn't thought about that aspect of him at all. Romeo was the annoying snob who'd claimed the second-most-prime office and who ruined Teddy's designs with bulky tech stuff. It was immaterial what— or rather, who—floated his boat. Except...over the past twenty-four hours, Teddy had learned that his previous assumptions about Romeo were off base. And hey, shock! Romeo was a human being with wants and needs. And desires.

"Are *you* into other dudes?" Teddy asked.

"Some of them."

A blush heated Teddy's skin. "I didn't mean—I wasn't trying to—"

"I'm pan. I've been attracted to people of various genders. Um, not that I've dated that many of them. I haven't…" He looked away as his voice trailed off.

"I get it. Work sucks up all of your time."

Although Romeo looked as if he wanted to say something, he just pressed his lips together and gave a small nod.

The conversation had gotten surprisingly personal, and it made Teddy uncomfortable. Anyway, they needed to be concentrating on Joyce and her mysterious tests.

"I'm glad you're understanding. I promise I'm not going to sexually harass you. I'm not interested in anyone anyway."

Romeo tilted his head. "But you said—"

"I'm done with anything remotely resembling romance. It never works out for me. I'm spending the next five to ten years focusing entirely on my career, and I can worry about love later, when I'm established." He'd made that resolution shortly after Gregory broke up with him, and it had made a lot of sense at the time. It *still* made a lot of sense. Romance was overrated—fine for Hallmark movies, yes, but this was real life, where True Love was about as practical and attainable as pet unicorns.

"You can't do both?" Romeo asked. "I mean, people do manage to have work and personal lives."

"I don't." Teddy hadn't yet removed his coat, so he shoved his phone into the pocket and announced, "I'm going for a long walk, okay? I'll probably catch something to eat somewhere. See you later tonight." He left before Romeo could respond.

Seattle was an interesting city but a hell of a lot hillier than Chicago. By the time darkness fell, Teddy's thighs ached. Clearly he'd been shortchanging his time on the StairMaster. He'd stopped twice for coffee—including a visit to the original Starbucks, because why the hell not?—but hadn't eaten anything. Although he was hungry, he felt too restless to sit for a meal. So he walked up endless hills and then back down again, ignoring the fact that the mist was giving him clown hair.

The weird thing was that he wasn't sure *why* he felt so unsettled. He kept trying to tell himself it was due to Joyce Alexander and her upcoming mysterious tests. That certainly merited unease. But what kept streaming through his brain like a YouTube video on repeat was the conversation with Romeo. During which Romeo revealed he was pan and single, and Teddy announced his plan to remain steadfastly unattached.

It was a good plan; Teddy was positive of that. It made total sense. Why waste time and energy on heartbreak when he should be putting energy into enriching his bank account and building a professional reputation? Sure, the concept of love was attractive, but the reality far less so. Love hurt, and Teddy was no masochist.

Except…loneliness didn't feel so great either. It was easy to forget that fact while engaged in his routine at home: work, exercise, eat, sleep, repeat. But now that he was two thousand miles away with time on his hands and Romeo in his bed, well, his outlook had shifted.

And the agonizing truth was that Romeo was…intriguing. Smoking hot, yes, but also smart and complex and even secretly sweet. He was, in fact, the kind of guy Teddy could really fall for. If falling were an option. Which it wasn't, because they worked together, and because Romeo was way out of Teddy's league. And because Teddy didn't want to fall for anyone.

He found himself wandering into another Starbucks. This one was enormous, with tasting menus and a steampunk-hipster vibe. Although he didn't really need any more caffeine, he browsed the menus until they overwhelmed him. Then he discovered that an Italian restaurant inside the building sold pizzas by the slice. Perfect. He bought a thick wedge of margherita and, because he was feeling somewhat contrary, hot tea.

He spent some time arranging and rearranging his little meal on one of the long tables, hoping to get the perfect shot for Instagram. He might not be lounging on a beach in Thailand with a guy who looked like a model, but he wasn't stuck at home either. He'd spent the morning with Joyce Alexander, and he was going to see her again the next day. Gregory couldn't say that, could he?

"Ugh." Teddy gave up on the photography and took a bite of his pizza while it was still hot. Gregory. What did Teddy have to do to evict that jerk from his brain?

As it turned out, the food was good, and Teddy's stomach was thankful that he'd stopped ignoring it. He bought and ate a second slice, this one with roasted eggplant, and he drank more tea. He attempted to avoid brooding.

And then he had an odd thought. Romeo was alone in Seattle too. Maybe he was happy about that—or maybe he wished he hadn't been abandoned. Like Teddy, Romeo didn't get much chance to stray from their low-ceilinged office in the Loop. What if he'd hoped to play tourist a little bit with some company at his side?

Great. Now Teddy had added guilt to his emotional bouillabaisse. It didn't taste good.

The hotel was downhill from the fancy Starbucks, which his legs appreciated. Along the way, he realized that his feet were sore, his nose was running, and he really wanted a warm, dry bed.

Romeo sat at the desk in their shared room. He glanced over when Teddy entered but quickly turned his attention back to his laptop screen. A small assortment of paper food containers sat beside the computer.

"You're not starving," Teddy observed while hanging up his coat.

"Grubhub. You?"

"Pizza."

The meaning of Romeo's answering grunt was unclear.

Teddy spent a few minutes contemplating how to make his one remaining outfit—which he'd planned to wear on the plane ride home—suffice for a meeting with Joyce Alexander. He'd opted more for comfort than style, and that was a problem. He couldn't see himself wearing jeans and a button-down to her house, even if the shirt was a totally amazing Eton floral-and-bird pattern he'd scored at his favorite thrift store. He draped his scarf around the shirt experimentally, but the gray-and-navy-checked cashmere didn't work at all with the shirt's bright colors.

Dammit. His herringbone jacket also looked shitty with the shirt. He should have gone shopping this afternoon instead of tromping around aimlessly. Seattle likely had some awesome clothing resale shops, and he could have found something more suitable. But now it was too late, and there wouldn't be time for a retail expedition before Joyce's driver picked them up at eight tomorrow morning. Could he get away with wearing the same trousers he'd had on today? Joyce would certainly notice, and then—

"Are you almost finished?"

Teddy looked up from the unsatisfactory arrangement of clothing on the bed to discover Romeo glaring at him. "What? I didn't say anything," Teddy said defensively.

"No, but you're moving around a lot. And sighing. I told you before: I get distracted really easily."

Distracted from what? "What are you working on anyway?"

"I'm studying for the tests."

"Studying?" Teddy scoffed. "How can you study if you don't know what the test is going to be on?"

"Well, I can predict it won't be on the War of 1812 or the periodic table of elements. It'll be about the vase, of course. So I'm boning up on the specs."

Teddy skipped the adolescent joke about "boning up,"

even though he really wanted to say it, and instead gathered his clothing from the mattress. "I think she already knows as much as she wants to about the vase. She has something else in mind."

"Since I'm not psychic and I can't study every conceivable subject in one night, I'll concentrate on the specs."

"Suit yourself." It came out sounding snottier than Teddy had intended, and also ironic, considering that he was struggling to, well, literally suit himself for the next day. He quickly returned his clothes to the closet and scuttled into the bathroom, where he eyed the tub. His apartment had only a shower, and his legs still ached. "I'm taking a bath," he shouted through the closed door.

The answer came back clearly enough. "Suit yourself."

Chapter Nine

"This isn't the route we took yesterday." Teddy squinted suspiciously at the back of the driver's head.

"We have a different destination today."

"Where?"

The driver didn't answer.

It was very much like a scene in an action-suspense film—the type where Matt Damon or Daniel Craig would show up any minute to save the kidnapping victims—except Teddy couldn't think of a single reason why anyone would want to abduct him. His parents and grandma could barely afford the house they shared in Palm Springs, so a ransom was out of the question, and he doubted that a nefarious rival high-tech vase manufacturer wanted to torture industry secrets out of him and Romeo.

Traffic was heavy, so it took forever to crawl out of the city and into a strip-mall-infested suburb. Romeo didn't say a word, his attention focused on his phone. He'd been asleep by the time Teddy emerged from the bath the previous night, and this morning he'd awakened before Teddy. Romeo had said very little as they got ready, and Teddy couldn't tell whether he was angry at him, nervous about the test, or simply uninterested in conversation.

At long last, the driver turned into a vast and nearly empty parking lot and stopped at the front door of a sporting-goods store. "Please go in."

"Joyce is meeting us *here*?"

"You'll receive more information inside."

Well, great.

According to the posted schedule, the store wouldn't open for another hour, but a smiling young woman opened the door from inside. "Come on in. I'm Tish." She wore track pants, a polo shirt, and a lanyard around her neck, and she had an enthusiastic bounce to her step. Teddy expected her to blow a whistle and order him to run laps. Instead she led them to the back of the store. Along the way they passed a few other employees but no other customers.

"Where's Joyce Alexander?" Teddy asked when they arrived at the shoe section.

Tish blinked. "Who?"

Romeo shot Teddy a triumphant look, clearly pleased to have proof that he wasn't the only person on the planet who'd never heard of Joyce. "We thought we'd be meeting her today," Romeo explained to Tish.

"Oh. I don't know anything about that. Sorry. My boss just told me to get you guys outfitted."

"Outfitted for what?"

She grinned. "Adventure!"

With that completely unenlightening explanation, she helped Teddy and Romeo choose hiking boots and special hiking socks, which Teddy hadn't even known were a thing. She then took them to pick out shirts and pants—not at all stylish, but they were moisture wicking, which she claimed was a benefit. They got thermal underwear, and knit caps and gloves, and puffy rainproof jackets in orange and gray. Wherever they were going with all this stuff, they'd be dressed as identical twins.

True to character, Romeo remained mum as their purchases accumulated, although he did look increasingly worried with each additional item. Finally, when Tish handed each of them a pair of sunglasses, he shook his head. "Um, these are pretty expensive."

"I know, right?" she said with a laugh. "You guys are so lucky! My boss said top-of-the-line all the way."

"But I can't—"

"It's all paid for, dude. Man, I wish someone would do that for me. I couldn't afford a spree like this even with my employee discount."

Romeo appeared relieved, an emotion Teddy shared. All these items would have made his credit card bleed. And Tish wasn't through with them, as it turned out. She handed each a large blue daypack.

"Heavy," Teddy observed as he took his.

"All kinds of gear in there. Filled water canteens. A bunch of nutrition bars. Sun protection. First aid kits. TP and a spade." She shrugged. "Pretty much everything you're gonna need."

"Need for *what*?" Teddy chose not to speculate on why he might require toilet paper and something to dig with. It didn't bear thinking of.

But Tish only grinned.

Teddy and Romeo used the dressing rooms to change into their new gear and stuffed their street clothes into a store shopping bag. Teddy felt ridiculous in his outfit, but of course Romeo looked stunning, as if a runway model had taken up a second job as wilderness guide. Then again, Romeo looked stunning in everything— including boxer shorts.

"Are you uncomfortable?" Tish tugged at Teddy's collar. "Does something not fit right?"

"No, it's all great."

She bypassed the cash registers and piloted them back to the front door, where she shook their hands. "I hope you guys have an amazing time!"

Their stone-faced driver put the backpacks and street clothes into the trunk of the Rolls, then motioned Teddy and Romeo into the back seat. "Enjoy your breakfast, sirs." And sure enough, while they'd been inside shopping, he'd somehow produced thermoses of coffee and bento boxes stuffed with sliced fruit and a delicious egg-sausage-and-veggie concoction. Whatever Joyce had planned for them, at least it didn't involve starvation.

It did, however, involve taking them even farther out of the city, into an area with lots of trees. Teddy eyed the hills suspiciously. He didn't trust them. It was possible Joyce had a country home here, although that didn't make much sense since the house they'd already visited was hardly urban. Even if rich people needed more than one country house, the homes in this area looked decidedly modest. Older farmhouses, mostly, some of them with horses grazing behind white picket fences.

The driver turned onto a tree-lined roadway that led not to a house but a park with picnic tables and the type of bathroom that probably housed a lot of spiders. "Here we are," the driver announced before getting out of the car.

Teddy and Romeo exchanged bewildered looks. "What the hell?" said Teddy.

"Is Joyce an outdoorsy person?"

"Not that I know of."

"Maybe…we're supposed to find flowers appropriate for our vase?" Romeo obviously doubted his own hypothesis; after squinting, he shook his head. "Not too many flowers in February."

"I think we should get out of the car. Then we'll find out what's going on."

But neither of them made an immediate move. The plush interior of the Rolls was comfortable and safe. Outside lay the unknown. And lots of green stuff.

They might have remained there forever, but the driver opened Romeo's door. "The sun sets before 5:30 tonight. You should get going."

Sunset? That was ominous.

They got out and put on their new jackets and back-packs. The driver handed Teddy a compass and Romeo a laminated paper. "If you follow these directions prop-erly, it's an eight-mile loop."

"What is?" asked Teddy despite a dawning realization.

"Your hike."

"I don't—"

"Ms. Alexander has requested that the two of you complete this hike today. I'll be waiting for you here when you're done."

"*This* is the test?" Romeo asked. "What does this have to do with Reddyflora?"

"Sir, my job is simply to drive and give you her in-structions."

Well, shit. Teddy knew he could refuse. Even if that meant the driver abandoned him, they were hardly in uncharted wilderness. He could possibly even call for a Lyft back to the city. But that would surely mean fail-ure. Joyce wouldn't back the project, Teddy would lose his job, and Romeo…he'd be screwed too, wouldn't he?

"Let's go," Teddy growled.

Remembering the toilet paper that Tish had men-tioned, Teddy shuddered and stopped in the bathroom first. No spiders in evidence, but there were a lot of webs, plus a large beetle in one corner that might or might not have been dead.

They set out side by side, with Romeo reading in-structions that led them down a short paved path, across a narrow road, over a quaint wooden bridge, and finally onto a dirt trail softened with leaves and fallen evergreen needles. The ground felt nice under Teddy's new boots. Moss-covered trees reached into the blue sky, creating an intimate space on the trail, while oversized ferns and various little shrubs covered the ground. Teddy very much hoped none of those pretty leaves were poison ivy, poison oak, or anything else in the poison family.

"Do you do this often?" Teddy asked after a few minutes. "Hiking, I mean?"

"This is my first time."

"Mine too. Unless you count when my parents took me to the arboretum when I was a kid. And that's not the same."

"I've never even done that." Romeo stepped gracefully over a fallen tree branch.

Although it would have been nice if one of them had experience in the great outdoors, it was comforting to know that Romeo was as out of his element—literally— as Teddy was.

"No Boy Scouts for you, huh?"

Something tightened in Romeo's expression. "No."

"Me either. Dad tried to sign me up, but I did one bout of summer camp before resigning. I had, uh, other extracurricular interests."

"Such as?"

Teddy didn't usually discuss this, but he couldn't exactly back off since he'd raised the topic. "Art classes, mostly. Some drama stuff. Guitar. And dance, but it turned out my balance sucks and I have all the grace of a drunken rhinoceros. That's an exact quote from my ballet teacher, by the way."

Romeo laughed, but not unkindly. "I hear the life of a dancer is pretty rough anyway."

"Yeah, I saw *Black Swan*. And I don't look good in a leotard. I'm too stubby."

That made Romeo snort.

They proceeded steadily uphill—much to the disgruntlement of Teddy's thighs—and came to a fork in the trail, with a weathered sign announcing they were at May Valley Loop. Romeo consulted their instructions. "We go left."

"You know, we're probably only a mile in. We could sneak back to the beginning, hide behind some trees, and then pop out in a couple of hours and say we did the whole trail."

"What if Joyce quizzes us on what we saw?"

"Yeah," Teddy sighed. He didn't truly want to cheat anyway, but this exercise seemed pointless.

As it turned out, the left fork became steeper—so much so that Teddy's breathing grew rough as he struggled to keep up with Romeo's longer legs. What the hell was the deal with all the hills anyway? Why did Washingtonians insist on living and recreating on them, when they could instead find a nice, reasonable plain where you could see forever and you weren't at risk of skidding on the damp leaves, tumbling down the slope, and breaking your neck?

"What did you do instead of Boy Scouts?" Teddy hoped his panting wasn't too noticeable.

Romeo didn't answer right away. "Most of the guys in my neighborhood played sports."

"Did you?" Teddy could picture him speeding down a track or cutting through a pool in a pair of Speedos that barely— *Nope. Don't go there.*

"Nah. I was the nerd who read science fiction and begged my teachers for extra computer time."

For some reason that image appealed even more than Romeo the athlete. He'd probably gone through a gangly phase as a teen, before he grew into his body. And he'd probably been awkward and shy, unlike Teddy, who'd been awkward and belligerently extroverted, as if a loud voice and brash demeanor might protect him from bullying and boost his own self-confidence.

They came to a tiny stream, hardly more than a trickle, really. Teddy's bathroom sink had generated a bigger body of water than this, back when it developed a disastrous leak last July. But Romeo paused to crouch and gaze at it. "I bet this comes from snowmelt at higher elevations. I wonder if it runs all year."

"It's really small."

"Yeah, but it forms its own ecosystem. I bet if we could analyze some of this water it'd be full of all sorts of critters."

"Like great white sharks?"

Romeo flashed him a grin. "Unlikely. It's not salt water."

In the very unlikely event that Teddy had been taking this hike by himself, he might not have even noticed the tiny stream, and he certainly wouldn't have stopped to inspect it. But there was Romeo, acting as if it were the most fascinating damn thing in the universe, and that made the stream interesting to Teddy too. It was as if proximity to Romeo made Teddy's world open up in unexpected ways.

"I guess we should move on." Romeo stood and wiped his hands on his jeans even though he hadn't touched anything. They continued up the trail for ten or fifteen minutes.

The sky had clouded over without Teddy noticing, and now a light rain began to fall—hardly more than a mist, really. He debated whether to pull up his hood, but Romeo hadn't, and Teddy didn't want to look like a wimp. He'd endured blizzards, fierce lightning storms, tornadoes, and humidity levels high enough to soften iron. A little falling water wouldn't melt him. He sniffled, though, and wondered if Tish had packed some Kleenex.

"This is a long walk." Teddy knew that sounded more like a complaint than an observation.

"Not really. Sometimes on my days off, when the weather's nice, I like to walk around Chicago. Just...you know. Take in the sights."

"Yeah, and sometimes I walk to work. But Chicago's flat. And it has way less nature."

"True. Although, you know, Chicago has some nature too. If you know where to look." A bit of wistfulness had crept into Romeo's voice.

"Brookfield Zoo?"

Romeo shrugged. "I guess. But we never went there when I was a kid. It gets expensive if you have five kids."

That hadn't occurred to Teddy, whose family was smaller. Anyway, his parents weren't much interested in animals and believed that zoos were only for young children, so he'd rarely visited. "So where's all the nature? Lake Michigan?"

"Dad would check out guides from the library—bugs, plants, birds—and we'd go to parks and see what we could find. Did you know there are four thousand coyotes living in Chicago?"

"Coyotes?" Teddy looked around quickly, as if one might jump out from a behind a tree. If there were that many coyotes in a metropolis, how many lived here in the forest? And then there were other predators. Bears. Wolves. Mountain lions. Elk, maybe? Teddy didn't know whether elk were dangerous to humans, but he knew that moose were; he'd seen videos of them attacking people. But he had no idea whether there were moose in the greater Seattle area.

Teddy pictured himself mauled to death by beasts. That might make the headlines back home. *Local Man Gobbled by Grizzly*. Maybe Gregory would even hear about the incident, and then he'd feel guilty for dumping Teddy so rudely. And be impressed by his—sadly now demised—adventurous spirit.

Romeo patted Teddy's shoulder. "I think we're pretty safe here."

Think wasn't the same as *know*, and besides, Romeo

wasn't from here and so he had little basis for that assurance. It was nice that he was trying, though.

"It's funny," Teddy said. "I never would have pegged you for a nature lover."

"I don't know, I guess the science part of it appealed to me. Like, if you look closely enough at things, if you really study them, they make a lot of sense. Like ferns, for instance." He knelt beside the trail to point out one of the plants in question.

"Ferns."

"Just sort of some frilly, leafy things, right? Except did you know that they're some of the earth's oldest plants? Some species have stayed basically the same for almost two hundred million years."

Teddy blinked. "Wow. Impressive." Actually, he was more impressed with Romeo's knowledge than with the ancient history of forest plants.

"You know where I always wanted to visit? The desert."

"Like…the Sahara?"

Romeo laughed as he stood upright. "I'd be satisfied with the Mojave. My parents gave me a book about American deserts for my birthday when I was eight, and—" He stopped with a wince. "Sorry. This is dumb."

Teddy planted his hands on his hips and frowned. "I want to hear about your book." Which he did. He liked the way Romeo's expression turned all soft and his eyes lit up.

After a brief pause, maybe to see if Teddy was serious, Romeo continued. "It wasn't a children's book, but one meant for a general adult audience. So I had to look up a lot of the words. But it contained all these gorgeous photos and maps and essays on plants and animals and rocks. It was all so completely different from where I lived. And maybe a lot of people think the desert is empty, but it's actually full of all kinds of life, each of them perfectly adapted for the challenging environment."

"That's really cool."

"You don't have to humor me, Teddy."

Teddy didn't know whether to be indignant at the accusation or just sad. He hadn't treated Romeo nicely, but he'd never been outright mean. Had he?

"I'm not humoring you," he said softly.

Romeo nodded with his lips pressed together. "Okay." He seemed to relax a little. "I always wanted to go camping in the desert. Joshua Tree National Park, maybe. Technically, it contains two deserts: the Mojave and the Sonora."

"You can, you know. Go camping wherever you want, I mean."

"Work."

Teddy waved a dismissive hand. "We'll get our product launched, Lauren will pay us big fat bonuses, and you can take a nice long vacation." That was a bit optimistic, maybe, but he wanted to keep a positive attitude. In fact, with that idea in mind, he resumed walking. There wouldn't be a launch and bonuses if they never finished this hike.

With his longer legs, Romeo caught up right away. "Where will you vacation?"

Thinking of Gregory and his beachside selfies, Teddy tried to imagine himself somewhere with palm trees, but it didn't appeal. Okay, what about New York to see some shows and do some shopping? Or Paris, maybe, where he could stun the locals with his two years of high school French. Or...the desert.

The truth was, he couldn't see himself enjoying any of those places alone. Not that he had anything against solo travel; a lot of people surely appreciated that sort of freedom and independence. But he doubted he'd be one of those people. If he was going to travel, he wanted a companion to talk to, someone to share experiences with. Someone whose own delight would echo Teddy's own. Someone to help him see things through different eyes.

"I'd stay home," Teddy said.

"Yeah? How come?"

They came to a fallen tree, its bark badly eroded. But it was still a place of life, home to mosses and little plants and probably a zillion bugs. Teddy took care not to crush anything as he stepped over.

"Teddy?"

"I guess I'm just a homebody," Teddy said with only a partial serving of truth.

"Nothing wrong with that. I bet your place is really nice."

Surprised at the compliment, Teddy almost tripped over a rock. "It's...petite."

"But cozy, right? And perfectly decorated."

"Well, not perfect. I don't have a Googie smart vase."

Romeo's laughter echoed among the branches.

They paused at the next fork so Romeo could consult Joyce's instructions. Teddy dug out an energy bar and his canteen, but before he could partake of either, he glanced down at his feet and leapt back with an undignified squawk. "What the fuck is *that*?"

The creature in question—which he'd very nearly stepped on—was a sickly yellow-green color with blackish spots, gleaming with slime, and seven or eight inches long. It moved very slowly along the trail, leaving a line of shiny goo. Teddy thought it looked like the type of alien that would crawl into your ear and take command of your brain, forcing you to reshape the Earth's environment so its species could colonize.

Romeo bent to peer at it. "That's a slug."

"No. It's Captain Zrgomaf from the planet Xyton Two, and it's about to immobilize us with its paralytic-slime gun."

"It's a mollusk. It eats decaying stuff."

"Thank you, Biology Man. It's gross."

"It probably thinks you're gross, with your dry skin and fuzzy hair, all those appendages and white teeth." Romeo was crouching, his finger almost touching the creature. The slug didn't seem to care. "I think slugs are interesting. The slime keeps them from desiccating, and it's really cool from a chemical and structural standpoint. Did you know slugs are hermaphrodites? Plus their penis-to-body ratio is bigger than almost any other animals— and they usually eat each other's penises after they mate."

"Ugh." Teddy stepped farther away. "I think I'd prefer alien control rays, thanks. How did you become an expert on slugs anyway?"

"Nerd, remember? I dug my science classes." Romeo poked the slug very gently with one finger.

"Ew. Don't touch it!"

"Why not?" He did it again. And then to Teddy's absolute horror, he picked the thing up and set it on his upturned hand. "I'm just going to move the poor little fellow off the path so nobody steps on it. *It*. Man, that sounds too cold for a living creature. What pronouns do you suppose are appropriate for slugs?" He seemed completely sincere with this question.

"I usually just ask people which pronouns they prefer. I think that's polite."

"Agreed. But I can't very well ask our friend, can I?" Romeo walked to the edge of the trail, bent, and with utmost care urged the slug onto a wet leaf. It crept along, apparently untraumatized by the encounter.

Romeo looked down at his hand, which was coated with slug goo. He started to reach for his backpack strap but stopped suddenly, a mischievous grin lighting his face. "Oh, Teeeeeddy," he crooned. He stepped toward Teddy with his palm outstretched.

"Agh!" Teddy scrambled backward, away from the slimy hand of doom. "Don't you dare!" But Romeo advanced, so Teddy retreated—until his heel landed on a patch of mud and he slipped. For a perfect, brief moment he thought he'd regain his balance.

Then he fell hard and yowled with pain.

Chapter Ten

"I am so sorry," Romeo said for the tenth or eleventh time. Teddy kept telling him it was no big deal, that Teddy's innate klutziness was as much at fault as Romeo's faux threat, but Romeo remained distressed even as he wrapped an Ace bandage around Teddy's swollen ankle. "Is that too tight?"

Teddy winced as he moved his foot experimentally. "No, I think it's okay." He tried to settle more comfortably on the fallen log, but he'd also bruised his ass when he fell.

"Sit tight, okay? I'll go get help."

Naturally, there was no cell service, so Romeo would have to walk the two and a half miles back to the trailhead, summon assistance, and lead them back here.

Which meant Teddy would be alone for perhaps two hours, feeling stupid. "No. You finish the hike. I can walk back by myself—nothing's broken."

"I'm not going to abandon you!"

Teddy warmed at Romeo's declaration but shook his head. "There's no point in both of us failing the test."

"I am not leaving a wounded man alone in the woods just so I can impress a rich lady that I'd never heard of." Romeo folded his arms firmly.

The rain had increased to a steady drizzle. Teddy tied his hood under his chin and gingerly stood. He could walk, sort of, as long as he didn't put too much weight on the bad foot. It hurt, but not agonizingly so. "Let's go," he said, shoulders heavy with defeat.

But first Romeo insisted on taking Teddy's backpack, and then he found a sturdy stick, broke it to a suitable length, and held it out. "Makeshift cane?"

"Sure. Why not?"

The stick helped, in fact, especially on the steeper bits. Still, they made slow progress downhill, with Teddy stopping often to rest. The forest, which had seemed so interesting before, was now just huge and uncomfortable. And if those killer coyotes showed up now, he'd never be able to outrun them.

During one of Teddy's pauses—he'd found a log to sit on—Romeo frowned at him. "Really, Teddy. Stay here and I'll bring help."

"No."

"You don't trust me?"

"I'm absolutely positive you're not going to leave me to

the elements. You wouldn't even finish the hike when I told you to. I just..." He shifted uncomfortably. "I don't want to sit here alone."

Not that he was seriously worried about being attacked by wild animals, although apparently even a slug was capable of taking him down. He knew that if he had to wait, his mind would go to all sorts of miserable places, and then he'd feel completely ridiculous when a rescue squad showed up. It was bad enough that he was failing the test; he didn't need to get park rangers and EMTs involved.

With help from his stick, he regained his feet. "Let's go."

Although he looked doubtful, Romeo didn't argue. They continued making their slow way back. Sometimes Romeo offered an arm to help steady him, and he never once displayed anything other than kindness or concern.

By the time they neared the trailhead, Teddy was exhausted, sopping wet, and gritting his teeth against the pain. But they made it, and there was the fancy Rolls Royce, just as the driver had promised. He popped out of the car as soon as he saw them and came running over. "What happened?"

"Sprained ankle," Teddy replied tersely, not pausing in his shuffle toward the car. He really, really wanted to sit somewhere soft and warm. No. What he wanted was to strip out of the stupid hiking gear and climb into a bed with lots of pillows and a fluffy down comforter, then swallow a couple medicinal shots of cinnamon whiskey and tumble into a sleep so deep he wouldn't dream about his impending joblessness.

Romeo helped him to the car, his strong arms steadying Teddy as he lowered himself into the back seat. Romeo handed him an energy bar and canteen and then buckled him in before going to the other side of the car and scooting in beside him.

Meanwhile the driver had been on his phone, presumably to Joyce. He returned to the car in a businesslike manner. "I'm taking you to urgent care and then back to your hotel. Ms. Alexander will contact you later."

"Fine." Teddy leaned back and closed his eyes. It was too late now to worry about failure.

As Teddy had predicted, his ankle was sprained but not broken. The urgent care doctor, a cheery man with a sexy Indian accent, told Teddy to keep it elevated and apply ice packs every couple of hours. "Advil for pain, and rest as much as you can."

"I'm going to have to walk at least a bit. Work and airport."

"Of course. A brace will help."

The brace in question was black, stretchy, and supportive. It also reminded Teddy of the light-bondage gear he had hoped would spark up his relationship with Gregory. Teddy had ordered a bed restraint kit and blindfold, but when he'd tried to install the kit, the straps kept tangling or refusing to adjust properly, and he'd given up before Gregory even arrived. He kept the blindfold, though. It was handy for blocking the early morning sunlight that beamed through his thin curtains.

It was dark when they exited the Rolls in front of their hotel. The driver insisted they take all the hiking gear with them, although Teddy was certain he'd never use any of it again. If he wanted to feel outdoorsy in the future, he'd stick to nicely groomed arboretums in low-topography states.

Teddy's phone rang as they arrived in their room. He collapsed onto the bed with a groan and answered the call on speaker. "Hello, Joyce. I'm sorry—"

"How are you feeling? Sprains can be quite painful."

"I'm okay, thanks. I just need to baby it a little."

"Will you be able to engage in the second test tomorrow?"

He sat up abruptly, ignoring the various twinges. "Second test? But I thought after today—"

"Yes. Today was not as successful as we might have hoped. But two assessments remain. Tomorrow's will be less physically challenging but will require some standing and walking. Are you capable?"

A second chance. For that, he'd be willing to gnaw off his foot. "Sure. Of course."

"Excellent. My driver will pick you up at two o'clock. That will give you some extra time to recuperate."

For the first time since he'd fallen, optimism peeked through the gloom. Maybe her tests weren't pass or fail. He and Romeo had managed over four miles on their hike, so that could mean they'd earned partial credit.

"Can you tell me now what you were testing us for today? Because I still don't get it."

Her laugh sounded genuine. "Of course, darling. There are qualities I believe members of a successful team must possess. Today I was looking for fortitude."

"Oh." Yeah, his score on that must have been pretty abysmal. He hadn't even made it halfway around the loop. "Um, you know that Romeo was doing fine, right? He would have finished the hike if he hadn't needed to help me."

Romeo gifted Teddy with a slow smile that was as sweet as maple syrup. Heated maple syrup, because… there was almost certainly a glint in Romeo's eyes. The type of glint that warmed Teddy's skin and turned his heart into a flock of butterflies.

"Teddy?"

He almost dropped the phone. "Uh, sorry, Joyce. The connection faded for a sec there."

She clucked her tongue. "That never happened when we all used landlines. Anyway, as I said, today was forti- tude. I'll give you a bit of a preview about tomorrow—it involves intelligence."

"Oh. Well, thanks for the heads-up." Not that it would do any good. It wasn't as if he could take a magic smart pill in the meantime.

"Darling, in a short while my driver will leave a debit card for you at the hotel reception desk. Please use it to treat yourselves to some nice meals. And do some clothes shopping as well—I realize that when you packed you didn't expect to stay this long."

"Wow. That's really generous of you." And a relief for him.

"Don't be silly. We all know I possess unreasonable amounts of money. Now, you boys have a good time, and you rest your foot. Two o'clock tomorrow."

He set the phone on the bedside table and looked at Romeo, who hadn't lost that something in his eyes. In fact, that something had grown and taken shape, and now its identity was unquestionable: attraction. The same type of attraction that Teddy had been fighting since they arrived in Seattle. Hell, be honest: since long before that. In Teddy's somewhat limited experience, this was a look that led rapidly to groping and the shedding of clothes and stroking and thrusting and sweating and...regrets and silent coldness soon afterward.

"I guess we're not out of the game yet." His voice came out hoarser than usual, and he sniffed as camouflage. He had, after all, spent hours outside in the rain.

Romeo licked his lips, which was downright *mean*. "Yeah. Guess not."

"What do you think she's going to make us do to prove we're smart?"

"No idea, man."

With a sigh, Teddy leaned forward to unlace his boots. At which point Romeo hurried over, batted Teddy's hands away, and did it for him, removing the one on the injured foot with exquisite care. Teddy, who'd never once in his life entertained a medical kink, found Romeo's actions so unbearably sexy that he nearly injured himself yanking the comforter up over his lap. Seemingly oblivious to Teddy's condition, Romeo remained kneeling at the bedside. "How's it feeling?"

For a wild moment, Teddy thought Romeo was referring to a part of his anatomy that, while also somewhat swollen at the moment, would not be relieved by ibuprofen. Then common sense prevailed and he gave a shaky laugh. "It's fine as long as I don't walk on it."

"I put your ice packs in the mini fridge. They just barely fit in the teeny freezer."

"Thanks."

Romeo still hadn't moved. One of his hands lay on the comforter. Not quite *on* Teddy, but almost. He was so close that Teddy could smell him: a pleasant combination of pine needles, hotel shampoo, and peanut butter, the latter thanks to their energy bars. He likely tasted good too. Oh, and the nape of his neck was undoubtedly soft and warm, and his chest—

"Dinner."

Romeo blinked at him. "Huh?"

"We should discuss what to do about dinner."

"Uh, yeah." Romeo slowly rose, which was both a shame and a relief. "We can order in so you can rest your foot. Or I can go out and get us something."

"You don't need to be stuck inside tonight just because I am."

"Wasn't planning to go out anyway."

Although Teddy shouldn't have cared whether Romeo stayed with him tonight, he *was* happy. He liked having Romeo around, despite the increasing temptation to throw himself into his strong arms.

Romeo brushed his hands together as if he'd made a decision. "I'll go get us something."

"Sounds good. And we can clothing shop in the morning."

"Okay." But Romeo's expression had closed down. Teddy had no idea why. And before he could ask, Romeo was striding meaningfully toward the desk. He sat down and started typing at his laptop. "Any specific requests or no-gos for dinner?"

Teddy thought about that for a moment. "You know what? I could really go for a big bowl of pho." He wanted comfort food, and Vietnamese broth and noodles would hit the spot for sure.

"Really?"

"You don't like pho?"

"No, it's great." Romeo shrugged. "I expected you to want something…fancier."

That made Teddy frown. Sure, he liked to splurge on a meal now and then, but more often he was a sandwich or pizza kind of guy. Or noodles. Why would Romeo think otherwise? Jesus, did Teddy put on airs that made him come across as a snob? He wasn't one; he couldn't afford to be. But even if he were as rich as Joyce Alexander, he'd still appreciate the simpler things in life. In fact, he was proud of his ability to put together a nice outfit or attractive décor on a tight budget.

"I'm cool with whatever you want," Teddy said.

After a pause, Romeo nodded and stood. "I'll be back," he said with a very bad Schwarzenegger accent. Then he put on his coat and left.

★ ★ ★

Romeo returned with huge bowls of pho with steak and brisket, along with spring rolls and lemongrass chicken over rice. They laid everything out atop the bed for a gleeful if precarious picnic. "My mama would skin me alive if she knew I was eating like this," Romeo said. Then he pitched his voice higher and waved a finger. "'You are *not* acting like that in a nice hotel, Romeo Blue. Uh-uh.'"

Teddy laughed so hard he almost spilled his soup. "My mom probably wouldn't care. My dad would worry about damage costs, though. But hell, he'd have never checked in anywhere as nice as this." He deepened his voice for his imitation. "'The La Cucaracha Motor Inn will be fine, son. Just ignore the meth cookers and the prostitutes.'"

"A little tight with his money, huh?"

"Oh man, like you wouldn't believe. I love him and he's overall a really good person. But he used to spend hours every week with the grocery ads, making a list of who had what the cheapest, and then he'd make a circuit of, like, five or six different stores to get everything. I'm fairly certain he has never paid full price for anything in his life. Plus he kept the house temps at arctic levels in the winter and in the summer refused to turn on the AC until we were all three minutes from heatstroke." He smiled as he said this. Yes, Dad had sometimes driven him nuts when Teddy was a kid, but like Mom, he'd supported Teddy in all his childhood artistic endeavors—as long as they didn't cost too much. When

Teddy came out to his parents during his junior year of high school, they'd both hugged him long and hard and told him they loved him. They were good parents even if they didn't fully understand him.

"Do your folks live in Chicago?" Romeo asked as he wrapped noodles around his spoon.

"Not anymore. They retired a couple of years ago and went off with my grandma to California. Mom was tired of winter. How about your family?"

"My dad died when I was twelve."

Shit. "I'm so sorry." Teddy wasn't sure whether to offer a hug. It likely would have resulted in spilled food, so instead he awkwardly patted Romeo's shoulder.

"Thanks. It was a long time ago. Mama used the insurance money to buy us a house, uh, somewhere better. He would've been happy about that."

They ate for a few minutes, and when the silence grew heavy, Teddy ventured another question. "You said you have sisters?"

Romeo's grin returned. "Four of 'em. I'm the youngest. And no, growing up with all that estrogen wasn't painful at all." He giggled over his obvious untruth like a naughty child, which made Teddy laugh too.

"Just the one little brother for me. He's two years younger than me and as butch as you can possibly imagine. He's a forklift operator in Kansas City."

"Does he give you shit for being gay?"

"I think he was a little embarrassed by me when we were kids. But he got over it." He'd apologized for it one Thanksgiving when Teddy was twenty-four, which had taken a lot of guts. They were too different from each other to be very close, but they got along fine.

The discussion after that turned to mild office gossip and then talk of what they'd do with their spare time if they weren't chained to work for such long hours. They both vowed that they'd have better exercise routines. Teddy wished he could go to museums and plays. Romeo said he'd play more video games and catch up on several years' worth of reading. He didn't say anything about wanting to go to clubs or out on dates, which was interesting.

Eventually they returned to speculating about the next day. "What if Joyce makes us take the SATs or something?" Teddy fretted.

"She said something about you needing to walk a little, so probably not."

"Oh, right." Teddy tried to imagine an IQ test that involved physical movement, but couldn't picture it. He was going to have to go into the second test as blindly as the first. "Well, at least you don't have to worry about it."

"What do you mean?"

"I mean you're gonna ace whatever she gives us."

Romeo paused with the last spring roll in midair. "What makes you think that?"

"You're super smart." Duh.

Romeo ducked his head, but not quickly enough to hide a broad, shy smile. Then he laughed and tossed the spring roll at Teddy—who missed the catch, of course. The spring roll bounced off a pillow and onto the floor.

★ ★ ★

Not long after dinner, they each did their nighttime ablutions. Teddy's ankle was still tender, but the rest, ice, and bandaging definitely helped. It was a little too early for sleep, but neither of them felt like working. So they lay propped on pillows in bed—which smelled faintly of fish sauce and lemongrass—and binged *Watchmen*. Apparently Romeo had been a big fan of the comic series, but he loved the TV show even more. Teddy had never seen either of them, but he had to agree that the show was great.

"Want to watch another episode?" Teddy asked after the third was over.

"Neither one of us is going to be very smart tomorrow if we're sleep-deprived."

True enough. But it was so nice to simply hang out with someone, commenting on the actors and plotlines and passing back and forth a box of Milk Duds that Romeo had magically supplied. This was the kind of evening Teddy had secretly dreamed of when he was dating Gregory, but which had never materialized. Teddy had tried a few times, but Gregory had complained that the apartment was too cramped and he was bored.

Romeo didn't say anything about being bored.

After a certain amount of pillow fluffing and blanket rearranging, they turned off the lights. But Romeo was right *there*, with nothing between them but Romeo's boxer shorts and Teddy's corgi pajamas. Silently but sternly lecturing himself—*fall asleep, dammit*—Teddy struggled to remain still.

"Teddy?" Romeo's voice, hardly more than a whisper, sent a pleasant frisson down Teddy's spine.

"Yes?"

"Um…could you do me a favor?"

Rub myself in scented oils and prostrate myself at your feet? Write a poem about the beauty of your mouth? Gaze at you in adoration as I hum you a lullaby? Done. "Sure."

"Tomorrow, with the clothes shopping…could you help me pick some stuff out?"

A wave of happiness hit Teddy so hard he had to hug himself to keep from floating away. Surely Romeo must have felt the blush that spread over Teddy's cheeks. "I'd love to," he managed with an almost steady voice.

"Thanks." And whether by intention or accident, Romeo moved his hand until his fingers touched lightly against Teddy's. They fell asleep like that.

Chapter Eleven

Romeo took a long shower in the morning, and Teddy made good use of the time, digging deep into the internet. By the time they were ready to leave the hotel, he had a short but carefully curated list of shopping destinations. After a brief stop to pick up the debit card and then a longer stop for coffee and breakfast sandwiches, they walked a few blocks to the first shop, which was just opening. Teddy didn't limp too badly.

"A resale shop?" Romeo seemed surprised by their destination.

"Yep. Is that a problem?"

"No. I spent my first two decades wearing mostly stuff from Goodwill. But we have Joyce's debit card, remember?"

Teddy took Romeo's arm and brought him to a halt. "It's not about the money. I mean, usually that's a good chunk of why I buy clothes resale. But also... I don't know. This way is more creative. You can mix up eras, designers, styles. Create something that's unique."

"I have no clue how to do that."

"But I do." Grinning, Teddy hauled him into the store.

It was a lot of fun picking things out for Romeo—so much so that the store owner, a fortyish woman with sleeve tattoos, joined in. It was as if Romeo were their own private fashion model. Of course he looked good in pretty much everything, and he dressed and redressed according to their commands without complaint but with a good shot of bewilderment.

"How'd you know this was going to work together?" he asked, staring at his reflection in a mirror.

"It's my superpower."

In the end, they didn't have to go anywhere else. Teddy found three workable ensembles for himself and, better yet, three amazing ones for Romeo: a nicely cut dove-gray Italian suit with a rose-colored silk T-shirt; a pair of dark denim jeans with a mustard button-down, a vintage gray waistcoat, and a blue-and-green-striped tie; and black trousers with a lightweight blood-red cashmere pullover and bright paisley scarf.

"That one makes him look like a rock star," the shop owner opined. Teddy agreed.

Despite the sore ankle, Teddy was almost skipping when they left in search of lunch. He hadn't enjoyed himself that much in ages. "Thanks for being my dress-up doll," he said to Romeo.

"No, thank *you*. I'd never have tried..." Romeo sighed when they stopped to wait for a crossing signal. "I told you, Mama and my sisters tell me where to shop so I can look successful and...sophisticated, I guess. And I go to those stores and let the people there pick out stuff for me."

"You always look nice at work."

Romeo shot him a sideways look. "*Nice*. Yeah, okay. But I'm like a mannequin in a mall window—boring. You make me look *interesting*. The kind of dude who might show up in a magazine spread of successful entrepreneurs or drop in to chat with Trevor Noah on *The Daily Show*. But you also make me look like me, which is pretty damned cool."

Teddy floated on that praise all the way through his charred-corn quesadilla.

After a quick stop for boring underwear and socks, they went back to the hotel to change. That took longer than it should have because Romeo kept pausing to admire himself in the mirror. Which gave Teddy the excuse to admire him too. And then they took some photos so Romeo could send them to his mother and sisters, all of whom replied with a chorus of texts that made Romeo blush and grin. "Titania wants to know if you'll give her wardrobe advice too."

"Titania?"

"Youngest sister. The others are Portia, Cleopatra,

and Reagan." He shrugged. "My parents had a thing for Shakespeare."

"So Romeo really is your name?"

"Do I seem like the kind of guy who'd call himself Romeo if it wasn't?"

He had a point. Now that Teddy knew him better, he couldn't imagine Romeo taking such a fanciful pseudonym. "Well, you lucked out. They could have stuck you with Iago or Hamlet. Or Petruchio."

Romeo raised his eyebrows and quirked his lips. "Worse, you say? Wanna know my middle name?"

"Yes. I most definitely do."

"Valentine."

It took a moment for that to sink in. "Romeo Valentine Blue?" At least he managed not to laugh.

"Yep."

"Oh my God."

"Now, I want you to picture what it was like for me—the kid who wanted to hide in the corner where nobody'd notice him—when every teacher said my full name during roll call."

Teddy winced. "Ow."

"Yep."

"You must have been one tough kid."

Romeo barked a laugh. "Not even a little bit. I used to fake being sick so I wouldn't have to go to school. I'm pretty sure Mama was completely onto me, but she let it slide as long as I kept my grades up."

"Ah. Not tough but smart. But then, I already knew that."

Although Romeo waved a dismissive hand, he looked pleased. "Speaking of smart…"

"We better get our butts in gear. Yeah."

The driver was waiting for them in the Rolls, as expressionless as ever. Teddy wondered if that had been a qualification in the job description. *Wanted: One chauffeur, experience necessary. Those with emotions need not apply.* But then, as Teddy was getting into the back seat, the driver surprised him with a question. "How is your ankle today, sir?"

"Better, thanks. You're not going to make us do rock climbing or skiing today, right?"

Oh my God. The guy's lips twitched slightly. "You'll be sticking to solid, flat ground today."

This drive was much shorter and didn't end among farms and trees. Instead they were surrounded by hip restaurants, upscale salons, fancy boutiques, and the types of apartments and condos Teddy would aspire to if he relocated to Seattle. The driver pulled to the curb, and for a giddy moment Teddy thought he was going to take them into a paint-and-sip place. That would be okay. Even though Teddy wasn't so great at the sipping part, he could produce a painting that wouldn't sear anyone's eyeballs.

But no, their destination was next door, behind a solid wood entry that read simply Perplexicate. What the hell was that?

The interior confused him further. It looked like somebody's vision of a steampunk library: lots of wood paneling, dusty old books, mismatched antique reproduction furniture, and random brass gadgetry. Two women in their early twenties stood behind a small counter whose front was decorated with an assortment of clock faces and gears. Both wore black T-shirts with the Perplexicate name and logo.

"Messieurs Blue and Spenser," the driver announced to the employees before waving Teddy and Romeo forward.

Both women were staring openly at Romeo; not that Teddy could blame them. Romeo had a celebrity's name and looks and had just been ushered in by a guy in a chauffeur's uniform. But the women recovered quickly, smiling and offering welcome.

"I'll be waiting when you're done," the driver said before walking out the door. Teddy was briefly distracted, wondering what the guy did while he waited. Did he enjoy sitting around like that, or did he spend the time seething and plotting revenge? Maybe he just practiced keeping a blank expression.

As one of the women led them down a hallway, Teddy tried to concentrate on the task at hand. He was surprised when they entered a room lined with lockers. "Coats, cell phones, and wallets in a locker, please. Take the key with you."

"What are we doing that we can't take our phones and wallets?" Teddy demanded.

Her eyes twinkled. "Adventure!"

Oh hoorah. Just like yesterday. *Look on the bright side— at least we get to keep our pants on.*

Once Teddy and Romeo had followed orders and pocketed their locker keys, she took them farther down the hall and around a corner, stopping in front of a door marked only with the letter X. She waved a keycard, hanging from her lanyard, in front of the knob to disengage the lock.

She pushed open the door to reveal…a medical exam room. There was an exam table covered in paper, a cabinet and sink, and a few items of unidentified equipment. The beige walls held a video screen, an illustrated chart of the human muscular system, and two large framed prints of waterfalls. Teddy shifted his feet uneasily and hoped his relief about remaining clothed hadn't been premature.

"Um…" Romeo said. He didn't look any more comfortable than Teddy.

But their guide remained chipper. "Okay. In a sec, you're gonna get a video introduction. The clock starts when the video does. You get one hour. Just push that button near the door—" she pointed "—or call out if you want a hint. You can ask only three times, so use that help wisely."

"An hour to do what?" Teddy asked.

"Escape, of course." Laughing, she exited the room and closed the door behind her.

"Oh, shit," Teddy said with a noisy exhale. "Escape room."

"Have you ever done one of these?"

"No. I'm really bad at—"

Before Teddy could explain how poorly he did at figuring things out while under pressure, the wall-hung video screen crackled to life, showing what looked like a news anchor at his desk. The man looked nervously at a sheaf of papers in one hand. "Breaking news! We're receiving reports of people being attacked by roving packs of animals in multiple locations. Authorities advise everyone to remain inside behind locked doors and await further instructions. I repeat—"

Crashes, growls, and multiple screams came from off camera. The image tilted, as if the camera had been knocked askew, leaving only the anchor's arm in frame. The arm flailed, the screams grew louder, and then the anchor was yanked completely out of view. A moment later, blood spattered the lens.

"What are we supposed to—" Romeo stopped when the screen showed a man with his hair messed up and parallel claw marks across his shirtfront.

"Wolves!" the man shouted. "Packs of wolves and they're killing everyone. They're— Ahhhh!" Something large and furry landed on him, knocking him out of sight. The screen turned to static, then went blank.

Teddy took a deep breath. "We have slightly less than one hour to figure out how to get out of here. And, I guess, battle the wolves."

"How do we do that?"

"No idea."

A big clock on the wall ticked loudly as Teddy and Romeo wandered the room, aimlessly searching for clues. Teddy picked up a newspaper that was sitting on a chair. It was the science section, which he supposed was important. But nothing jumped out at him from the headlines.

"What's it say?" Romeo had been opening and closing the books on a shelf.

"Nothing relevant. Swimming Neanderthals, altruistic parrots, a volcano crater in Laos."

"Let me see." Romeo strode over and grabbed the paper.

"Hey! I was—"

"Supermoon."

"What?"

Romeo pointed at the page. "This article says there's supposed to be a supermoon tonight."

"So?" Teddy suddenly noticed that Romeo's arm was touching his. They'd been close before. Hell, they'd been close in *bed*, and with fewer clothes on. But for some reason the proximity was more…significant now.

And maybe Romeo thought so too, because the newspaper hung loosely from one hand as he stared intently into Teddy's eyes. Teddy angled himself toward Romeo and tilted his head up. God, Romeo had the most beautiful eyes! And that jawline. And those lips, slightly chapped, which practically begged for Teddy's tongue. And—

"Werewolves," Romeo said.

Teddy took a step back. "Huh?"

"The wolves. I bet they're werewolves. 'Cause there's a full moon."

"Oh. Yeah." Teddy shook his head to clear it. "Okay, so werewolves are attacking. What are we supposed to do about it?" He took the newspaper back.

"Silver bullets?" Romeo marched over to the cabinet and tried to open a drawer, but it was locked.

"We'd need a gun too, but I think that's too simple.

Escape room problems have multiple layers. Anyway, silver bullets won't get us out of this room."

Romeo jiggled the drawer and then opened the cabinet, revealing supplies including cotton swabs and latex gloves. "We could shoot the lock open."

"But a few silver bullets won't help against hordes of weres."

"What does work, then?"

Teddy tossed the paper back on the chair. "I don't know. You're the one who says he loves science fiction."

"Right. Sci fi—that's space ships and aliens. Werewolves are… I dunno. Horror? Paranormal?"

Ten minutes had passed already and they'd made almost no headway. It occurred to Teddy that maybe there were hidden clues, so he dropped to his knees and looked under the exam table. Nothing. Not even a cobweb. "Didn't you watch monster stuff on TV when you were a kid?" he asked as he got to his feet—with more difficulty than usual due to the bad ankle.

Pausing in his examination of the boxes of latex gloves, Romeo threw him a look over his shoulder. "We didn't have a TV."

"No TV? What were you—Amish or something?"

"We were poor," Romeo said, scowling. "My parents worked really hard, but they had shit jobs because neither of them graduated high school. And they were convinced that the best way for their kids to have a better life was education, so they banned television and pushed us to read instead."

Feeling guilty about his stupid joke, Teddy offered an apologetic smile. "They sound like amazing parents."

"They were. Mama still is. All five of us went to college." Romeo was methodically checking every box and bag in the supply cabinet. "Reagan's a dentist, Cleo's an actuary for an insurance company, and Titania's a lawyer. Portia, she got married after college and stayed home after she had a couple of kids. But then she got divorced, and now she's working on her PhD in economics. She's gonna be a professor." Romeo said this proudly, his chin high. "Portia lives with me and Mama, and we help take care of her daughters."

"Ah." Teddy remembered how great Romeo had been with the children on the plane and now understood why he was so driven to succeed at Reddyflora.

"And none of that is helpful regarding werewolves." Romeo sighed.

Stumped for ideas, and with the clock still ticking loudly, Teddy got back on his knees. This time he looked on the underside of the chair seat. "Aha!" he crowed, pulling tape off a key and waving his find in the air.

Romeo loped over, grabbed the key, and successfully unlocked the drawer.

"What's inside?" Teddy struggled to rise.

"A notebook."

Now it was Teddy's turn to crowd close so he could read too. The first few pages contained handwritten lists of medical supplies—bandages, tongue depressors, needles—which didn't seem very helpful. But then came something like a diary entry in which the author claimed to have discovered a serum that would allow people to change their physical shape and become animals. The author planned to test the serum on some patients, apparently. A page in the notebook had a list of dates and names.

Romeo pointed to the first date. "This is one day before the newspaper."

"Got it. The mad-scientist doctor gave someone a shot and now all hell's broken loose."

"Right. But if he created the serum, maybe he made an antidote too." Romeo turned another page, but the rest of the notebook was blank.

There was nothing else in the drawer, and no other locks for the key. Teddy and Romeo cast around for more clues but found nothing. Finally, Teddy glanced at the clock—thirty minutes already gone!—and huffed. "Time for a hint." He pushed the button next to the door.

"Need some help?" The voice of one of the employees came through a speaker in the ceiling.

"Desperately."

"Maybe you should try making a phone call."

Teddy glanced at the beige phone affixed to a wall. "We tried that. Nothing happened. Not even a dial tone."

"Sometimes the answers can come in a flood." She giggled.

"A flood? What does that mean?"

"Do you want to use your second hint?"

Romeo shook his head vigorously. "No, not yet."

Dead silence.

"Okay, flood," Teddy said thoughtfully. "Water?" He

turned the faucet handle on the sink, but nothing came out. There was nothing in the sink either and no clear way to get to the drain. When he checked the cabinet underneath, he saw that the sink wasn't hooked up to a water source or drainpipe. "That was not a useful hint," he grumbled.

He turned to seek Romeo's agreement and found him staring at one of the waterfall photos. Teddy hadn't given them much thought, assuming they were just intended to mimic the soothing artwork often found in doctors' offices.

"I think we need a phone number," Romeo said, chin in hand. He tried to remove the print from the wall, but it was firmly attached. He leaned in closer to the picture.

Not to be outdone, Teddy parked himself in front of the other waterfall, which also proved inseparable from the wall. Numbers. Was there tiny print somewhere? Not that he could see. He growled in frustration. "This is stupid. It has nothing to do with our work. I think we should—"

"Go pick up the phone."

Huffing his annoyance, Teddy stomped over to obey. "Still nothing," he reported after picking up the receiver.

"It's the...the streamlets. Their width might be binary code. Put in these numbers. Um, one. Zero. One." Romeo went to the other picture. "Zero. Zero. Zero. One."

"How do you know which order—" But before Teddy could complete his question, a buzz and a click came from one wall. A hidden door behind the muscle chart sprang open. He and Romeo scurried over and mildly jostled each other in the doorway, seeking a better view.

"Wow. I guess we know what happened to the good doctor," Romeo said. The open door revealed a closet, empty except for an old-fashioned doctor's bag and a lab coat that had been shredded into large pieces.

"The doc's werewolf guinea pig ate him?"

"Nah, no blood. I think the doc *was* the guinea pig. She—or he—injected themselves with the serum."

That made sense. The bag contained a flashlight, some AAA batteries—which didn't fit the flashlight—an empty plastic syringe, and several plastic vials full of purple liquid. Teddy clicked the flashlight on and off, but nothing happened. "Is there anything else in here?" He walked into the closet, intending to check the single shelf. But even if he stood on his toes, straining his ankle in the process, he was too short to see.

"Let me look." Romeo stepped inside.

It wasn't a tiny closet. It was bigger than either of the two in Teddy's apartment and, unlike them, wasn't stuffed full of clothing. But it was pretty cramped for two grown men, and when Teddy moved slightly to one side just as Romeo did the same, they ended up pressed against each other, chest to chest.

Teddy couldn't stand it one minute longer. He reached up and ghosted a finger along Romeo's lips. Romeo responded with a strangled sound, then wrapped his arms around Teddy and kissed him.

Teddy kissed him right back.

Chapter Twelve

Romeo tasted delicious, like coffee and the spices from his lunch. But more importantly he felt delicious: warm and solid and breathtakingly real. Teddy was vaguely aware that his hands had settled rather firmly on Romeo's butt, and that Romeo didn't seem to mind a bit. But the kiss was more important than the grope. Teddy never wanted it to end.

Inevitably, though, they had to breathe. They broke off the kiss but remained holding each other. "I thought you didn't want this." Romeo's voice was wonderfully rough, and Teddy felt Romeo's heartbeat racing as fast as his own.

"Wha'?" Language felt too difficult at the moment and thinking was out of the question.

"You said you weren't interested in… You said you want to stay unattached."

Teddy was going to argue that a single kiss in a closet hardly made for a meaningful relationship. But he and Romeo were still tightly embracing—Teddy's hands still on Romeo's ass, in fact—which meant they were rather literally attached, at least for the moment. And Teddy didn't want to let go.

"You've been tempting me," he said stupidly.

"Like an incubus?"

"Pretty much."

Romeo's chuckle felt good. "For how long?"

Honesty was best. "Since the minute we met. Only… I thought you were a jerk who hated me."

"You don't think that anymore?"

Teddy squeezed him a little more tightly. "This is a weird way of showing hate."

"What about the jerk part?"

"I…" Teddy struggled for the right words. "I'm sorry. I made some wrong assumptions and I misjudged you. You're definitely not a jerk."

With a noisy sigh, Romeo rested his head against Teddy's. God, that felt good. His lips were tantalizingly close to Teddy's ear.

"I didn't think you were a jerk," Romeo whispered. "Just kind of prissy and pretentious. I figured you'd think even less of me if you knew where I really came from. If you knew I still live with my mother."

Teddy's heart, which had been light and bubbly a moment ago, now felt leaden. "Jesus, Romeo. I'm sorry I came across that way. Honestly, I think you're damned amazing, and I kinda envy how close you and your mom are."

Romeo laughed lightly, his breath tickling Teddy's skin. "I've been lusting after you since we met. But even if I hadn't been worried about you judging me, I'm absolutely no good at…connecting with someone."

"You connected pretty well just now."

Teddy couldn't see Romeo's smile but he heard it in his response. "I guess I did." And then, as if to prove the point, he kissed Teddy again.

Teddy was even more enthusiastic about this one and kissed right back. What followed was the most intense make-out session he'd ever experienced—especially while remaining fully clothed. If there had been a Kissing Olympics, he and Romeo would have been gold medalists for sure, even though they hadn't practiced at all. Teddy felt as if he had a skull full of champagne bubbles and, where his heart should be, a mouse running very fast on its exercise wheel. Kissing Gregory had never been like this. God, Teddy was going to pass out soon because all his oxygen was gone and his blood was cavorting below the belt, and he didn't care one bit because this was perfection, it was Nirvana, it was—

"Do you guys need another hint?"

They startled so violently that Romeo hit his head on the shelf and then stumbled into Teddy, whose weak ankle gave out. Teddy collapsed to the floor with Romeo on top of him.

"Guys?" Now the voice through the speaker sounded concerned.

"Uh, yeah," Romeo called back as he tried to disentangle them. "Please." He gave Teddy a hand up, at which point they overbalanced and nearly fell out of the closet. Which was such a funny thought that Teddy started to laugh, making them miss what the woman said next.

Romeo shot him a quick glare. "Sorry. Could you repeat that?"

"I said, one way to make hidden messages appear is with grape juice."

Good to know, Teddy supposed, but what did that— Ah! He dove back into the closet and retrieved the vials from the medical bag. Sure enough, when he uncapped one of them, the unmistakable scent of Welch's filled his nose. "Hidden messages where?" he asked, looking around. Maybe he should just fling the juice here and there to see what appeared. There wasn't much of the liquid, however.

"Paper," Romeo said firmly. "Tania and I used to make invisible ink with lemon juice. Then you'd hold the paper over a lightbulb to see the message." He scanned the room for a moment before making a triumphant noise, springing forward, and poking at the paper on the exam table. "It looks different right here. Bring over the juice."

Easier said than done because Teddy was hobbling. He made it without mishap, though, and when Romeo carefully spilled a vial of juice, fuzzy letters appeared: XPMHV UPMMI

"What the hell does that mean?" Teddy squinted at it, but that didn't help.

"Could be an access code for something."

Teddy limped over and tried it on the phone. Nothing. He couldn't find another object in the room with anything resembling a keypad. He was about to say so when Romeo blew a raspberry. "Atbash!" he said.

"Is that a swear word I've never heard?" Teddy was fairly certain he'd heard them all.

"No, it's the name of a cipher. Hang on." Romeo spent a few moments looking at the letters and, apparently, counting off something in his head. Then he hooted triumphantly. "Closet floor! It says closet floor."

"I'll take your word for it."

Romeo had already sped back into the closet and was now on his knees. A moment's scrambling had the rug pushed aside, revealing a metal hatch underneath. When Romeo opened it, he exposed a space with thirteen flat plastic squares, each a different color.

"I think it's another kind of key," Romeo said. "See? The tiles slide around." They did, sort of like one of those square puzzles where moving the tiles around formed a picture or put the numbers in order. In this case, however, there were only two parallel rows.

Romeo moved the tiles, seemingly at random, and nothing happened. So Teddy knelt next to him—nudging him a bit to the side—and looked more closely. It felt good to get off his sore foot anyway, and now he was snuggled side to side with Romeo. Which distracted Teddy for a few seconds, until the obvious revealed itself. "They're complementary colors in the RGB model."

"Yeah?" Romeo grinned delightedly.

"Yep. Like this." Teddy moved the tiles back and forth until red was over cyan, orange over azure, yellow over blue, and so on. It reminded him of a frustrated and fruitless week he'd spent trying to solve a Rubik's cube. Here, though, he finally had all the colored pieces arranged, with the white tile hanging out by itself.

Nothing happened.

Romeo tapped the red. "Are they in the right order?"

"I know my complementary colors."

"Right. But how do you know red and cyan are first?"

Teddy scratched his head. "Because red's the first color in the rainbow's ROY G BIV."

"But it's possible they could be in a different order."

"I guess. How'm I supposed to know? You're the smart one."

Romeo huffed. "Well, this smart one can't calculate the number of permutations in his head, but it's a lot. No way we have time to try them all."

Time! Teddy leaned out of the closet and nearly panicked when he saw the clock. They had eleven minutes left. Shit. "I'm going to ask for a hint."

"It's our last one."

"Do you have a better idea?"

"No," Romeo said, apparently defeated. He looked so sad that Teddy couldn't stop himself from leaning over to kiss his cheek, all chaste and comforting. Except

Romeo turned his head at the last second, and his lips met Teddy's. The smooch wasn't at all chaste. Teddy's libido had been idling ever since they made out, and now it accelerated smoothly into high gear, as if eager to get him to the finish line.

"Eight minutes," Teddy said in a strangled voice when they paused.

"Right." Then Romeo raised his voice. "Another clue, please?"

Apparently it wasn't necessary to push the button; the woman answered right away. "Try pushing." She sounded annoyed.

Romeo and Teddy pushed: the tiles, the floor, each other—when they got in each other's way—the doorknob, and the back of the closet wall. That last push turned out to be the right move. The wall swung open, revealing an entire new room. They climbed through.

"Well, shit," Teddy said.

This room was bigger than the first and full of way more stuff. It was supposed to look like a laboratory: beakers and test tubes and scales, a whiteboard scrawled with equations, mysterious instruments, and a bunch of other objects that gave Teddy an unpleasant flashback to high school chemistry class. In which he'd accidentally caused a fireball that nearly incinerated himself and his lab partner.

"I think," Romeo said quietly, "we're supposed to find the werewolf antidote. And then an exit."

"We're never going to manage that in six minutes."

"And we're out of hints."

"Yeah."

Romeo sighed loudly before shrugging. "Might as well, then," he murmured. And he swept Teddy into his arms for the type of kiss that usually existed only at the ends of sappy movies. Teddy secretly loved those movies, and now he swooned with abandon. The only things missing were a surging orchestral score and a majestic wind, but he could survive without them as long as he had Romeo.

Which wasn't going to be much longer, was it? They'd head back to Chicago, listen to Lauren fire them, and go their separate ways. Romeo was brilliant and would surely find another tech job right away. Teddy would likely end up working in someone else's store.

"What's the matter?" Romeo had broken the kiss but continued the embrace.

"Workplace romances are terrible ideas. But soon we're not even going to have a workplace."

"We made it into this room. Maybe Joyce will give us partial credit."

Although Teddy nodded, he wasn't hopeful. He and Romeo hadn't come anywhere near solving the puzzle, and they'd only made it this far with help from the hints. They'd done very little to demonstrate their intelligence, which had been the point of the game.

And it was Teddy's fault again. Yesterday he'd screwed things up by hurting his ankle. Today he'd been dumb and distracting. Romeo would have done better if he'd been alone. He would have aced both tests.

The two of them spent a couple of minutes idly pick-

ing items up and setting them down, and then an ob-
noxious buzzer sounded and a hidden door popped open.
Both of the employees stood there, peering in. "Time's
up," one of them said, completely unnecessarily. "Want
us to show you the solution?"

Teddy didn't care, but Romeo nodded. It turned out
that Romeo was correct about what they were supposed
to accomplish, but they'd still been about six steps away
from getting there. At the rate they'd been going, it
might have taken all day.

"Sorry you guys didn't win," said the shorter woman
as she walked them to the lockers. "I hope you had fun
anyway."

Romeo nodded. "We did."

And that was no lie. Apart from the looming spec-
ter of failure and joblessness, the experience had been
enjoyable. The puzzle itself was kind of cute and, well,
there was all the making out, which had exceeded Teddy's dreams and expectations. Plus, Romeo was great to
hang out with even when they weren't kissing. He kept
his cool under adversity, he wasn't afraid to express his
feelings, and he wasn't obnoxiously competitive.

The employee was smiling at them. "You know, we
have date night puzzles for couples. The themes are a lot
more romantic than werewolves."

"We're not—" Teddy began and then stopped. They
weren't a couple. They'd just kissed a few times was all,
and they certainly hadn't discussed anything beyond that.
Yet he felt a strong connection to Romeo, as if the world

would spin more smoothly as long as they were together. As if they were complementary colors.

Jesus, that was stupid.

Their driver awaited them, of course. He looked relieved that no new injuries had occurred, but he didn't ask about the escape room. Maybe he'd already had a report, or maybe he didn't care. It was his boss's test, not his.

Even though it was early for rush hour, traffic had worsened while they'd been occupied. The Rolls inched forward while Romeo poked at his phone and Teddy gazed out the window. His thoughts had wandered to somewhere dismal and hazy, when he felt something touch his pinky. He turned his head to find Romeo smiling at him—and Romeo's hand against his on the plush seat. Teddy smiled back.

Chapter Thirteen

Back at the hotel, the driver announced that he'd be picking them up at nine the next morning. He claimed ignorance of the final test and then departed.

They were about halfway across the lobby on their way to the elevator when Teddy stopped and grabbed Romeo's elbow. "Have you ever been to Seattle before?"

"No."

"Me either. We have some time today, and there's no use stressing about tomorrow. Want to play tourist?"

Romeo's smile could have lit up an arena. "Yeah."

With the help of a visitors' guide that Romeo found on his phone, they did exactly that. They wandered through the main branch of the public library, which was a weird and interesting building. They took the monorail to Seattle Center and spent an hour at the Museum of Pop Culture—also a weird building. Romeo could easily have spent much longer there, oohing and aahing over the sci-fi exhibits, but the museum closed. So they went across the way and spent another hour admiring the Chihuly glass sculptures.

When that closed too, they gazed up at the Space Needle speculatively. Its design was Googie influenced, which he hoped was a good omen. "Might as well?" Teddy said hopefully.

Romeo chuckled. "Might as well."

Thanks to a clearing in the weather, the nighttime views were fantastic. Romeo and Teddy took selfies together, and then Romeo bought one niece a silly Space Needle hat and the other a plastic Space Needle bank, and he was so thrilled over these gifts that Teddy wanted to kiss him senseless. They boarded the monorail for a ride back downtown, walked down the hill to Pike Place Market, and found a fancy French restaurant with a view of the water. "Joyce can treat us tonight," Teddy announced, and Romeo agreed.

They pigged out on mussels, oysters, and crab. On Teddy's dare, Romeo ordered escargots, and they both decided snails tasted mostly like butter. They got a bottle of wine. Teddy sipped one glass while admiring the way Romeo moved his hands whenever he became excited about a topic—his favorite authors, his mother's cooking, his adorable and brilliant nieces. He showed Teddy photos of the girls, and they were very cute indeed. Back at the office, Romeo had been stiff and closed off. Aloof.

But now he opened up beautifully, his expression softening with happiness and his eyes glittering.

"So, why Reddyflora anyway?" Teddy asked while dipping a piece of baguette into the escargot sauce.

"What do you mean?"

"Someone with your skills, I bet you could've landed a job with some big tech company. A sure thing instead of a maybe. Doing something more important than making vases."

Romeo didn't answer right away. He poked at a crab leg, his mouth pursed thoughtfully. "I'd be less likely to fit in somewhere like that."

"Because…?"

"I grew up poor. My parents worked hard and gave us everything they could, but every month they had to worry whether they could make rent, groceries, and the other bills. And I didn't attend any fancy private schools. Two years at City College because it was cheap, and then I transferred to U of I."

Teddy, who'd earned his degree at U of I Springfield, cocked his head. "There's nothing wrong with that."

"No, there isn't. But at a big tech company, I'd be with people who'd gone to MIT, Stanford, Cal Tech…" He engaged in further crab dissection. "Anyway, I aspired to more than corporate drone, you know? I didn't want to be one of a hundred people clacking away at keyboards."

Baguette still in hand, Teddy leaned forward. "You wanted to be creative and stand out instead of trying to blend in."

There was that smile again. It made Teddy want to

burst into song and dance on the tabletop. He'd never made anyone smile like that before.

Romeo grabbed Teddy's bread and took a bite. "How about you? Flower fixation?"

"Actually, I'm a little allergic," Teddy admitted. "But this was such a great opportunity. So much more exciting than arranging store displays and arguing with the owner about whether coupons are effective sales generators. They're not, by the way—not if you're going for a high-end vibe."

Finishing the bread and leaning back in his seat, Romeo fixed Teddy with a piercing look. "What's your dream job? If you could do anything at all."

"It's stupid."

"Dreams are never stupid, but ignoring them sure is," Romeo responded smugly.

"That sounds like a quote."

"My mama's. So what's your dream?"

Teddy sought courage in the only form available: the remaining wine. He poured himself a healthy glassful and took a long swallow before speaking. "You know that shop we went to this morning?"

"Of course."

"I'd love to own a place kind of like that."

Romeo didn't scoff. Instead he leaned forward, his attention so complete that Teddy felt it like a caress on his skin. "Tell me more," Romeo said. "What do you mean by *kind of*? I want details."

Teddy downed the rest of his glass, which he knew would be a mistake eventually. That amount of alcohol might have little effect on most adults, but it would lay him out. "I want to spend hours every week scouring thrift stores and estate sales and resale shops for treasures. Not just clothing, but also décor and small pieces of furniture. I want to present my carefully curated collection in a space that's inviting but not intimidating. I want customers to come in so I can help them put together exactly the right look for themselves or their homes. I'll mix and match eras and styles to create something that makes them feel unique and beautiful. I don't want to be Joyce Alexander. I don't care if I'm featured in magazines, living in a mansion, or riding in a chauffeured Rolls. I just want my pretty, cozy storefront and devoted customers."

He'd never thought through these wishes so completely—not until now as he said them aloud. But as the words left his lips, there wasn't a lie among them. He almost expected to find his heart, still beating, lying on the empty oyster platter in front of Romeo.

Romeo reached forward and took Teddy's hands. "That's a wonderful dream. You'd be amazing at it. Look what you did for me in just one little shopping excursion!"

Wow. Teddy's family members loved him, but they'd always shot down his ideas. Gently—but rather thoroughly. *Oh honey, retail ownership is hard. Wouldn't you be better off with the security of a steady paycheck?* Or *You'd practically work yourself to death for razor-thin profit margins and no retirement plan.* But Romeo? He believed in him.

Teddy gently pulled his hands free, picked up his napkin, and pretended he needed to wipe his mouth. It took several moments to steady his voice. "Thanks. It's not a realistic goal, though."

"Why not?"

"Money. I have none. Finding a space, building up inventory, advertising...those require initial capital. Right now, there's not much left over after rent every month. I'll be a hundred and eighty before I save enough."

Romeo gave a little nod. "Which is why you're hoping Reddyflora does well. Stock options and bonuses."

"Yeah."

The wine was already going to Teddy's head. He could feel it curling along the neurons, tickling them, goading them to behave in ridiculous ways. The only question was how the neurons would react. Would he end up dancing on the tables in this nice restaurant or sobbing underneath them? Only time would tell.

"What's your dream?" he asked, hoping to maintain a steady course as long as possible.

"Independence. I want to work someplace where I can do what I want—within parameters, of course—and not have people in suits bossing me around all day. I want to create something new and different, something that gets people's attention. Not chunks of boring code that get buried in the middle of boring software that does boring things."

All that good food felt heavy in Teddy's stomach. "Reddyflora *is* your dream."

"Yeah. I guess it is."

Shit. And Teddy's incompetence with Joyce's tests was

ruining that dream. And…it looked as if crying under the table was today's call. He hid his face behind his napkin.

"You okay?" Romeo's voice was rich with concern.

"My, uh, ankle hurts."

There was no way Romeo believed that. Teddy hadn't complained about the ankle all day, and right now he was sitting down, for chrissake. But all Romeo said was, "Of course. Let me just flag down the waiter."

After they'd paid—thank you, Joyce—Teddy's long-dormant theatrical skills came in useful as he limped dramatically out of the restaurant to their waiting Lyft. The hotel wasn't far, so riding there was kind of silly, but he couldn't very well suggest walking now. Not when he was grievously wounded.

The cool outdoor air did nothing to sober Teddy up. If anything, it made him dizzier, as if the light drizzle were made of booze that soaked into his skin. He tripped on the sidewalk outside the restaurant and would have landed on his face if Romeo hadn't caught him. Romeo smelled now of the sea—or maybe that scent was Elliott Bay, a block distant.

"I don't know if I trust the ocean," Teddy told Romeo. "Too much salt. Too many tides. I like my water less… up and down. Like Lake Michigan."

Smiling, Romeo helped Teddy into the back seat of the waiting Subaru. "Lake Michigan has tides. They're just too small to notice."

"Too small," Teddy echoed sadly. That would suck. Here you were, a mighty body of water, but you didn't get the cred that the oceans did. You were just a lake, albeit a great one. You didn't get mermaids or kraken or even sharks. Just trout, and they weren't very impressive except for dinner.

Romeo slid into the seat next to him and Teddy toppled against his shoulder. He was allowed to do that on account of being injured. "Poor Lake Michigan," Teddy said.

"Okay."

"My parents took us on a dinner cruise in the lake when I was four. I screamed 'cause I thought we were gonna sink. Dad had to carry me on board."

"Did you stop screaming then?"

"After he bought me a Coke. I wasn't usually allowed to drink pop. Made me hyper."

Romeo wormed his arm around Teddy's middle and gave a light squeeze. "I've never been on a boat."

Teddy considered wiggling around to look at him but decided he was too comfortable. "Never?"

"Not so much as a canoe."

"Are you afraid you'll sink? Is it a phobia? They can do something about that. It's called…" Teddy scrunched up his face as he tried to remember, but his brain mostly sputtered. "Desalinization? No, now we're back at lakes and oceans again. Desolation? That's me when this is all over. De…de…"

"Desensitization. And no, it's not a phobia. It's just something I've never done. I'd like to someday." Romeo kissed the top of Teddy's head, which made Teddy sniffle because it was so sweet and tender.

"Stupid ankle," Teddy muttered, knowing even while inebriated that he was fooling nobody.

At the hotel, Romeo helped him out of the car and across the lobby. Inside the elevator, Teddy pressed all the buttons, earning a glare from a middle-aged man in a suit.

"Why'd you do that?" Romeo asked. He sounded amused instead of angry.

"What if someone on one of those floors wants to go up but forgets to—" Teddy mimed poking something and sort-of-accidentally almost poked the scowler instead.

"You don't want them to be stuck," said Romeo.

"Better stuck outside an elevator than in one, but both are bad. I carry my scooter up the stairs instead." His poor scooter, abandoned in an apartment in Chicago. It would have enjoyed zooming down the hills of Seattle.

The middle-aged man got off before them, shooting one final angry look on his way out, and they had only two more stops to their floor. Their room was a long way down the hall. Really long. And twice Romeo had to shush Teddy, who thought the acoustics called for a musical interlude. "Hotel California" didn't seem apt since they were in Washington, so he settled on "Heartbreak Hotel" instead.

"But this isn't Lonely Street," he pointed out as Romeo unlocked their door.

"Nope. We're on Second Avenue."

"Dunno that song."

Romeo's laughter was better than music anyway.

Although the hour wasn't especially late, Teddy was tired. Plus the room was beginning to spin—like the Space Needle, only faster—and the bed seemed like the safest place. The *only* bed, which he got to share with Romeo.

"Sleeping together is underrated," he announced.

Romeo, hanging up their coats, glanced over. "Oh?"

"Not sex. That's not underrated. Or overrated. It's... X-rated?" Teddy giggled at his own joke and collapsed onto the mattress. "I guess sometimes it's also overrated. Like with Gregory. He was boring."

"I'm sorry to hear that."

Teddy tried to remove his boots. They were Jeffery-Wests with pointed toes and an iridescent blue scaled-leather finish. Way out of his price range if he hadn't found them in pristine condition at one of his favorite consignment shops.

"*Sleeping* together," he said. "Like, being asleep in the same bed. That's underrated." The boot came off suddenly, hitting the floor with a thunk. He'd need to be more careful with the other foot, the injured one.

Romeo, who'd smoothly removed his own footwear, began stripping off the rest of his clothing. "Yeah? What do you like about it?"

Romeo's increasing nudity was a distraction. Teddy had to blink several times before he answered. "You're warm and you smell good. And you're cute when you're asleep. Cute awake too, but in a different way."

"Well, I like sleeping with you too. You're good company."

Teddy grinned.

In the end, Romeo had to help him with the second boot. Teddy managed to get most of his own clothes off but decided the pajamas were too much effort. He snuggled between the sheets in his underwear, waiting for Romeo to finish brushing his teeth. After Romeo doused the lights and got into bed, it was perfect. It was everything Teddy wanted, at least for tonight.

Well, maybe not everything.

He scooted closer.

"Not-sleeping in bed together is also good," he suggested hopefully.

Romeo chuckled. "Unless it's with what's his face. The ex."

"Let's forget him. But I bet you—"

"And you're going to hold that thought, Teddy Spenser. All we're doing tonight is sleeping."

Teddy cringed with embarrassment. "Oh. Sorry. I thought—"

Romeo caught Teddy's arm before he could slink back across the mattress. "You thought correctly. Look. I don't hook up often, okay? And never with someone…"

When the pause stretched on, Teddy tried a prompt. "Someone who screws things up so much for you?"

"No." Romeo gave Teddy's shoulder a gentle punch. "Someone special, okay?"

Just like that, Teddy felt like dancing on a table after all. Too bad there wasn't one handy. "I'm special?"

"Yeah. And you're also wasted. If we're gonna do this, let's be in our right minds, okay?"

Although that was disappointing, it also carried the implication of hope for the future. "I could drink some coffee."

"That doesn't work. Nothing's going to sober you up but time."

Teddy wasn't sure they had time. Tomorrow was the last test, whatever that might be, and then they'd have to fly home in disgrace, and Teddy would be totally broke. But even worse, Romeo would lose his dream job.

Teddy opened his mouth to explain all of this, but before he could get a word out, his phone rang.

Chapter Fourteen

"It's not too late, is it, darling?" Joyce's voice over the speaker was as clear as if she were standing in their hotel room.

"No," Teddy lied. "Not at all."

"Good. I hope you boys had some fun this evening."

A mix of emotions, along with the alcohol and fatigue, roiled within Teddy. *Polite and coherent. Try for polite and coherent.* "We saw some sights and had a great dinner. Thank you."

"Wonderful. And you'll be ready at nine, yes?"

"Of course. Um, tomorrow is—"

"A surprise, darling."

Great. "How should we dress? Do we need any supplies?"

"Casual is fine. You'll be remaining indoors. No supplies needed."

That didn't really narrow it down, but no use pushing her. "Okay, thanks. Um, about today—"

"We'll discuss it tomorrow." She hung up before he had a chance to explain that the escape room failure was all his fault.

Teddy lay there in the darkness, listening to Romeo breathe, trying to process the sudden shifts his life had taken in the past few days. The alcohol didn't help, but even sober he would have been overwhelmed. Maybe his existence in Chicago was kind of a grind, and maybe he'd been a little—well, a lot—lonely. But at least he'd possessed a predictable routine. Now in the space of only a few days, he'd learned that Romeo wasn't an asshole and was, in fact, sweet and fun to hang out with. Teddy had gone hiking, sprained an ankle, failed to get out of an escape room, ridden in a Rolls Royce, eaten escargots, been to the top of the Space Needle, had tea with Joyce Alexander, and placed his and Romeo's jobs in jeopardy. And, oh God, he'd kissed Romeo.

"Workplace romances are a bad idea," he finally whispered, almost hoping Romeo had fallen asleep.

"I guess."

"That won't be an issue when I get us fired. Or if Reddyflora goes belly-up because of me."

"You're not—"

"And my pledge to give up romance in favor of work, that wouldn't apply anymore either."

With a sigh, Romeo rolled over to face Teddy and

settle a warm hand on his bare shoulder. "Are you intending to fail tomorrow's test?"

"No. Just trying to see the silver lining."

Romeo replaced his palm with his lips and gave Teddy a dry little kiss. "Go to sleep, Teddy."

"Can't. Mind's too swirly."

Romeo's answering chuckle warmed Teddy like an electric blanket on his soul. "Figures," Romeo said. "Even your thought waves have interesting patterns."

If only the patterns weren't so confusing.

Teddy woke up too early, spent half an hour doing a gentle workout in the fitness center, and snagged coffee and bagels before returning to the room, where Romeo had just emerged from the bathroom. Droplets glistened on his skin, and he was wearing boxers again.

"How's your head?" Romeo asked, taking his coffee cup with a smile.

"Fine. Two drinks get me wasted, but I don't get hangovers."

"Lucky!"

"I guess."

Romeo strode to the closet and peered inside for a long moment before turning to make puppy dog eyes at Teddy. "Help."

It wasn't especially difficult to pick out an outfit among Romeo's three new ones. Teddy suspected the request was more about making him feel useful than getting Romeo suitably attired, but he played along. Naturally, Romeo looked delicious in his new cashmere sweater, but he eyed the scarf doubtfully. "It's not that cold out-side."

"Good, because that's not going to keep you warm. It's there for form, not function." Teddy fussed with the silk folds around Romeo's neck. "You didn't protest yes-terday when we bought it."

"I guess I got...caught up in the moment."

Teddy straightened a tassel. "If you don't want to wear it, don't. You look fantastic without it. But go see your-self in the mirror first."

Romeo obediently crossed the room. He stood awk-wardly in front of the mirror at first, but then his shoul-ders loosened and his expression relaxed. "I look good."

"Duh. But do you feel good? The point of clothing shouldn't be to impress other people; it's to make you feel great." He laughed self-consciously. "Sorry. You didn't ask for a lecture."

"I gave you one of Mama's sayings last night, so that earns you a lecture in return. Tell me something, though—what made you choose this scarf for me?"

"It's pretty." After a pause, Teddy decided to reveal the whole truth. "It's a little feminine, I think. Not some-thing many men would wear. But on you...it emphasizes your broad shoulders and nice muscles and makes you appear brave and adventurous and unique."

Romeo dropped his gaze to his feet. "I'm not any of those things."

"I disagree. But more importantly—when you wear that scarf, do you *feel* brave and adventurous and unique?"

"I guess…yeah. I do." Romeo straightened his stance and raised his gaze. "I really do."

He kept the scarf on.

They met their driver promptly at nine, and this time Teddy recognized the route. They were returning to Joyce's house. He wasn't sure whether that was a good or bad thing, but at least outdoor activities had been ruled out. That was a decidedly good thing because it was raining steadily, leaving the world awash in grays and muted greens.

Joyce greeted them at the door and ushered them inside. As soon as Romeo took his coat off, she made a delighted cooing noise. "That scarf! It's as if it were made for you, darling!"

"Teddy picked it out for me."

She gave Teddy an approving nod. "Well done! I'm not sure it's something I'd have been brave enough to try, but the two of you have pulled it off so well."

Teddy basked a little in the praise—from Joyce Alexander!—as she led them through the house. Today she wore wide silky palazzo pants in a pastel floral print, along with a lacy cream blouse. A collection of silver bangles jingled on her wrists. An elegant but understated ensemble that was probably her version of loungewear.

Her kitchen was as spectacular as he would have predicted: wooden floor of wide dark planks, white cabinetry with intricate molding, and acres of pale marble countertop. Teddy didn't know much about kitchen appliances but guessed hers were top-of-the-line. The walls were pale taupe, and the only bright colors came from huge glass vessels filled with lemons, oranges, and limes. Ornate chandeliers lent the room plenty of light, making everything gleam.

"Are you ready for today's challenge?" Joyce asked, stopping in front of a refrigerator that was half the size of Teddy's apartment.

"About yesterday—" Teddy began.

"Yesterday is gone. Thankfully without bodily injury. We're focusing on today."

Shit. Maybe he'd try to explain later. She needed to understand that their failures had not been Romeo's fault.

Seemingly oblivious to Teddy's turmoil, Joyce laced her fingers. "Today's test involves creativity. A critical skill in almost any endeavor, yes?"

A few of Teddy's nerves settled. He could do this—he was a creative guy. Even his teachers had said so, back when he'd been failing exams so miserably. One teacher had given him a B on a history test because, she said, although his essay was uniformly incorrect, he had demonstrated wit and originality. Maybe he knew nothing about the causes and consequences of the Cold War, but he could entertain with a dumb little story about a married couple fighting over control of the thermostat.

"Today I'm going to ask something special of you," Joyce continued. "It's self-serving as well, so I hope you won't mind. As I'm sure you're aware, today is Valentine's Day."

Teddy hadn't been aware. The holiday held little significance for him, and he'd lost track of the dates since leaving Chicago. But he nodded knowingly and saw Romeo do the same.

"Usually my husband Ron makes us dinner on occasions like this. He's a wonderful cook. But I'm going to break from tradition because this presents a perfect opportunity for you to demonstrate your creativity."

After a quick glance at Teddy, who gave a tiny shrug, Romeo cleared his throat. "Um, opportunity?"

"Yes! You're going to plan and prepare a dinner for me, Ron, and my boyfriend, Dave."

The whole husband-and-a-boyfriend thing caused such a stumble in Teddy's brain that it took a moment for him to notice the rest of the sentence. "Dinner?"

"A romantic dinner for three, yes. You can begin now by planning the menu. Once you have a list of ingredients, run it out to the car and Dave will do your shopping. Then—"

"Dave?"

"My driver and boyfriend," she said with a touch of impatience. "And you've met my husband Ron as well, the first time you were here. He's my household manager and cook. I realize our arrangement is unconventional, but it works for us."

Wow. Teddy couldn't manage even one serious relationship, and here was a woman in her seventies with *two* of them, each man a good two decades younger than her. It was very impressive, but saying so would be incredibly rude. "I see." He tried for an approximation of Dave's poker face but probably failed. Well, at least he was relieved he and Romeo hadn't said anything damning when they were in the Rolls.

"And once we get the groceries?" Romeo, bless him, remained on task.

"Then you prepare the meal. No need to serve it—I won't ask you to wait table as well." She laughed as if this were amusing.

Teddy's mind was now a horror-stricken blank. "Wh-what do you want us to make?"

"That's where your creativity comes in, darling! I prefer to take dinner fairly early, so let's plan to eat at six. I have quite a lot of work to complete today and won't see you until then, but you have free access to everything in the kitchen. I believe you'll find it well equipped. Oh, and make sure to fix yourselves some lunch as well. A pair of starving chefs just won't do."

She swept out of the room, leaving Teddy and Romeo to goggle, speechless.

Teddy was the first to break the silence. "I can't cook."

"At all?"

"Misshapen pancakes, burnt hamburgers, clumpy pasta. I mean, I can manage to heat premade things, but I doubt that will impress Joyce."

"How do you survive?" Romeo appeared stricken.

"I eat out. Or I do soup, sandwiches, and stuff I can nuke. Honestly, that's about all anyone could do in my kitchen." He had two drawers, three cabinets, a dorm-style fridge, a two-burner stove with minuscule oven, a teeny tiny microwave, and about four inches of counter space on either side of the sink. "Please tell me you know how to cook."

Romeo squinted and shifted his feet. "Um…"

"Oh God. Really?"

"I *do* know how. Mama taught me. She taught all us kids. It's just that…"

"What?" That came out louder than Teddy intended, and he lowered his voice. "Just pick a couple of your best recipes, okay?"

Frowning, Romeo shook his head. "Look. My parents came from a tiny little place in Mississippi that you've never heard of. Population about five hundred. They got married, moved to Chicago, and did their damnedest to help their children succeed."

"And they did," Teddy said gently. "You and your sisters have all done so much."

Romeo gifted him with a brief smile. "Yeah, we have, but that's not my point. Mama still cooks the way *her* mama did, and I'm sure her mama before her. Catfish. Fried okra. Collard greens. Black-eyed peas. Biscuits and gravy. Cornbread. A sweet potato pie you'd trade your soul for. And that's what she taught us. I don't regret any of that. But it's not what a famous rich white lady in her fancy-ass mansion wants to eat on Valentine's Day."

Teddy traced a finger along a vein in the marble. All those foods sounded delicious. He couldn't remember the last time he'd had a good home-cooked meal, and the mental image of a very young Romeo sitting at a table with his family made him envious. Neither of Teddy's parents enjoyed cooking, so they'd done a lot of takeout and premade grocery stuff even though that twisted his father's thrifty heart. Teddy hadn't been deprived, but he'd rarely had the chance to enjoy a warm kitchen filled with good smells and friendly chatter.

But he wasn't Joyce Alexander, was he?

"I guess you're right," he said slowly.

"So what do we do?"

"Look up recipes on our phones. You know your way around a kitchen at least, and we can follow directions. How hard can it be?"

Chapter Fifteen

As it turned out, it could be very hard.

The first challenge was finding acceptable recipes. They agreed on parameters: elegant and interesting, do-able within their time frame, and excluding overly exotic ingredients.

Beyond that, however, the negotiations broke down.

Romeo, who claimed little confidence in his cooking skills beyond his family's recipes, pushed for a few simple dishes. "They can be fancy, though," he said. "Shrimp cocktail, a nice steak, maybe—"

Teddy mimed a huge yawn. "We're being tested on creativity, remember? That's gonna earn us an F-minus. We can't afford to flunk this one." A note of desperation had entered his voice. No, not a note. An entire god-damn chorus.

"But we won't pass if we screw up the meal."

"Then we need to make sure we don't screw it up."

They glared at each other before returning to their phones. Occasionally one of them would throw out a suggestion, only to be shot down by the other. Meanwhile, the clock was ticking.

"How about if we pick a theme?" Teddy finally offered. "That's creative, right?"

"Like what?"

"Well, Valentine's Day, I guess, but maybe that's too obvious."

"Probably. We could pick a country—maybe one that's a little more unusual for Americans. Uzbekistan? Mauritania? Suriname?"

"Hmm." It was a good idea in principle. Teddy was fairly certain he'd never had foods from any of those countries. In fact, he had no idea what dishes might be involved. "I think this violates our exotic ingredients rule."

Romeo sighed heavily. "Yeah."

Then brilliance struck—or at least Teddy hoped so. "Flowers!"

"What?"

"We're Reddyflora—so how about if we make things that include flowers as ingredients? That's kind of Valentinish too."

Although Romeo looked skeptical, he didn't say no. "How do you cook with flowers?"

"No clue. We can google it."

"But it's February."

Oh. Yeah. This problem hadn't occurred to him. Teddy's succulents—may they rest in peace—had been his only houseplants, which is why he occasionally used fake foliage in décor. "Maybe...florists? I don't know. It's Washington, not Illinois. There's plenty of green stuff around right now, so maybe there are flowers too."

Romeo was scratching his lip, which wasn't a good sign. But then he gave a small shrug. "Let's come up with a list and see if Dave can come through for us."

It took them another long period to agree on a menu. Eventually they settled on chive flower flatbread, a smoked salmon salad with greens and flowers, herb and flower pasta, and lemon lavender tartlets. "At least we have the lemons already," Teddy pointed out.

Romeo didn't seem much cheered.

While Teddy made a dishearteningly long list of ingredients, Romeo checked the fridge and cupboards to see what was already available. After an extended rummage he exclaimed, "I think this is a pasta maker!" Teddy would have been more reassured had the statement been worded with greater confidence.

Because Romeo was still poking around in drawers, Teddy took it upon himself to get the list to Dave. The rain had intensified, but as promised, Dave was sitting in the Rolls not far from the back door, waiting for him.

"That took you a long time," Dave said as he took the paper. Apparently now that his secret identity was revealed, he'd decided to become a little chattier.

"We put a lot of thought into it."

Dave took so long to peruse the list that Teddy got into the passenger seat to avoid getting waterlogged. Oh, that dashboard was gorgeous! That lovely curve, the gleaming wood, all of those dials and buttons uncluttered by modern lights and digital readouts. He realized he was stroking the dash like a lover and quickly dropped his hand to the seat.

"Flowers," Dave finally said.

"It's a theme. Will she like that?"

"I'm not allowed to divulge that information."

"It's a dinner, not a spy mission." But after a long pause it became clear that Dave wasn't going to crack. "Can you get everything on the list?"

"I can try."

Teddy let out a relieved breath. "Make sure the flowers don't have any chemicals on them. You guys are going to be eating them."

"Wouldn't do to poison Joyce Alexander." Although Dave said it with a straight face, Teddy suspected it might have been a joke.

"Um…do you think this shopping trip is going to take you very long?"

Dave gave him a steady look. "Flowers. With no chemicals on them."

Right. Teddy thanked him, gave the dashboard one last pet, and returned to the deluge.

When he got back to the kitchen, he discovered Romeo clad in a frilly yellow apron and elbow deep in flour. He had flour on his nose too. He was so adorable that Teddy couldn't help himself—he scooted up behind him and leaned fully against Romeo's back, wrapping his arms around Romeo's middle for good measure.

"Kinda hard to knead when you do that." But Romeo sounded more amused than annoyed.

"But I neeeeded to do it."

Romeo groaned at the awful pun. It had been a fairly honest statement, however: Teddy had been overcome with the urge to…snuggle. Which was weird because he'd never thought of himself as a cuddler, not even when he was dating. He and Gregory had complained to each other about how other couples got all gross and cutesy, with their gratuitous touchy-feely and their pet names. He and Gregory had always looked great together, but they'd never been handsy.

Now though? Teddy yearned for an oversize couch with lots of pillows, a roaring fire, big mugs of hot cocoa, a couple of fluffy throw blankets; maybe even a purring cat. And Romeo, squished up against him all warm and sleepy. Dozing in front of a dumb movie perhaps. With snow falling thickly outside the windows and nobody having to go anywhere for the rest of the day.

Agh. Must be the remnants of the previous night's wine.

Teddy supervised while Romeo pushed and tugged at what looked like a ridiculously large mound of dough. Teddy didn't point that out at first, because what did he know about making flatbread? But after a while Romeo stopped, took a step back, and cocked his head. "That doesn't look right."

"There's a lot of it."

"And it's supposed to double by the time it's finished rising."

An image formed in Teddy's mind of a beige blob inexorably overflowing the counter, taking over the entire kitchen, and spreading toward the door on its way to conquer Seattle. "Are you sure you did the recipe right?"

"I followed it exactly." He gestured with his elbow toward his phone, which he'd propped on the jar of limes, safely out of range of the flying flour.

Teddy picked up the phone and peered at the text. Nothing looked untoward. Except… "Shit."

"Shit what? What's wrong?" There was an edge of panic in Romeo's voice.

"Did you read the fine print? It says this recipe makes enough for six large flatbreads. We don't need six. Nobody needs six. Why would the recipe be for six instead of a reasonable number like one? Who is this recipe for?"

Romeo ran his fingers through his hair—a bad idea since they left a flour track—and chewed his poor abused lip. "I guess we could use part of it and throw the rest away."

"That's wasteful, isn't it?"

"So you want to bake it all?"

Teddy did not want to bake it all. There was nothing creative about burying Joyce Alexander in flatbread, not even if it was floral themed. Besides, it wouldn't fit in the oven. He gently pushed Romeo out of the way, removed roughly one sixth of the blob and set it aside, and carried the remainder to the trash can under the sink. It was a very ordinary trash can, nearly identical to the one that took up all the space under his sink in Chicago. He would have expected Joyce to have something more upscale, maybe a designer garbage can.

Teddy's stomach suddenly reminded him that it was lunchtime. Dave wasn't back yet, and there wasn't much he could do to assist Romeo, so Teddy assembled a couple of turkey sandwiches and plated them up with some little apples. In one cabinet he discovered a trove of Pringles cans, which shocked him more than the trash can. Did Joyce, of all people, eat Pringles? He put some of them on the plates.

They ate at the pretty white table tucked under a window overlooking the water. They didn't talk much, but it was nice nonetheless. It made Teddy realize that although he went out to restaurants with friends now and then, he never had company for his meals at home. He liked sitting with Romeo over sandwiches.

"What are you thinking about?" Romeo asked before crunching his way through a chip.

"That I'm an idiot." Although he wasn't sure whether he was more foolish for vowing to eschew romance—or for now wanting to break that vow. Especially when he was perfectly aware that he had no future with Romeo.

"I don't think so."

"Thanks."

"No, I mean it. You don't give yourself enough credit." Teddy snorted. "You should see my grades. I made it through school thanks to a few close scrapes and a couple of sympathetic professors."

"I got almost straight As. Summa cum laude. But I can't even dress myself without other people's help. Want to hear more of my mama's wisdom?"

"Sure." Teddy figured Mrs. Blue must be a pretty smart person to have done such a good job raising her kids, and he wanted all the wisdom he could get.

"When I was a kid, I'd get upset because I sucked at sports and I was just…awkward around everyone. I used to come home and cry over it, Teddy."

Teddy reached over and patted Romeo's hand, wishing he could time travel just long enough to give young Romeo a comforting hug and tell him that someday everything was going to be all right. "I cried when I realized I was never going to make it to Broadway," Teddy admitted.

"But you found your light somewhere else. That's what Mama calls it. She says everyone's got their own light, and instead of envying someone else's we should each do our very best to shine. You shine bright, Teddy Spenser." Romeo stroked his scarf, which he'd draped over a chair to save it from the flour. "So bright I'm almost blinded."

Teddy might have remained there, gaping, for the rest of the day. Or he might have hurdled the table, tackled Romeo, and torn those new clothes right off him. Luckily Dave entered the kitchen, laden with fabric grocery sacks. A hint of annoyance may have shown near the corners of his eyes, but if so, Teddy couldn't really blame him.

"Got everything but the squash blossoms," Dave announced, setting the bags on the island. "Not available this time of year."

That was disappointing but not an utter disaster. They could sub something else. "Thank you," Teddy and Romeo said in unison. Dave gave a regal nod and left the kitchen for parts unknown. Maybe he sat in the Rolls all day, regardless of what was scheduled. If Teddy had to be stuck in a vehicle for hours on end, he'd choose that one too.

The flatbread was still rising, in theory. It didn't look any different to Teddy. Maybe rather than rising gradually, it would bloom all at once, having reached some magical yeasty apex. In any case, since Romeo was now the more experienced of them when it came to making dough, Teddy appointed him chief pasta maker. That left Teddy to prep the flowers and juice the lemons for the tartlets. They'd opted for premade tartlet shells, hoping that wouldn't count as cheating. Making tiny piecrusts from scratch felt well beyond their limits of skill, time, and patience.

Nothing in the universe was cuter than Romeo in that apron—Teddy was positive of that. Romeo concentrated on the pasta dough, his brow furrowed and his tongue sticking out a tiny bit. Those long fingers working the flour mixture so dexterously got Teddy thinking about how they'd feel on his bare skin, stroking here and there, digging in a little during the more intense moments. Teddy wanted to suck on them and watch them leave damp tracings down his belly and over—

"You're staring."

Teddy blinked a few times to clear his head. "I, uh, I'm sorry."

"You weren't thinking about flatbread."

"No." There was no use lying. Romeo's eyes glittered with something other than a love of baking, and he licked his lips with decadent leisure.

"I'm not going to drink tonight," Teddy announced.

"I'm not sure I'd have the self-control to resist you again even if you did drink."

The kitchen was suddenly much too warm even though the oven wasn't on. Teddy got himself a glass of water and guzzled it. Then he filled another glass, carried it over to Romeo, and held it to his mouth with a wicked grin. "Your hands are too messy to hold it yourself."

"Hmm." Romeo never moved his gaze from Teddy's face as he drank, and Teddy watched with rapt fascination as Romeo swallowed. Who knew hydration could be such a turn-on?

Teddy set the glass on the counter and stood on his toes, intending to kiss whatever parts Romeo would allow. But Romeo danced a step backward and shook his head with a smile. "Remember where making out got us yesterday?"

"Trapped in an escape room."

"Yep."

Fine. The kissing could wait.

Teddy dedicated himself to the herbs and flowers: sorting, washing, drying, and removing leaves and petals. It made for a pretty project, and an aromatic one. But due to his slight allergy, he ended up having a sneezing fit and had to use paper towels to blow his nose.

The pasta dough had to rest for only a brief time. But then came the tricky part, which was feeding it through the machine. This stymied Romeo, who swore a lot under his breath. But then Teddy realized the machine was similar to one he'd used for clay in one of his childhood art classes. As it turned out, pasta making used essentially the same techniques. After a little practice, Teddy managed to make reasonable-looking noodles.

Then he attempted to add the flowers.

He might have been okay if he'd had an extra pair of hands, but with only two, he kept dropping things or smooshing the sheets of dough. Romeo tried to assist, but that meant they were standing pressed together, their arms entwining, which led to even worse pasta disasters.

There were some noodles in the end, but they sported numerous weird blobs and the flower petals were unrecognizable smears of color. There would be nothing Insta-worthy about this dish. "Maybe it'll taste okay anyway," Romeo said hopefully.

"If anyone's brave enough to eat it."

While Teddy put together a pistachio pesto sauce—scattering shells everywhere; he'd neglected to request the unshelled kind—Romeo tackled the salmon salads. "I think I'll assemble these directly onto the plates. We can keep them covered in the fridge until it's time to dress and serve."

"Good idea."

And it would have been, except as Romeo was carrying the carefully composed plates to the fridge, he slipped on a shell Teddy had missed during his cleanup efforts. He was able to keep his balance, but all three dishes landed on the floor with an ear-splitting crash.

Romeo and Teddy stared in horror at the mess. China shards everywhere, mixed in with pieces of rosy salmon, green lettuce, and bright flowers. Thankfully nobody came running to investigate.

Teddy knelt, picked up a broken piece of china, and examined the pattern. "Spode," he concluded with a sigh.

"Joyce probably didn't buy it on sale at Target, huh?"

"Antiques."

Teddy had a momentary fantasy of running out of the house, calling a Lyft, and scouring the city for replacements. But there wasn't time, and he didn't have a clue where to begin. There was an excellent chance he'd never find this particular pattern anyway. "We're going to have to tell her."

"Yep."

And then another thought struck Teddy. "Was that all of our salmon?"

"Yep."

"We could ask Dave to get us more."

Romeo cocked an eyebrow. "Do you want to tell him why? 'Cause we'd pretty much have to."

"No," Teddy replied with a sigh. "I guess we'll just serve pasta and flatbread. And dessert." Damn. The salads had looked so pretty—infinitely better than the pasta.

They cleaned up the colorful mess, setting aside the shards even though the plates were clearly unsalvageable.

Then Romeo checked on the flatbread dough. "It's been over two hours, hasn't it?"

Dread curled in Teddy's stomach. "Yeah. Why?"

"It's supposed to be doubled by now, but it looks exactly the same."

Maybe Romeo was mistaken. Teddy had a look for himself and...nope. Not doubled. Not changed at all as far as he could tell, and it didn't have the soft, somewhat spongy texture the recipe described. "What's wrong with it?"

"Dunno. I think I killed it."

"Maybe it's mad at us for throwing five-sixths of it away."

Romeo frowned at him. "Bread dough isn't sentient."

"How do you know? Maybe it has a yeasty consciousness of its own, and its ambition is to become beautiful baked goods everyone will enjoy. But this one is sulking." Teddy was fully aware how ridiculous this was, but absurdity seemed like a better option than despair. "Do you think there's some way to improve its mood?"

"I don't know how to cheer up yeast."

Teddy poked the dough a few times and then sighed. "We should've made your mother's recipes. They would have been delicious. The theme could have been love-infused Southern home cooking."

"Too late now."

And the clock was ticking.

Chapter Sixteen

Working together, they mixed the filling for the tartlets. That was blessedly simple, although Teddy drew blood from an abraded fingertip as he grated the lemon zest. He then got a little lemon juice in the wound. "Ow!"

Romeo turned quickly from the sink, where he'd been washing dishes. "Your ankle? Maybe you should sit down."

"Ankle's fine. I have acid eating away at my flesh."

The recipe said to let the filling chill thoroughly before using, which would have been a good thing to have noticed several hours ago. "Why don't they have reverse microwaves to make things cold really fast?" Teddy wondered aloud.

Romeo mentioned blast chillers and then launched

into a long explanation about thermodynamics that might have been fascinating under other circumstances but did nothing to solve their immediate problem. Teddy stuck the bowl of filling in the freezer and hoped for the best.

Joyce's oven was fancier than either of them was accustomed to, and it took them a while to learn how to operate it. Teddy wasn't convinced they hadn't accidentally launched some rockets in the process, but at least they'd also achieved the desired temperature to bake the tartlet shells. Romeo carefully slid the baking sheet inside and Teddy set the timer.

The flatbread dough remained stubbornly inert.

"I'm just going to use it anyway," Romeo announced. "It's still dough, right?"

"Maybe it'll rise when it bakes."

While Romeo attempted to roll the dough into submission, Teddy chopped the scallions, chive flowers, and onions for the topping. His eyes watered, of course, and while attempting to wipe away the tears he aggravated the grating injury, but at least he hadn't lopped off any fingers. "My hands are going to smell like onions forever," he lamented.

"I know how to fix that."

"Another of your mother's pearls of wisdom?"

"Of course. Look in those drawers until you find a stainless steel spoon or fork."

Naturally, Joyce's tableware was silver. But Teddy found a stainless spoon among the mixing utensils. "Got it," he said, waving the spoon in the air.

"Go rub the spoon under cold running water."

"That's weird. How's that going to help?"

"Chemistry. Sulfur from the onions bonds with the metal."

It worked, which was nice, but that wasn't what made Teddy smile. He'd never dated anyone who knew the slightest thing about chemistry or could tell him how refrigerators worked. Not that he and Romeo were dating, of course. But Teddy found that store of knowledge endearing, and he was also charmed by the way Romeo shared it without acting like a know-it-all or making Teddy feel dumb.

"Your light shines bright too," Teddy said.

Romeo beamed and opened his mouth to say something, but stopped with a frown. "Shouldn't those shells be ready by now?"

"Shit!" Teddy sprinted to the oven and looked at the timer. It read 60. "Oh God." Instead of 7 minutes, he must have set it for 70. He looked around frantically for an oven mitt, found one, and pulled the shells out.

Romeo was still battling the flatbread. "How bad?"

"Scorched. Not completely burned, though."

"Can you sort of scrape off the scorched bits?"

"I can try."

It was a delicate operation. Too much scraping and the shell cracked or crumbled. He lost three shells that way, but that left nine—enough for three people. Overly browned parts remained, but the filling would hide most of them. He slid the cookie sheet into the fridge so the shells could cool.

"This isn't working," Romeo lamented. "Dough's too stiff."

"You got it sort of flat, though. I don't think the overall shape matters. I've had restaurant flatbread that was irregular." Teddy tried to inject a cheery note into his voice. "It looks handmade this way. That's creative."

Romeo's scowl said he wasn't convinced. But he spread olive oil on the thing anyway, and distributed the topping over that. Then he increased the oven temperature. "We have thirty minutes," he pointed out. "What's left?"

"Bake the bread, fill the tartlets, boil and sauce the pasta." That sounded doable.

"Are we supposed to set the table too?"

"I don't think so. They probably want to eat in the dining room." It was too bad. Making an attractive table setting was something Teddy had confidence he could do well. But Joyce hadn't shown them the dining room. The only parts of her house they'd really seen were the room where they first chatted, the kitchen, and the powder room just off the kitchen. Presumably the dining room was nearby, but Teddy didn't feel comfortable exploring on his own.

"I guess we could finish washing up now, while the oven heats."

"Good idea."

The plan was for Romeo to wash and Teddy to dry and put away. A good plan, except it meant they were standing close together again, and this time when Teddy angled upward for a kiss, Romeo didn't step away. He set a half-scrubbed bowl in the sink and reached for Teddy, getting Teddy's shirt wet and soapy. Teddy knew they were being terribly unprofessional, and he didn't care. He also didn't care that Joyce could walk in on them any second. Worldly cares dropped away with Romeo in his arms.

Romeo nuzzled Teddy's neck, making him shiver, and cradled Teddy's face in his big palms, tracing a damp thumb along Teddy's cheek.

"How have you done this to me?" Teddy asked, leaning hopelessly into the touch.

"Done what?"

"A few days ago I thought I hated you. And now—"

"Hated?" Romeo arched an eyebrow. "I don't think you knew me well enough to hate me."

"I didn't know you at all. My loss."

"Mine too." Romeo gave his cheek another stroke. Teddy never would have thought such a simple bit of contact—and so far above the belt—could be so erotic. But oh God, it truly was. His eyes rolled back in his head and an embarrassing moan escaped him.

Chuckling, Romeo let him go. "I think we'd better finish prepping dinner."

He was right, of course, but Teddy grumbled nonetheless as he finished drying. When Romeo slid the flatbread into the oven, he bent rather more than he had to, and that ass waggle was definitely gratuitous.

"I should have dressed you in Spandex, like a member of an eighties hair band." Teddy sighed.

"Would that have been appropriate?"

"Absolutely not. But it would have been magnificent."

Romeo laughed. But when he closed the oven and turned to face Teddy, his expression was earnest. "Do you know something amazing about you?"

"Um...no."

"I can be completely myself in front of you. I don't have to pretend I'm someone else or worry you're going to think I'm weird. I've only ever felt this way around family before."

A lot of things had happened during the past several days, but Romeo's words shook Teddy more than everything else combined. He had to grab the counter for support, and for once in his life, he couldn't say a word, although he might have squeaked a little. He liked Romeo just as he was, and *weird* was a compliment as far as Teddy was concerned. Who wanted normal? But since he couldn't manage to say any of this out loud at the moment, he simply stood and basked in the rare sensation of being...special.

Then his phone dinged, reminding him that their time was almost up.

Working swiftly, Teddy filled the tartlets. Romeo checked the big pot of salted water, nearly at a boil, and removed the flatbread from the oven. "I don't know about this," he said.

"Does it look awful?"

"Hard to tell. It seems really...solid."

"At least you didn't burn it."

It was almost six o'clock, and Teddy had just lowered

the pasta into the pot when Joyce swept into the room wearing one of her vintage maxi dresses. Pastel pink with lace on the bodice and skirt, it should have looked much too young for her, but it didn't.

"You're lovely," Teddy said with genuine enthusiasm.

She twirled like a girl in a prom dress. "Thank you, darling. I haven't worn this one in ages. How's dinner coming along?"

"Ready in minutes." He waved toward the steaming pot to demonstrate. "We were wondering how you'd like us to serve it."

"Let's place it in serving dishes and we can carry everything in together."

Dishes. Ugh—that reminded him. Wincing, he pointed at the sad pile of broken china on one corner of the counter. "We broke three of your Spode salad plates. I'm so sorry! Of course I'll pay for the damage, or when I get home I'll find replacements, or—"

"*I* broke them," Romeo interrupted. "I was clumsy and dropped them."

"Only because you slipped on one of my pistachio shells."

Joyce regarded them both, ignoring the plates. She didn't seem surprised or upset at the revelation, just thoughtful. "Don't worry about it. Accidents happen, especially in the kitchen. I knocked a Waterford vase off a shelf just the other day. Let's serve dinner, shall we?"

Teddy doubted the Waterford story but appreciated the effort to make her guests feel better.

"What serving pieces do we need, boys?"

Romeo answered. "A big bowl and two platters."

"Interesting. All right." She removed the requested items from a hutch near the table. Not Spode this time but equally pretty, with a lacelike blue-and-white pattern around the edges. Teddy wondered if she'd deliberately chosen pieces with a solid white serving area—better to examine the food.

While Romeo drained the pasta and topped it with pesto, Teddy arranged the tartlets as attractively as possible. They were kind of cute, at least with the burned parts gone or camouflaged. But when he handled the flatbread, he was dismayed by its weight and the solid thud it made when set on the platter. It was like a warm, irregular, onion-scented brick.

"Are we ready?" Joyce asked.

Heavy with trepidation, Teddy handed her the tartlets. He hefted the flatbread, Romeo took the pasta, and they followed behind her in a short, terrified parade.

The dining room was ornate but not overdone: floor-to-ceiling bow windows with water views, pale blue walls with intricate gold molding, a floor of gleaming dark wood, and an enormous crystal chandelier. The long table, a modern design in clear Lucite, was a nice counterpoint to the more traditional décor of the room. The chairs were champagne-hued fabric rimmed with silver-toned wood, and massive candles flickered in several silver candelabras.

Ron and Dave—handsome in Armani suits, navy and black respectively—sat across from each other near one end of the table with an assortment of cutlery, dishes, and glasses in front of them.

"Dinner," Joyce sang.

Teddy felt nauseous.

Joyce set the tartlets on the table and gestured for Teddy and Romeo to follow her lead. Then she took a seat at the head of the table and surveyed the meal. It would have looked sad in Teddy's charmless miniature kitchenette. In this beautiful setting it looked full-on pathetic.

"Tell us what you've prepared for us," Joyce prompted brightly.

Romeo, who looked as if he'd swallowed his tongue, cast Teddy a desperate look. So Teddy took a deep breath and forged ahead. "We've gone with a floral theme. Because we're Reddyflora, of course, but also in honor of the holiday. And we've opted for a light meal because so often we're all tempted to overindulge a little during winter. Um, not that you've overindulged, but, um…it's a theme." He'd never been any good at extemporizing, and a raging case of nerves wasn't helping.

Seemingly oblivious to his distress, Joyce gave a regal nod. "Tell us about the individual dishes, please."

"The main course is flower-and-herb pasta with pistachio pesto."

"Ah, the source of the wayward shell." Her lips crooked slightly.

"I'm afraid so. Um, Dave did a fantastic job sourcing all the flowers for us. Thank you, Dave. We appreciate it."

Miracle of miracles, Dave actually smiled.

Onward. "Along with that we have a chive flower flatbread."

"Clever!" she said.

"And for dessert, lemon and lavender tartlets." Even as the words left his mouth, he felt his knees almost give. The lavender! He'd forgotten to sprinkle the florets on top, which meant the tartlets had no flowers at all. Maybe Joyce wouldn't notice. After all, the tartlets might have lavender essence in the filling, right? Oh God.

"Thank you," Joyce said. "Now, if you'll excuse us, we're going to enjoy our meal. There's a car waiting for you just out that door—" she pointed down a hallway "—and the driver has been instructed to take you anywhere you'd like, so you can have a nice dinner as well. I hope you don't consider it rude of me to evict you like this." She shrugged and gave a roguish smile. "Valentine's Day, you know."

Teddy didn't want to be in the room when they attempted to eat. Relieved, he nodded. "Of course. Thank you for the opportunity."

Romeo mumbled his thanks too.

"I'll contact you tomorrow," Joyce said, reaching for the pasta bowl. "Your flight leaves around noon, I believe. We'll talk before then."

Assuming the dinner didn't kill her, and her companions.

The waiting Lincoln Town Car was very nice—certainly tons better than Teddy's scooter—but a bit of a letdown after the Rolls. "Where to?" asked the driver, a thin older woman with smile crinkles at the corners of her eyes.

Teddy turned to Romeo. "What are you in the mood for?"

Romeo's answering look was so scorching that Teddy gasped. He gave the driver the address of their hotel.

Chapter Seventeen

They didn't exactly sprint to the hotel elevator, because that would be undignified. It was more like— Okay. They ran. And Romeo pushed the button approximately a hundred times, yet still it took the elevator forever to reach the lobby and slowly open its doors. They jostled inside.

"If you push all the floors this time I'm going to die," Romeo announced. He looked serious.

Teddy had no intention of pushing all the buttons. In fact, if elevators came with warp-speed buttons, he would have engaged one. He didn't manhandle Romeo during the ride up, but only because he knew there must be a security camera and he didn't want to give any voyeurs their nightly thrill.

On their own floor at last, they burst out of the elevator and raced down the corridor, which had lengthened by at least five miles. Once they were at the door of their room, the damned thing wouldn't open no matter how many times Romeo swiped the card, and now it was Teddy's turn to die, and— Oh.

"You're trying to open the door with Joyce's debit card."

Romeo stared at the plastic in his hand as if he'd never seen it before, so Teddy gently pushed him out of the way and swiped his own key card. It worked on the first try.

Good God, they were finally inside.

Coats and shoes still on, they crashed their bodies together and, lips locked, stumbled awkwardly to the bed. *Their* bed, in which Romeo was no longer a disliked near stranger or an off-limits object of desire, but rather a warm and willing and wonderful man.

With far too many clothes on.

"Forget Spandex," Teddy grumbled as he struggled with the buttons on Romeo's coat. "I should have dressed you in nothing but a toga. One good tug and boom! Naked."

Romeo was working on Teddy's coat too. "Kinda cold for that."

"It's practically tropical compared to back home."

At last their coats and Romeo's scarf were off, thrown to the floor and soon followed by Teddy's vest and Romeo's sweater and undershirt. Teddy unbuttoned just enough of his shirt to tug it off over his head and toss it aside.

Then they paused. They'd seen each other shirtless already; in fact, they'd seen each other pantsless too. But that had been different, because back then they were just looking. Now they could touch. And, Teddy realized with a shiver, taste.

He pushed Romeo back onto the mattress, straddled him, and began to nibble and lick. He started with Romeo's ears and the tender stretch of his neck, worked his way to the collarbones, and settled in on his nipples. Pebbled and salty, they felt pleasant against his teasing tongue, and Romeo arched underneath him with satisfying moans.

"You're good at this," Romeo said, voice already roughened.

"I was afraid I was out of practice."

"Hang on."

For a terrible moment, Teddy thought he'd done something wrong. But no, Romeo was smiling up at him, pupils wide with desire. "It's been a while for you, huh?"

Teddy, who wasn't even sure how long it had been—many months at least—nodded.

"Yeah, me too," Romeo said. "So let's slow this down, okay?"

Right. Because it might very well be their *only* time. But that didn't bear thinking of, so Teddy nodded again. "I can try."

"Lemme see you strip."

If Teddy had been standing, his knees might have buckled at the gentle command. It was sexy. And playful. And flattering—that a man as beautiful as Romeo wanted boring ol' Teddy to put on a show. And it was only four and a half little words but they made Teddy's pulse race.

He had to take off his boots first, and that part wasn't sexy. Maybe there was an erotic way to remove laced footwear, but if so, he wasn't versed in it. Once he was rid of them, he stood a few feet from the bed and slowly slid his hand down his chest and belly. And then, eyes never leaving Romeo's face, he unbuttoned his trousers.

Romeo licked his lips and palmed his own bulge through the fabric of his jeans. A flash of envy shot through Teddy, but then he realized he could play that game too. So he massaged his aching dick with one hand and teased a nipple with the other.

"You're good at this too," said Romeo.

"I'm a man of many talents."

Teddy continued to play with himself for a few minutes, which felt nice enough. The best part, though, was seeing how every tiny movement he made brought a spark to Romeo's eyes or a subtle shifting of his expression and posture. It was funny that Teddy had once thought him closed off, when now Romeo sprawled before him open and wanting.

When Teddy unzipped his pants, the metallic sound was like a punctuation between his heavy breaths. The trousers dropped to the floor, puddling at Teddy's feet. Stepping out of them might have been simple enough under ordinary circumstances, but with his sore ankle, he was afraid he might fall. Landing flat on his face would *not* be alluring. He tried a slightly complicated maneuver instead, twisting around to use a nearby chair as support but sending a coy glance over his shoulder and waggling his ass, as if showing off his butt had been his primary intention.

The slight charade paid off when Romeo groaned. "I'm having regrets about slowing down."

Cackling evilly, Teddy rid himself of the trousers and gave his hips a few undulations.

He was wearing navy-blue Hanes briefs. Underwear was one item he couldn't buy at thrift shops, and throwing away twenty-five or thirty bucks for little scraps of fabric and elastic had felt wasteful, especially when nobody else was going to see them anyway. Now Romeo *was* seeing the Hanes, but if disappointed, he certainly didn't show it.

When Teddy turned back around, he saw that Romeo had unfastened his jeans and stuck his hand inside, stroking himself as he watched Teddy. Strictly speaking, that might have been cheating. But since Romeo jacking himself to Teddy's little show was incredibly, meltingly erotic, Teddy wouldn't complain.

He was, however, eager to get his own hands on Romeo.

One sock came off easily, and he threw it aside. The other, however, was wrapped in his brace. He bent to remove it, but Romeo stopped him with a noise. "Keep the brace on if you want."

"It looks dorky."

"It looks like it's keeping you from hurting, which is what's important."

Oh God. That was it—that was the exact moment when Teddy realized he was falling hard and fast, and at the end he was going to suffer worse than a hurt ankle.

Because even now, when the air was so sexually charged it crackled, Romeo was more interested in how Teddy felt than whether he looked perfect.

No, no, no. A serious thing with Romeo was not in the stars, and Teddy needed to get that message into his brain—into his heart—pronto.

"You really don't care whether a scene is Instagrammable, do you?" Teddy said it because if he didn't say *something*, he was going to cry. And that would ruin the mood.

Corners of his lips raised, Romeo shook his head. "I don't have an Instagram account. I'm not a fan of social media. Anyway, I don't want to take photos right now—I just want you."

Shit. Yeah. That head-full-of-helium and heart-three-sizes-too-big feeling? That felt great even as Teddy tried and failed to fight it. Warmth filled him, along with the conviction that he could never have too much of Romeo's sweet, intelligent, wonderfully nerdy company.

You only get him until you leave Seattle, remember? Fine. Fine. But that meant Teddy *did* have him, at least for a little longer.

So why was Teddy way over here when Romeo was over there?

Giddier than the time he scored a flawless vintage Aquascutum trench coat for fifteen dollars, Teddy yanked off his briefs and launched himself onto Romeo. "I want you too," Teddy said between kisses. "Desperately." He didn't add the important words—*and forever*—because that was impossible.

Well, for now he had Romeo, and that was a delight.

Romeo had his hands, those lovely hands, all over Teddy. Caressing, squeezing, exploring. Teddy, however, concentrated on what he could do to Romeo with his mouth. What would make Romeo arch his back and cry out? Oh, *that* would. And *that*. Because it appeared that Romeo was incredibly sensitive to touch, his entire long, perfect body one erogenous zone. And that was with some of the most interesting parts still covered in denim.

"Clothes off!" Teddy didn't wait for Romeo to give him a strip show, instead taking matters into his own hands by tugging jeans and boxers down—past narrow hips, strong thighs, and long legs. Romeo's loafers slipped off easily, and Teddy was too impatient to care about his socks.

Teddy took a good long look at what he'd just revealed. "Oh my God."

Romeo beamed at him. "Yeah?"

"Uh-huh." That was about as much as Teddy could manage. His mouth had gone dry at the vision on the bed.

"I don't, uh, do much manscaping." Romeo waved at Teddy, probably indicating his waxed chest and closely trimmed pubes.

"If I don't, I'm a dead ringer for Sasquatch. But Jesus, Romeo, you're perfect exactly as you are." And not just because he looked beautiful, but also because he *was* beautiful.

Dammit, Teddy was in way over his head.

Hoping he looked sexy and not walleyed besotted, Teddy lay full-length on top of Romeo. Even though Romeo was several inches taller, they fit together well, skin against skin as if they'd been designed for each other. Romeo was warm, his heartbeat strong, his body solid where it ought to be and giving in all the right places. And oh! Those fingers playing along Teddy's spine and down to his ass as if Teddy were a computer keyboard and Romeo was programming him to ecstasy.

But then Romeo went still. "I didn't bring rubbers or lube."

"Me either. Had no idea we'd need them."

"We could find a drugstore..."

Teddy lightly booped Romeo's nose. "If you think I'm getting off you now and putting on clothes, you are sadly mistaken. I bet we can manage without." He undulated his hips to prove his point. That felt so good that he did it again. And again. By which time he'd forgotten what point he was trying to make, and probably so had Romeo, who was gasping and clutching him close.

They were noisy, but nobody complained. Teddy grew more intoxicated than he ever had on alcohol, absolutely drunk with the sensations that flooded him and the power he held to make Romeo writhe and moan. The best part of all was when Romeo chanted his name—"Teddy, Teddy, Teddy!"—over and over like a wonderful spell. And Teddy knew in his heart that for tonight at least, Romeo wanted *him*. Not just a convenient lay. Not someone who'd look decent in selfies. But him specifically. Teddy Spenser. Who felt as if he'd been yearning for exactly this for his entire life.

"Oh God—Teddy!"

Afterward they lay tangled together, sweaty and out of breath, Romeo running his fingers through Teddy's messy hair. "Can I terrify you by admitting something?" Romeo asked softly.

"Um…okay."

"I've never had a real boyfriend."

Teddy, whose brain was still flying on endorphins, asked, "You've had pretend ones?"

Romeo tickled Teddy's ribs. "I'm spilling my guts here, dude. I mean I've never been in a romantic relationship with anyone. I've been on first dates, and I slept with some of them. But I've never…" He sighed heavily, and Teddy snuggled even closer.

"I get it," Teddy said. "My track record's not much more extensive. But man, I cannot understand why anyone would give up on you after one small taste."

"Well, maybe because with everyone else, I've played a part. Badly. 'Cause unlike you, I was never part of the thespian crowd. And I told you: you let me be me."

This was a more deeply personal conversation than Teddy had expected. But honestly, if you couldn't get real with the person you'd just had sex with, the man whose taste still lingered on your tongue, then who could you confide in? "Maybe I played my part too well," Teddy admitted. "Maybe I even fooled myself." *And now I realize I'm kinda addicted to you.*

"What are we gonna do about us then?"

"As in *us* us?"

"Yep."

Teddy rolled onto his side and faced Romeo. "Man, when you open up, you're open. I dunno. I'm... Tomorrow we have to fly back to Chicago and face a big scary future. We're going to be jobless. We're going... Shit. I don't know where anything will be going."

"But given your druthers, would you want to go there together?"

God, yes. It made Teddy's heart sing just to hear Romeo ask this, because that meant Romeo was envisioning this as more than a quick away-from-home fling. But reality showed its ugly face, reminding Teddy of probable future paths. Unemployment. A ring at the bottom of the Chicago River. An ex standing poolside, grinning beside his new squeeze. A heart broken and patched together, now with barbed wire strung around it.

"Teddy?"

"I would want to go there together," Teddy said, tracing the contours of Romeo's mouth with a fingertip. Because the moment called for tender truths, not bitter events yet to come.

"Good."

Then Romeo grinned and swatted Teddy's ass. "But right now I'm starving. We still have Joyce's debit card. Valentine's Day dinner for two?"

Chapter Eighteen

They tried a couple of upscale restaurants first, but they were fully booked, so Romeo and Teddy ended up at a casual Korean place. Their Valentine's Day meal—babimbap and lots of kimchi—was much better than the one they'd prepared. The dining room was crowded and noisy, the floor was sticky, and the spices made Teddy's nose run so badly that he used half a tree's worth of paper napkins.

It was the most romantic meal he'd ever had.

Romeo was funny and charming, and he went on at length about the relative benefits of *Star Wars* versus *Star Trek*. Teddy laughed so hard that he almost knocked over his water. And they kept touching hands across the table, just brief brushes, nothing remotely PDA-ish. But every one of them sent a thrill through Teddy's heart.

Walking back to the hotel, Teddy wanted to scatter pink glitter on the damp sidewalks and dance to love-song duets. Instead he simply smiled a lot. About a block from the hotel, he dragged Romeo into a drugstore. They giggled so much over their rubber-and-lube purchase that the older woman at the cash register laughed and told them to enjoy their night.

Which they did.

Teddy woke up as the sun rose and then spent a long time staring in wonder at the sleeping man beside him. Romeo had unfairly long eyelashes, no pillow creases on his cheek, and a complete absence of bedhead—unlike Teddy, who always awoke with hair that looked as if it had barely survived a hurricane.

Why couldn't the two of them stay right here in this hotel bed forever? They could get food delivered.

Sighing quietly so as not to wake Romeo, Teddy slid out from the covers, gathered his exercise clothes, and crept out of the room.

He had the fitness center to himself, allowing him to hog the elliptical and to pedal slowly on the stationary bike. Working out wasn't really the point this morning, not when he was slightly and deliciously sore from last night's adventures. He wanted to get his head clear, however, and this was a better option than tromping around in the rain. He listened to the Broadway soundtrack of *West Side Story*, reminding himself that he was not Maria, Romeo had never been a member of the Jets, and failing Joyce Alexander's tests was not the same as getting shot.

Not quite, anyway.

Romeo woke up when Teddy entered the room. They showered together, an activity neither of them had ever attempted. It was fun but awkward in the small space. A lot of water ended up on the floor. Good thing there were extra towels.

"I don't have room for all this new stuff in my suitcase," Romeo said, eyeing the clothing spread across the rumpled bed. "I guess I could toss the old stuff, but—"

"But it's perfectly good and that would be wasteful. I'm out of room too. Tell you what—you go find us some breakfast and I'll hunt down some cheap luggage. Meet back here in forty-five minutes?"

Romeo tugged him close and kissed the top of Teddy's head. "Deal."

Although Teddy was tempted to forget about suitcases and breakfast and flights and jobs and rent and futures, and instead just drag Romeo back into bed, he did the adult thing and hurried out of the room. His phone informed him of a Target about half a mile away, which was perfect. It wasn't even raining out, although the skies were gloomy.

He was tempted to buy identical pieces but decided that would be silly, so he opted for one large case in navy and one in purple. Then he detoured by the snacks section and bought some in-flight munchies to share. Cheaper than buying them at the airport, and Target had a bigger selection. The Valentine's Day candy was on clearance. Grinning, he picked up an enormous collection of truffles in a heart-shaped box printed with bright flowers and festooned with a garish pink bow. When he checked out, he used his own card, not Joyce's. He figured he was pretty much on his own at this point anyway.

He had just exited the store, dragging the suitcases behind him, when his phone rang. Shit. Awkwardly, he veered to the side of the building, nudged the suitcases out of the way of his fellow pedestrians, and looked at the screen. Joyce's number.

"Hello?" He tried to sound brave.

"Good morning, darling. I trust the two of you had a good evening?"

He blushed so fiercely that he was grateful she couldn't see him. "Uh, yeah. Thanks."

"Is Romeo there?"

"No. I'm out running an errand, and he's... I'm not exactly sure. Getting breakfast."

She made a thoughtful noise that he couldn't fully interpret. "Our dinner last night was—well, we ended up ordering pizza." She laughed as if this didn't bother her, but Teddy's heart thudded. It wasn't as if he expected anything different—he knew what a disaster the meal was—but knowing and having it confirmed were two different things.

"I thought the tarts were okay," he ventured.

"Not bad, although I didn't see how they fit the floral theme. The flavor of the pasta was all right, although it was gummy and not especially pretty. The flatbread—"

"Made a good doorstop."

Another laugh. "Yes. I do genuinely appreciate the effort, however. You and Romeo worked hard. You had some good ideas. It was the execution that was wanting."

He was almost wanting an execution right now. A firing squad sounded less painful than being rejected by Joyce Alexander. A young woman walking by with a big brindled dog cast Teddy a worried look and paused as if she were going to ask if he needed help. He gave her a wan smile and she nodded and continued on her way.

"I'm sorry," was all Teddy could say to Joyce. And he was.

"I know. Both of you have tried very hard with my ridiculous tests. You clearly want Reddyflora to succeed, and you're willing to give a great deal of yourselves to achieve it. I admire such tenaciousness."

That was an echo of all the teachers who'd told Teddy he was a hard worker even as they gave him a C out of pity. He sagged against the wall and waited for the axe to fall.

Maybe she expected him to say something, because she remained silent for a few moments before clearing her throat. Then she spoke in a serious tone. "I have good news and bad."

Back in their hotel room, Romeo was acting chipper over bagels, coffee, and fruit, which he'd spread across the desk. "Do we have time to eat before we head to the airport?"

"I think so. Joyce is sending Dave so we don't have to mess with rideshares or taxis."

"Cool. I won't mind one last ride in that Rolls."

Teddy nodded and then did a Vanna White gesture at the suitcases. "Let's pack first. Which one do you want?"

Romeo looked at them for a moment before grinning shyly. "Mind if I take the purple?"

"No, of course not. It's all yours." He meant that sincerely, although he'd thought for sure Romeo would go for the navy.

As if reading Teddy's thoughts, Romeo shook his head. "A week ago I wouldn't have picked purple, even though I like that one better. I'd have figured blue is safer. But that was before you dressed me in paisley scarves and retro suits."

Despite the misery secretly lodged in his chest, Teddy gave a genuine smile. "You've found your more colorful self."

"He's always been there. You just helped me let him out."

Shit. Teddy was *not* going to break down in tears. "Purple's all yours," he said a trifle brusquely. "But hang on. I got you something."

Romeo widened his eyes and waited as Teddy unzipped the purple suitcase and removed a large plastic bag. The snacks could wait for the flight—assuming either of them had an appetite by then—but not the heart. He pulled out the box of chocolates and handed it to an astonished Romeo.

"For me?"

"Who else?"

"You got me fancy chocolates."

Teddy scratched an ear nervously. "I know it's kind of dumb, but—"

"Not dumb. Romantic."

Over the years, Teddy had been called a lot of things, but romantic wasn't one of them. He'd never thought of himself that way either. But maybe that side of him had always been there, deep inside. Like Romeo's colorful self.

"It was on sale," Teddy said gruffly.

Romeo laughed, set the box on the bed, and opened one of the dresser drawers. He stuck his hand inside and emerged with…a plush toy. "For you. Also on sale." He handed it over.

It was a very soft bear with an earnest expression and a three-piece tweed suit, a red heart embroidered on its chest. "It's adorable."

"It's you. You know, Teddy. Bear. Teddy bear. And I can see you in that outfit."

Teddy stroked the bear with one finger. "And my ears do sort of stick out like this."

"I like your ears."

Setting the bear atop the box of chocolates, Teddy gathered Romeo into a crushing embrace.

If they hugged hard enough, maybe Teddy wouldn't hear the nagging little voice in his head—the one reminding him that this couldn't possibly last.

Chapter Nineteen

They had to pack in a hurry and wolf their breakfast, but they made it to the curb just as Dave pulled up in the Rolls. He wore his usual inscrutable expression as he hoisted their luggage into the trunk. Once they were all in the car and had pulled into traffic, Teddy couldn't remain silent. "I'm sorry about your dinner last night."

Dave laughed. "It's fine. I like pizza."

"Oh. Okay."

"It would've been worse if Joyce or I had tried to fix dinner. Ron's the only one of us who can cook. Joyce can sometimes manage toast successfully, but I'm not even allowed to make tea. Not after the time we had to call the fire department."

Dave's admission didn't help Teddy's situation, yet it

made him feel a little better nonetheless. "I'm glad you didn't starve last night."

"I had two of your tarts for breakfast. They're pretty good."

Romeo held Teddy's hand for the remainder of the ride.

The airport was a madhouse, with a long line to check their suitcases and another to get through security. By the time they weaved through the crowds to get to their gate, it was almost time to board. Romeo was visibly nervous as they stood there, scratching his lip and shifting from one leg to the other, so Teddy leaned in close to whisper. "If we were zillionaires and had a private plane, I'd suggest we join the mile high club."

As he'd hoped, that made Romeo relax a bit. "Probably not advisable on this flight, huh?"

"Probably not."

Miraculously the plane wasn't quite full and they again ended up with an empty seat in their row. Teddy sat by the window and Romeo by the aisle, and they lifted the armrests between them so they could scooch slightly into the center. No crying children or harried parents this time, although Teddy was glad they'd sat near that family on the way to Seattle. It had given him his first look at Romeo's real personality.

This time they had peace and quiet and a flight attendant who winked when he saw them holding hands.

"I still have some drink tickets from last time," Romeo said.

"You want to order something?"

"Not really." He cocked his head at Teddy. "You going to tell me what Joyce said this morning?"

Teddy hid his face in his hands. "Do I have to?" he whispered.

He'd known Romeo would ask eventually. Romeo knew Teddy had spoken to her. But it had been nice to hide his head in the sand for a while and avoid the subject.

Now, though, Romeo was waiting, and it wasn't fair to keep him hanging. Teddy uncovered his face and twisted his fingers in his lap. "Okay."

"Okay."

"Okay."

They sat there. Teddy pretended to look out the window, but there was nothing to see except clouds. The inside of Teddy's head probably looked just like that—gray and featureless and unpromising. At least that's how it felt right now.

Romeo tapped Teddy's thigh. "No parachute."

"Yeah." Heaving a sigh, Teddy turned to him. "Joyce is going to back the project. She thinks it's a clever idea, and apparently Dave, who's the family tech guy, told her the software concept is solid. They went over the specs we left them."

"That's really good news. So why do you sound like you're delivering a funeral announcement?"

Lungs, do your thing. Deep breaths, in and out. That worked okay, but his tongue remained stuck in the back of his throat, threatening to choke him. Or maybe

Romeo would choke him for drawing this whole thing out. Shit.

"Joyce says that based on what Dave has told her, you've done a fantastic job with the software. She thinks you're smart, diligent, and innovative—those are exact quotes—and that you have a promising career ahead of you."

Romeo gave Teddy's knee a squeeze. "Again with the nice words and the gloom-and-doom face. What did she say about you?"

"I'm creative with an excellent sense of style and a good feel for what people might like."

"I concur. So the bad news is?"

Teddy looked down at his lap. "Together we're a disaster."

"I thought we were pretty good together," Romeo said mildly.

"I thought we were *spectacular*. On a personal basis. But professionally? Joyce thinks we distract each other in a way that hides our best qualities rather than revealing them."

"That's bullshit." Romeo said it quietly, but his expression was fierce. "She gave us dumbass tests that have nothing to do with anything. What does tromping through a stupid forest in February prove? Or trying to stop an imaginary werewolf epidemic, for God's sake? Her tests were the problem, not us. We are *not* a disaster." He took Teddy's hand and kissed the back of it.

Honestly, Teddy agreed. Sure, maybe he and Romeo would have succeeded at their tasks had they been alone rather than together, but that wasn't important in the long run. He would rather sprain his ankle with Romeo than hike a hundred miles without him.

"She's Joyce Alexander," Teddy said. "She's certain she's right. And she's the woman with the money."

"But you said she's going to back the project."

"Yeah. With a caveat."

Romeo groaned. "I don't like caveats."

"She's only in if one of us goes."

"Which of us?"

Teddy's answering laugh lacked humor. "Either. She said either of us is fine—just not both of us."

"Then—"

"I guess Lauren's supposed to decide."

Romeo threw his head back against the seat and closed his eyes. "Shit."

It was Teddy's turn to kiss Romeo's hand. "Don't worry. She'll choose you."

"I don't— Why would you assume that?"

Teddy had given this considerable thought as he'd walked back to the hotel from Target. "For one thing, a big chunk of my job is done. I've designed the basic look of the vase and set up a solid marketing plan. For another, Lauren will have no problem finding someone else to take over the marketing at this point. She'd have a hell of a time replacing you, though. Your work is the heart of the project."

"Uh-uh. I'm just coding, man. You're the one making the vase beautiful—and that's the whole point of a vase, isn't it? And you're the one who can convince people that they absolutely must buy this vase or they're just gonna keel over and die."

Teddy didn't want to argue about it. "It's up to Lauren anyway."

"Guess so."

"I'm sorry that I—"

"Don't start that again. Whatever mistakes we made, we made together, okay?" Romeo leaned as close as his seatbelt permitted, but that wasn't good enough for Teddy, who scooted into the middle seat, buckled up, and leaned against Romeo's solid shoulder.

Neither of them slept, exactly, but they did doze, perking up enough to eat pretzels and drink water as the flight attendant came by. They munched on a few of their Target snacks as well. Teddy thought about how miserably cold it probably was back home, and how distant spring seemed. But he pictured a balmy day in early summer, before the humidity truly set in, when he could take Romeo on a day cruise in the lake. A few weeks earlier, Teddy had spotted a pair of Esteban Cortazar board shorts in one of his favorite resale shops. He hadn't bought them for himself—they'd only make his legs look stubbier—but with their mixed paisley print in oranges, yellows, and pale blue, they'd be spectacular on Romeo. Not too many people in Chicagoland were in the market for shorts right now, so maybe the store still had them. If Romeo liked them, he could wear them on their boat ride, and—

And that was all a pretty dream, but summer was months away. By then, Teddy might be nothing more than a vague and distant memory to Romeo. The guy who'd messed up with Joyce Alexander, who'd been a fun quick fling but nothing else. The guy who was probably spending the summer behind a cash register, ringing up clearance bathing suits and beach towels.

"Romeo?"

"Hmm?"

"Are we…" God, he shouldn't ask this. He should just let it be, because saying the words was like opening the door for disaster. But he couldn't stop himself. "Will you want to see me after we get home? Outside of work, I mean." Not that the work part would last much longer anyway.

Romeo looked stricken. "Of course! I thought I'd been clear about that."

"Sometimes people say things in the heat of the moment. Postcoital moments especially. But after the hormones wear off, good sense settles in."

"When I say things, I mean them. Even right after sex." Romeo squeezed Teddy's hand.

While doom and gloom still lingered nearby, some of the heaviness left Teddy's heart. "Okay."

"Um, maybe this is too much to ask, but since you've sort of raised the subject…"

"Ask away." *Because I'd give you anything.*

"Next Sunday will you come over to my house for dinner?"

Teddy's heart stuttered so badly, he wondered whether the plane carried a defibrillator. "Dinner?" he squeaked, although the meal itself wasn't the scary part.

"Yeah. Sunday dinner's a big production. I help Mama with the cooking, and my sisters and their families come over if they can. Course, Portia and her girls are always there because they live there, but the rest of the crowd usually comes too. Kids running around everywhere, everyone arguing over sports on TV, my brother-in-law Vic fixing someone's car, my nephew Andre—he's sixteen—mooning over some girl, everybody always waiting in line for the bathrooms. Good chaos, you know? And lots of good food. It's early afternoon, so really more like late lunch than dinner. Sometimes we have videogame tournaments and sometimes—" He stopped so suddenly that Teddy heard his mouth pop closed.

"What?" Teddy urged.

"Babbling. Sorry."

"Don't apologize. You love them, and that's beautiful."

Romeo snaked an arm around Teddy and pulled him closer. "So you'll come?"

"I've, uh, never done the family meet-and-greet thing." He'd spoken to Gregory's mother on the phone once, and that was it.

"Me either."

Great. "What if they hate me?"

"Jesus, Teddy. Why would they hate you?"

"Too male? Too white? Too…me. And I screwed up—"

Romeo squished him hard enough to make Teddy squeak. "For the last and final time, you didn't screw up any worse than I did. And further, my family knows I'm pan, they won't care about the shade of your skin, and as for you being you? The more you you are, the better."

Sighing heavily, Teddy nodded. "I'll come. I'll be a nervous wreck, but I'll come."

"Good. I'll bet you ten bucks that before dinner's over, my sisters will be interrogating you for fashion advice. Especially after they see what you've done for me."

Doubts and fears zoomed through Teddy's brain faster than a jet airplane. Why was Romeo offering this invitation and what did it mean about their future? The future that Teddy was so certain they didn't have. Maybe he knew that a family meal could go wrong easily, offering Romeo a good excuse for telling Teddy to get lost for good. Maybe Romeo wanted his mother and sisters to confirm that Romeo was way out of Teddy's league. No, that couldn't be right—Romeo wasn't cruel or conniving. He was a good person. Jeez, maybe he was just trying to be polite.

"Teddy?" Romeo's brows were drawn with concern.

It dawned on Teddy that he *wanted* to meet Romeo's family. If Romeo was representative of them, they'd be a wonderful group of people. Teddy managed a smile. "I'll look forward to it."

The cold hit Teddy like an icy mallet the moment he stepped outside the airport, stealing his breath and making him want to run back inside. Surely he hadn't been in Seattle long enough to lose a lifetime of Midwest acclimatization? But maybe the frigid temperatures weren't to blame. Maybe it was bitter, hard reality. Family dinner plans notwithstanding, Teddy and Romeo had a difficult near future to navigate.

But first they had to get away from the airport, and seemingly everyone else in Chicago was trying to do the same thing.

"People should be flocking to leave the city in this weather, not come back," Teddy complained.

Romeo nodded, but he'd seemed distracted ever since they landed. Then he shook himself. "You sure you don't want a ride? Mama won't mind."

"It's completely out of your way. I'll catch a cab." Besides, it would take time for him to work up the courage to meet Romeo's family.

"Teddy—"

"Do you want to talk to Lauren or do you want me to?"

"Go ahead."

"Okay." There were a million things Teddy wanted to say to him, but instead he pasted on a fake smile. "See you in the morning, I guess."

Romeo looked at him with a pained expression before letting go of his suitcase handles and grabbing him. Romeo's warm lips were a stark contrast to the icy air, and even encased in gloves, his hands felt wonderful on Teddy's neck and cheek. In a perfect world they could have stayed like that for hours. But the taxi line had inched forward, and Romeo's mother was probably waiting for him.

They ended the kiss and Teddy watched Romeo walk away.

Chapter Twenty

Teddy's studio apartment—barely larger than the Seattle hotel room—had only two winter temperature settings, depending on the boiler: tropical and arctic. He was relieved to discover that this was a tropical day, and he shed layers as soon as he was inside.

Clad in nothing but socks, underwear, and an undershirt, he took a quick look around. He'd left everything tidy, although he'd need to clean out the fridge since he'd been gone longer than anticipated. New life forms appeared to be evolving in the tiny vegetable drawer.

With his landlord's consent, Teddy had painted the industrial white walls a cozy greige instead. He'd salvaged and painted an old bookcase that, together with lightweight curtains in a Portuguese tile pattern, created a room divider to separate his bed from the rest of the room without making the sleeping area claustrophobic. His apartment didn't contain a lot of furniture or knick-knacks, but he'd chosen each item with consideration for both practical and decorative value. Even his diminutive kitchen had functional and aesthetic worth.

It was no waterfront mansion, but he liked his home. He'd be heartbroken if he had to give it up.

And God, he missed Romeo already.

Although he would have preferred running naked through Millennium Park to calling his boss, Teddy took a deep breath and dialed. Lauren picked up after the first ring.

"Hey, Teddy." Her voice was neutral, but that was usual for her.

"Hi. We're back."

"Great. No problems with the flight or anything?"

"No, it was fine."

"Great. Get your receipts to Skyler for reimbursement. It should take just a few days to get you repaid."

"I don't have many receipts. Joyce paid for almost everything except the hotel." Teddy sat on his love seat, a comfortable but basic Ikea model he'd spruced up with a vintage cotton bedspread from India and a couple of throw pillows.

"She mentioned that," Joyce said. "She also said that although she gave you guys free rein with her card, you were pretty frugal."

Teddy straightened a pillow tassel with his fingers. "So you've spoken to her already."

"She called me this morning."

"Congratulations on getting the project funded, Lauren. That's really fantastic." He pulled up all his acting skills on that one, attempting to sound sincere instead of gutted. He *was* genuinely happy for Lauren, who was a good person.

"Teddy, we need to talk."

Oh no—there they were. The four deadliest words in the English language.

"Okay," he replied evenly, although when he looked down, he had two loose strands of tassel caught between his fingers. He must have tugged them out. "Look, we both know how critical Romeo is to—"

"It's late and you had a long flight. Get some rest, okay? I'll see you in two days."

"Not tomorrow?"

"You had quite an experience in Seattle. You deserve a little downtime. And by then my nieces will be out of my hair."

She likely thought she was giving him a reprieve, so he managed a polite good-night before ending the call. It didn't feel like a reprieve, however, but rather like extended torture: the guy in the black hood turning the wheel on the rack very slowly. He'd prefer that the guy just crank that baby.

After patting the tassel apologetically and throwing away the ruined strands, Teddy nestled his new teddy bear between the throw pillows and got to work. He unpacked his luggage, folding or hanging the clean items and tossing dirty stuff into the hamper. His old suitcase nested conveniently inside the new, and with only a little effort, he slid them under the bed. There was just enough room beside the storage drawers he kept there. Cleaning out his small fridge took only a few minutes, and sorting through accumulated mail was also fast.

That left him with...nothing.

His job at Reddyflora had eaten up most of his time for over a year now. On the rare occasions when he was free, he liked to haunt resale stores—none of which were open this late—or catch a bite out. He wasn't hungry now, however, even though he'd had nothing but a bagel, some fruit, a teeny bag of pretzels, and a few assorted Target munchies. He could binge-watch *Project Runway* or *Stranger Things*, since he was far behind on both of them. But that didn't appeal to him either.

Books. He had some books on the Kindle his parents had given him for his last birthday. But his gaze skittered over the words, which might as well have been in Sanskrit for all the sense they made.

It was too cold to go for a walk, and he was too exhausted to hit the gym.

In the end he simply doused the lights and climbed into a bed that, although smaller than the one at the hotel, felt vast and far too empty. He fetched the bear from the love seat and tucked it under the covers next to him. Ridiculous damn thing for a man his age, but it helped him settle.

The insistent buzz of Teddy's phone woke him up, and it took a few moments for his eyes to unblur enough to read the string of texts.

You up?

Guess not. You're probably still on West Coast time.

I didn't sleep very well. Bed was too empty.

Well, text when you get up.

If you want.

You don't have to.

But I hope you do.

He sat up completely and began to tap with his thumbs, but stopped halfway through a witty, airy reply. That wasn't right. He was already feeling bad enough about the abrupt way he'd parted from Romeo at Midway. After deleting the whole thing, he tried to compose something charming and romantic instead. But his efforts fell flat, and the teddy bear gazed at him with disappointment.

"Fine," he said to the bear. Teddy called Romeo instead.

Romeo answered immediately, sounding alarmed. "What's wrong?"

"Nothing. You're the one text-bombing me."

"Oh. Sorry."

"Don't be. I like hearing from you. But hearing your voice is even better." Teddy shifted around a bit, propping himself on pillows and arranging the blankets just so. "How's everything at the Blue house?"

"We're doing all right. Mama made us waffles for breakfast. The kids loved the stuff we bought them at the Space Needle." Despite the positive words, Romeo's voice didn't sound happy, carrying about as much emotion as if he were reciting a grocery list.

"How are *you*, Romeo?"

"I'm okay."

Teddy wanted so badly to see him, and not through the soulless lenses of FaceTime. Dammit, he wanted to touch him. To smell him. To press his lips to Romeo's chapped ones. "It's all going to work out somehow." He wasn't at all sure of that, but maybe if he said it often enough, he'd convince them both.

"Yeah, I guess so. Hey, I told Mama and Portia all about you." Romeo's tone definitely picked up at that.

Teddy, on the other hand, felt his heart race. "Oh?" he squeaked.

"They're dying to meet you. Mama's already planning the menu for Sunday dinner."

"What exactly did you tell them about me?"

"That you're incredibly handsome and sexy, and you're great in bed, and—"

"Romeo!"

Even over the phone, the laughter warmed Teddy. It took Romeo a moment to calm himself enough to speak. "I told them you're amazing. Funny. Creative. That you take genuine joy in helping other people express their inner selves."

Well, now Teddy was thankful Romeo wasn't there, because that meant he couldn't see Teddy's eyes get a little misty. "You think that about me?"

"I know that about you, Teddy Spenser."

"Well, that's funny. Because when I'm with you—Well, you're sort of almost too perfect. It should scare me away. But when I'm with you, I feel like I can be my best self."

They were both silent after that, not because they had nothing to say, but rather because they'd just said important things that needed time to settle in. Teddy felt raw, but in a good way. A little like after a wonderful day at the beach, when you come home tired, overheated, and somewhat sunburned.

Eventually, though, Romeo cleared his throat. "You have plans for today?"

"No." Teddy almost invited him over, but stopped himself. "I think—I miss you. But I think we should spend today apart. We've got the whole Joyce thing hanging over our heads, and everything's happened so fast. Maybe we need..." He struggled to find the words.

"A little space to get our heads clear," Romeo offered.

"Yeah. Is that okay?"

"It's a good idea. I might send you a couple of texts, though."

Teddy smiled. "I might too."

He ended up spending the day in decadent repose. His apartment needed a little tidying, but that took about ten minutes—one of the advantages of living in a shoebox.

After that, he drank tea while reading design magazines online. Then he took several Buzzfeed quizzes in which he discovered his horcrux, scored beautifully on naming Pixar characters for every letter of the alphabet, and failed abysmally at identifying countries by their outline. At least he recognized Italy.

After a lunch of grilled cheese sandwich and canned tomato soup, he took a nap for possibly the first time since he was a toddler. It was glorious, and he vowed to do it more often. Then he binge-watched *Schitt's Creek*.

Teddy didn't exercise at all. Didn't step foot outside his apartment, not even to fetch the mail from downstairs. Didn't think about his failures in Seattle. Well, not more than two or three hundred times.

And all day, Teddy and Romeo sent each other texts. Nothing fancy or complicated. Sometimes they were funny memes about Chicago or office work, and sometimes they were simply quick little notes.

I've decided my scooter needs accessorizing. Haven't decided how yet.

Or Younger niece just accidentally but maybe on purpose broke older niece's favorite drinking glass. Did you hear the screaming?

Or I really think you should wear more green. Emerald, not hunter or olive.

Or Mama wants me to teach her to play Red Dead Redemption because, and I quote, "Cowboys are sexy." Save me.

Or I think if we had the time, I'd like to take a cooking class with you. Would you be up for it?

A little after ten, Teddy found himself slumped in the loveseat, longing for Romeo's voice. Well, longing for a lot more than that, but a FaceTime call would have to suffice. Romeo picked up at once, smiling into the phone. He was propped up in bed, with pillows and a somewhat battered wooden headboard behind him. "What's up?" he asked.

"I missed you." That sounded a little pathetic—or at least Teddy thought, until he saw Romeo's pleased reaction.

"Yeah? Me too."

"I don't mean to be clingy. But we were together, like, almost every minute, and now you're there and I'm here and that's…not the same." Oh, good one, Teddy. Such a way with words. He should have stuck to texting.

But Romeo only nodded. "Definitely not the same. It was your idea to stay apart today, remember."

"I know. And I still think it was the wisest thing. But that doesn't mean it makes me happy."

"Mama likes to say— You up for another of her pearls of wisdom?"

Teddy settled even more deeply into the cushions. "Always."

"Mama says sometimes you gotta do the right thing, not the easy thing. I'm fairly sure she didn't invent that, but it's one of her favorites."

The right thing. Not too long ago, Teddy had been positive that keeping his nose to the grindstone while remaining steadfastly single was the right thing to do, but now his world had been turned upside down and his course was no longer clear.

Except there was one thing he *did* know—one thing that was definitely right. "I need to tell you something."

"Uh-oh." Romeo seemed to be trying for a joking tone, but his eyes were worried.

"This is on me, not you, okay? I'm not telling you what you have to do or even asking you to make any decisions. But you need to know that as long as we're… doing whatever it is we're doing, I won't be seeing anyone else. No hookups, no dates, no nothing. Not that I was leaping from bed to bed anyway, but now…it's only you."

Romeo looked at him solemnly for a moment before nodding and giving one of his soft, sweet smiles. "It's only you, Teddy."

After ending the call, they sent goodnight GIFs and sleepy emojis. Teddy crawled into bed with a healthy dose of optimism about his personal future—his future with Romeo—despite his dread over what would happen in the morning.

Light sleet was falling when Teddy woke up, and no matter how much he tried to psych himself up, he couldn't face taking his scooter. He called a Lyft instead. *Might as well go out in relative style.*

He arrived at the office building when Romeo did, well before normal business hours. If that had happened only a week ago, Teddy would have assumed Romeo was sucking up to Lauren. Or maybe wanting to sneak in and mess around with the project before anyone else got there. But now he knew better, especially when he caught sight of Romeo's poor chewed lips.

"You need some ChapStick," Teddy said as Romeo held the front door for him.

Romeo came in behind him, and before Teddy could trudge to the stairs, Romeo grabbed him and dragged him to a little nook behind the sandwich place. "Missed you," he breathed into Teddy's cheek.

Teddy wanted to collapse against him in a sobbing mess but confined himself to a sniff—which could have been attributed to the weather. "Me too. There's probably a security camera pointed at us right now, though."

"I don't care. Do you?"

"No."

"Okay then." Romeo kissed him gently and thoroughly, and for a few seconds Teddy could almost believe everything would be okay.

"You taste like maple syrup," said Teddy.

"Pancakes for breakfast. Mama was awake early."

Teddy smiled against him. "That's nice."

"She's been going on about you."

"Yeah?" Teddy leaned back so he could look up at Romeo.

"Yep. She and the kids ate half the candy you gave me, Portia yelled 'cause I let the girls have so much sugar that late at night, and I told all of them how amazing you are."

"Amazing?"

"Stop fishing for compliments, Teddy. Let's get this over with."

Teddy grumbled as they tromped up the stairs. "Compliments are better than calamity."

The main room of the Reddyflora suite stood empty, with Teddy's cubicle dark and forlorn in the corner. But the door to Lauren's office stood open, spilling warm light toward them. "Is that you, Teddy?" she called.

"And Romeo," Teddy answered.

"Come on in."

Dressed in a navy pinstripe suit and crisp white blouse, she sat behind her minimalistic desk. A blank pad of paper and Montblanc pen waited in front of her, while an oversized cup steamed gently nearby. Tea. Teddy noted its slightly floral scent. "Sit down, please." Her face was as carefully composed as her voice.

Teddy and Romeo obeyed.

"I want to begin by apologizing," Lauren said. "I honestly thought she simply wanted you to pitch the product in person. I had no idea she'd subject you to those… trials."

Teddy sat up a little straighter. "If you'd known, would you have refused?"

A slight vee appeared between her carefully shaped brows. "I don't know. But I would at least have forewarned you and let you make a more informed decision about whether to participate."

That seemed fair. And if that had happened, Teddy

would have willingly boarded the plane, although with considerably more trepidation. He nodded his acknowledgment.

Romeo, however, shifted in his seat. Instead of one of his usual midrange black suits, he was wearing the lovely gray one that Teddy had chosen for him. "That woman's tests were asinine," Romeo said. "The project's promise and our value as employees have nothing to do with whether we can make flatbread."

Lauren picked up her pen, peered at the nib, and set it down again. "I know. I suppose when you're old and rich and famous, you feel like it's okay to indulge in eccentricities, even at other people's expense. If you ask me to, I'll try to find funding elsewhere. But there's no guarantee I'll succeed."

Romeo's eyes widened and Teddy snapped his head back as if struck. "If you turn Joyce down, where else could you go?"

"Honestly, I have no idea. But none of this is fair to either of you. The two of you have worked incredibly hard for Reddyflora. We wouldn't have come this far without you. I'm not willing to throw you to the wolves just because Joyce Alexander wants me to."

Teddy knew that without Joyce, Reddyflora was effectively DOA. A fairy godmother was not going to magically appear and bibbidi-bobbidi them into solvency. And not only would he, Romeo, and Lauren be unemployed, but Imani and Skyler and everyone else would also be left high and dry. Still, it was nice that Lauren offered to take that step for their sake.

"Take the money," Teddy said. Beside him, Romeo nodded in agreement.

Lauren sighed and let her shoulders droop. "Thank you for that. But you know what this means. I'm going to have to—"

"Fire me." Teddy kept his chin high. "I know."

Romeo and Lauren both spoke at once.

"That's not—"

"She didn't—"

Lauren waved her hand at Romeo to quiet him. "You know that's not what Joyce said. She said one of you has to go, but she left the decision to me."

Now it was Teddy's turn to gesture at Romeo to hush. "But I know what the decision has to be. Look, let's assume for the sake of argument that the failures in Seattle weren't mostly my fault. I think they were, but whatever. And let's also assume that Romeo and I are equally valuable employees and would be equally hard to replace. Also not true. But even if it was, you need to fire me."

"Why?" Lauren set her elbows on the desk, clasped her hands, and leaned forward.

Teddy shot a quick look at Romeo, hoping he wasn't about to betray a confidence. "This is Romeo's dream job. Really. He loves what he does here and there's nothing he'd rather do. And me? Don't get me wrong, I like my job too. But if I could be granted a wish by the Employment Genie, this wouldn't be my first choice."

He'd thought she might be offended by his statement, but instead her expression softened a bit. She turned her gaze to Romeo. "Is that true?"

Looking miserable, Romeo gave a slight nod. "Yeah." Then his lips tightened. "But that doesn't mean you should choose me. I can find somewhere else to work. Maybe it won't be as great, but it'll be fine. And since I live with my mother and sister, it's not like I'm gonna end up on the street. But Teddy has to make rent, Lauren. And it'll be real hard for him to land a job anywhere near this good. He's got more to lose than me, so keep him."

Teddy didn't know whether he wanted to kiss Romeo or strangle him. Teddy was trying to be noble here, and Romeo was messing that up. But he was also willing to sacrifice something really important just so Teddy didn't end up folding T-shirts at Old Navy. That was pretty amazing.

"Well," Lauren said, leaning back in her chair, "I didn't expect this. I didn't even think you guys liked each other very much. I was worried about sending you to Seattle together."

"We were stupid," Teddy said firmly.

Romeo reached over to grab Teddy's hand. "We like each other. Actually..." He paused and, chewing his lip, turned his head to look at Teddy. Then Romeo grinned and faced Lauren again. "I *like* like him."

The sound that escaped Teddy was unclassifiable—some mutant combination of a squawk and a gasp. The L-word. What Romeo had just casually dropped wasn't the same L-word that Teddy had avoided even thinking. But it was an L-word word that floated around the room like a helium balloon, dropping glitter and rainbows and teeny tiny unicorns everywhere.

So what did Teddy do? He grabbed that balloon.

"And I *like* like him too," he said.

Romeo didn't make weird noises. He whooped with joy and leapt to his feet, dragging Teddy with him, and then wrapped him in the most crushing, wonderful embrace of all time. It felt amazing, even if Teddy couldn't breathe. Hell, who needed oxygen when he had Romeo?

How could Teddy ever have forsworn this? How could he have believed he didn't want this? Didn't *need* this? Because now his very cells sang with it, his entire being suffused with joy.

Lauren cleared her throat. When Teddy and Romeo reluctantly peeled apart, she was smiling. "Okay. You don't hate each other. I believe that." Her expression turned serious. "But unless you want me to turn Joyce down..."

"One of us gets the ax," Teddy said. It was harder to care about it now that he knew Romeo reciprocated his feelings.

"Yeah."

Romeo looked as giddy as Teddy felt, his eyes sparkling like disco balls. "You're gonna have to make that decision without us, Lauren. We have some business to attend to." He pulled Teddy toward the door by one hand; Teddy didn't put up a fight.

"I'll call you this afternoon!" Lauren yelled after them.

They got only as far as the hallway before they started making out. Romeo pushed Teddy up against the wall, caging him with his long arms and locking their lips together. Teddy countered with a double handful of Romeo's ass.

"This. Is not. Proper workplace behavior," Teddy panted after a while. By then he'd laced his fingers behind Romeo's nape and was snuffling at the juncture of neck and shoulder, wondering if it might be interesting to suck right there. Yes, it almost certainly would. A hickey would look nice under Romeo's dark skin.

"Whichever of us keeps his job should watch one of those anti-harassment videos."

Teddy gave Romeo an investigatory lick. Mmm. Salty. "Not feeling harassed here."

"Me either."

"But I also wouldn't mind going somewhere more private. A bed would be handy too."

"Handy," Romeo agreed. But handsy was more like it, because now he was palming Teddy's ass.

"Come over to my place?"

"God yes."

After a few more gropes, they moved apart. They were still straightening their outerwear when Imani stepped out of the elevator. She came to an abrupt halt when she saw them. "Um…"

"Don't worry," Teddy told her brightly. "We're going to get a room."

"You two?"

"Uh-huh."

"Must've been some weird shit going down in Seattle." She was still shaking her head as she entered the suite.

That brief interval had been just long enough for a

thought to push aside some of the schmoop in his head. "Romeo? If Lauren chooses me, I'm going to turn her down. I don't want to work here if you don't."

Romeo rolled his eyes. "I was going to do the same thing."

"So whatever she decides…"

"We're unemployed."

"Yeah." Normally that would have scared the shit out of Teddy, but Romeo had just publicly declared that he had feelings toward Teddy. Feelings Teddy reciprocated. Maybe losing a job wasn't such a big deal in the face of all that.

Except Romeo wasn't going to last, was he? Here was Teddy, falling, falling, but he couldn't expect Romeo to catch him. "This is all so confusing. A week ago we barely knew each other. I was stubbornly single and we both had a bright future ahead of us at Reddyflora. Now everything's up in the air and the future's a huge big question mark and none of this matters anyway 'cause you'll be sick of me pretty soon, and then—"

"Breathe, babe." Romeo clasped Teddy's shoulders, but it was the endearment more than the command or the contact that stopped Teddy's panic.

"Babe?"

"Do you mind if I call you that?"

"No! I… It's nice."

"Good. Now look at me. Concentrate for a second. Consider how far the two of us have come in less than a week."

"Way far," Teddy agreed. Not just Chicago to Seattle

and back; they'd found each other. *Seen* each other. Become willing to sacrifice for each other.

Romeo leaned his forehead against Teddy's. "Give us a few more weeks, babe, and we will conquer the world."

Chapter Twenty-One

Lauren and Imani looked up from their conversation near the copy machine. It was clear from their expressions that they'd been talking about Romeo and Teddy.

"I thought you had urgent business to attend to?" Lauren said.

Imani snickered. "Is that what kids are calling it these days?"

Teddy rolled his eyes and was preparing an appropriate retort, but Romeo spoke up first. "We have something to tell you before we head out."

"Yes?"

"It doesn't matter what you decide about who stays and who goes. Teddy and I are a team. If one of us leaves, we both do."

"It's bad enough to lose one of you. I don't want to lose you both!"

Lauren looked distressed, which spurred Teddy to use a calming voice. "But without Joyce, the project's probably never getting off the ground, and you've put too much into it to give up now. The rest of you will manage without us."

She set her jaw stubbornly and shook her head. "This is idiotic. I shouldn't have to choose between two highly valued employees and her money. I'm going to see if I can talk some sense into her."

"Good luck with that," Romeo muttered.

Teddy wasn't optimistic either, but he was strangely at peace with the whole situation, at least for now.

"Urgent business," Romeo reminded him, taking Teddy's hand. They beat a hasty exit.

Despite the celebrations Teddy's libido was throwing, the rest of Teddy fretted during the entire short journey to his apartment. Aside from his landlord and a plumber, the last man to walk through Teddy's door had been Gregory. Romeo might have come from humble beginnings, and Teddy had already warned him not to expect the Taj Mahal, but what if Romeo was disappointed anyway? Oh, he'd be polite about it. But he might find the space too confining, the décor too…too Teddy.

Teddy concentrated on breathing steadily while he unlocked the door and then shed his outerwear and collected Romeo's. "Feel free to look around. That should take you ten, maybe fifteen seconds."

While Romeo strolled around, Teddy stuffed everything into the closet. Then Teddy pretended to be fascinated by the takeout menu he'd found under his door. He definitely didn't watch as Romeo slowly examined everything, head cocked as if he were walking through a modern art museum. Sometimes he asked questions about particular items, wanting to know where Teddy had acquired them or why he'd chosen them. Romeo's exploration even extended to the bathroom.

"This is so cool!" Romeo was bent over, peering into the glass-front cabinet where Teddy kept his towels and hair products. "What was it originally?"

"An old medical storage cabinet."

"Like from a doctor's office?"

"Probably." Teddy had found it for twelve dollars at a salvage shop and decided to keep the scuffed white paint. He'd had to replace one of the glass panes, but that was easy and cheap enough. It had needed a thorough cleaning, of course, and a new set of casters for its legs. He liked the way it looked, and it was easy to move when he cleaned. It also added badly needed storage to his bathroom.

Romeo straightened up and shook his head slowly. "It's unbelievable what you've done with your apartment."

"Yeah?"

"It has so much character. It's like… I don't know. It feels like it's in another time, another country even, but it doesn't feel fake like a stage setting. It's a home."

Gregory had never asked where Teddy had found any of his things or why he'd chosen them; he'd just employed them as props for his selfies. Romeo, however, had just spent fifteen minutes giving Teddy's place a thorough inspection, seemingly interested in the provenance of everything.

Now that Teddy no longer feared that Romeo would hate his place, he remembered they had more immediate priorities.

"You know," Teddy said from the bathroom doorway. "If you open that drawer to your left you'll find rubbers and lube."

"Will I, now? Did you have something in mind, Mr. Spenser?"

"I'd rather have someone in bed."

Romeo blew a raspberry, then opened the drawer and pulled out the items in question. Waggling his eyebrows, he backed Teddy out of the bathroom, across a few feet of open floor, and up against the bed, toppling Teddy backward onto the mattress.

"Your bed is tall," Romeo observed as he covered Teddy's body with his own.

"Storage underneath."

"When I was a kid—" Romeo nuzzled deliciously at Teddy's neck "—I desperately wanted one of those loft beds with the desk underneath it. We never could afford it, though."

"You could get one now."

"Mmm." Romeo planted a series of kisses along his jaw. "It's lost its appeal."

"Yeah?" Teddy gave a little groan, but he pressed on. "What kind of bed do you dream of now?"

"One with you in it."

That was a dream Teddy would happily support.

Today he was more thankful than usual for overenthusiastic radiators. The apartment's sultry temperature allowed them to take their time undressing each other, with no need to dive quickly under the blankets. Somehow it seemed much more real to have Romeo naked in his arms here, in Teddy's home, instead of in a chain hotel room two thousand miles away. Here, Romeo seemed more truly his.

If Teddy were to tell his family about Romeo and how he felt about him, he knew what they'd say. *That's nice, dear, but it's much too soon. Don't rush into this.* They'd mean well. But it wasn't too soon. He'd been waiting for Romeo his entire life—even if he hadn't been aware of it. The question was whether Romeo had been waiting for him as well.

"That's some pretty loud thinking you're doing," Romeo said with a chuckle. "Want me to tone down the handsiness?"

"No!" Teddy pulled Romeo tight, demonstrating how much he'd abhor a toned-down handsiness.

"Good."

"I was thinking about you."

"Also good."

Teddy laughed. "It *is*. It's all good. *We*'re good."

His expression serious, Romeo locked their gazes and threaded his fingers into Teddy's unruly hair. "We are. We really, really are."

There wasn't much talking after that, unless moans,

pleas, and half-uttered blasphemies counted. Romeo was a tease in all the best ways, inching his palms up the inside of Teddy's thighs, blowing softly in his ear, flicking his tongue almost everywhere but the place that would send Teddy over the edge. Teddy had been reduced to a sweaty, writhing, desperate mess—and he never wanted it to stop.

The condom and lube were lost somewhere in the bedding, which could have meant a delay of game, except while Romeo searched, Teddy used the opportunity to play with that magnificent ass. Teddy's actions didn't exactly assist in the quest, but Romeo didn't complain.

Eventually, after the condom had been donned and the slick liberally applied, Teddy moved slowly inside his lover. Romeo didn't complain about that either. He was too busy gasping and clutching Teddy's hips.

"Romeo!" Teddy shouted as he climaxed.

From the other side of the wall, the neighbor's voice came faintly. "Wherefore art thou?"

Laughing and breathless, Teddy and Romeo settled in for a midmorning nap. Well, Romeo napped, anyway. Teddy remained awake, clutching Romeo's warm body even as hope and worry battled in Teddy's brain.

He and Romeo, they *had* something. It was tenuous but real, and Teddy felt it with every beat of his heart. Having didn't mean holding, however. There were still so many chances for Teddy to mess things up. Back when he'd been convinced his future involved career success and a life flying solo—less than two weeks ago—he might have been lonely. But he'd known what was coming. Now? Now was like running down the train tracks in a blinding blizzard. He might be led to safety. Or he might get run over.

Oh, but the run was so exhilarating!

"This was a fabulous idea," Teddy said, clinking his bottle of Tooth & Claw lager against Romeo's. The conversations of other cafeteria diners eddied pleasantly around them.

"Yeah? Not too dorky?"

"Not remotely. Man, I haven't been to the Field Museum since I was a kid. I forgot how much I used to love it."

Grinning, Romeo swallowed a bit of his beef stew. "Were you a dinosaur fan?"

"So-so. I was more into the mummies."

"My dad used to bring me and Reagan here on free admission days if he could get off work. She liked all the dead stuffed things, but my favorite was the gems."

Teddy was trying, with moderate success, to eat a meatball sub without wearing most of it. He finished a chew and swallowed. "I would have pegged you as a Museum of Science and Industry sort of guy. Lots of buttons to push, all the tech stuff. Oh, and the coal mine!"

"Yeah, I liked that too." Romeo shrugged. "But the Field was sort of special for the three of us, you know? My other sisters weren't interested, but the three of us would bring sack lunches and stay here until closing time. He'd explain signs to us when we didn't understand them and help us pronounce all the words, and before we left he gave us money to buy a little plastic statue from the Mold-A-Rama machines. I still have my collection. I wonder if Reagan does too."

Romeo's eyes reflected a heartbreaking mixture of sorrow, love, and remembered happiness. Teddy reached across the table to lightly touch the back of his hand. "You miss your dad a lot."

"It's weird how someone can be so much a part of your life and then one day without warning—bang! They're gone."

"He's not, though, is he? He's always going to be a part of your family."

"That's what Mama says." Romeo laughed softly.

"Well, she's right. You're remarkable. My favorite human, in fact. I'm sure your mom and sisters contributed to making you who you are, but so did your dad."

"Favorite human, huh?"

"Yep. One in seven billion."

They spent most of the day at the museum, even paying extra to see the 3D movies and the Hall of China. They'd intended to catch a Lyft back to Teddy's place, but when they stepped into the gathering dusk, sleet had given way to big fluffy snowflakes, the sort that often starred in Hallmark Christmas movies. It was too pretty to resist so, despite some risk to life and limb on the slick sidewalks, Teddy and Romeo decided to walk back through Grant Park instead.

"Magical," Teddy said when he saw the rapidly accumulating blanket of snow atop the dormant plants in the Lurie Garden. The city's skyscrapers rose in the near distance, sharp edges blunted by the weather. It was like walking through a giant snow globe. Yes, he'd seen snow falling plenty of times before, and usually he grumbled about it. But today he and Romeo were together, and the landscape was nothing short of enchanting.

Teddy scooped up a handful of snow, formed a ball, and threw it at Romeo, hitting him squarely in the back.

"Oh, you're gonna regret that!" With a wild whoop, Romeo bent, scooped, and returned fire.

War broke out. They slipped and shouted and screamed with laughter as they pelted each other, earning either wary looks or indulgent smiles from the few other pedestrians. Finally they collapsed on their backs next to each other, out of breath and thoroughly besnowed.

"Hot cocoa," Teddy said after a moment. He sat up and brushed his coat clean. "I think I have some."

"Capital idea." Romeo got to his feet and offered Teddy a hand.

The apartment's heat was almost too much, and they stripped to their underwear right away. While Romeo hung their damp clothing in the bathroom, Teddy heated water in a vintage Alessi teakettle. "Sorry I can't make it with milk," he called. "I need to go shopping."

Romeo stepped out of the bathroom, glowing and nearly naked. "I'll go with you if you want. We can catch dinner. Or get ingredients to make something."

"As long as flowers aren't among the ingredients."

"How about my mama's famous pork chops?"

Teddy cast a significant glance at his miniature kitchen. "You can make that here?"

"You have a frying pan?"

"Uh, yeah."

"Then I can do it," Romeo said confidently.

Before Teddy could interrogate him about particulars, their phones rang in tandem. Teddy turned down the heat under the kettle while Romeo rushed to retrieve their phones from the table beside the love seat. "Could it be Lauren?" Romeo wondered aloud.

Teddy's pulse didn't even race—it was probably tired out from all the racing it had already done with Romeo today. He grinned as they picked up the call simultaneously.

"I need you both here first thing Monday," Lauren said without preamble. Then she added, "Please."

"To clean out our desks?" Romeo asked.

"I just got off the phone with Joyce. She's flying in to meet with us."

Chapter Twenty-Two

They didn't waste the evening speculating about what Joyce Alexander might want. She'd meddled enough already. Instead Teddy and Romeo went grocery shopping, and then Romeo performed a magic act by baking cornbread and frying up some delicious pork chops.

"We should have made this for Joyce," Teddy said amidst licking his fingers.

"Her loss."

After dinner they squished together on the love seat, making out and watching episodes of the original *Star Trek*. There was a friendly argument over who was hotter, Chekov or Sulu, which ended in a draw. Teddy learned that Romeo gave excellent foot massages—as if he wasn't already perfect enough!—and Romeo learned that Teddy was absolutely capable of eating a second dinner when Mrs. Blue's pork chop recipe was involved.

They'd just finished Teddy's personal favorite episode, the one with the shirtless George Takei, when Romeo looked at his phone and sighed. "It's getting late."

"Please tell me you're spending the night here." Did that sound desperate? Yeah, probably. But who cared? Teddy didn't have the fortitude to face an empty bed.

Romeo grinned shyly. "Yeah? You want that?"

"We could hang out tomorrow too. You could sleep over again. Then it's Sunday and time for me to meet the Blues." Wow. That was…a lot, all said out loud like that.

"Right." Then Romeo winced. "I, uh…"

"If you want or need to leave, do it. I won't tie you to my bedposts, even if I really want to."

"I want to stay. Tying is optional but intriguing. It's just, um, Mama. I need to call and let her know I won't be home. I know I'm a grown-ass man, but I don't usually spend the night away, and she worries, and—"

"And it's sweet that you both care."

Romeo gave a heart-melting smile. "You really think that? You don't think I'm a mama's boy, or—"

"I think you love your mother, and if your thoughtfulness and consideration for her is any indication of how you'll treat your boyfriend, I'm a lucky man."

Oops. Now Romeo was wide-eyed, and Teddy wished he could rewind and take back that last sentence. The B-word part of it, at least.

"Boyfriend." Romeo said the word carefully, as if it were foreign and he wasn't sure how to pronounce it.

"Um, you can forget I said that. You're thoughtful and considerate, la la la la, you're a good son."

Romeo shook his head firmly. "Nope. You *said* boyfriend."

"I say a lot of things. You should have noticed that by now. Sometimes I can babble on for hours if nobody shuts me up, and God only knows what spews out of my mouth. I've always been like that. My first-grade teacher, Mrs. Solomon? She used to make me sit in a little desk at the back all by myself 'cause I was bugging the other kids, but even that didn't really work and—"

"Boyfriend." Romeo scooted impossibly closer on the loveseat, pressing himself firmly against Teddy. "That's an interesting word. A *good* word."

Teddy wasn't sure what apoplexy was, but he felt as if he might keel over from it here and now. "How good?" he whispered.

"Good enough that I might just mention it casually to Mama. If you don't mind."

Grinning, Teddy picked up Romeo's phone and handed it to him. Tonight they could celebrate their new status a little—tomorrow Teddy could worry about exactly what boyfriend might mean to them.

Because they had a free day, and because it was better than worrying, Teddy suggested a little shopping.

"Maybe we should watch our wallets," Romeo said. "Since we're probably both going to be minus a paycheck now."

"Yeah. But I bet I can make you look good for under

thirty bucks. Not that you don't look good now." Romeo happened to be naked as they were having this conversation.

"No way I'm taking that bet. I know I'll lose."

They went to one of Teddy's favorite thrift shops, where a grandmotherly clerk had taken a shine to Teddy and sometimes set aside good finds just for him. She smiled broadly when she caught sight of the two of them. "Teddy! I haven't seen you in weeks. Got a sweater you're gonna love."

"Thanks, Marie. But today I'm shopping for Romeo. My boyfriend." The last part was unnecessary, but it felt really good to say. He imagined cherubs flitting through the air and blowing trumpets.

"Boyfriend!" She looked Romeo up and down approvingly before grinning at Teddy. "No wonder you've been making yourself scarce."

While Marie interrogated Romeo, Teddy prowled the aisles in search of something perfect. He found a lot of things that were acceptable, but that wasn't good enough. This was Romeo, after all. Then he caught sight of his prey and pounced, although he felt a little apprehensive as he carried it to Romeo.

"Okay," Teddy said before Romeo could speak. "Full disclosure—this is supposed to be a woman's blouse. The buttons are going to be backward and the sleeves too short. But I bet you can handle the button issue, and we're going to give you a nice gray cardigan anyway, so your cuffs won't be obvious. These colors are going to be amazing with your skin tone."

He waited for Romeo to object to wearing a woman's shirt. Instead, he took the hanger and held it in front of his chest. "Yeah?"

"Oh, yeah," Teddy breathed, and Marie said something in Haitian Creole that sounded approving. The shirt was seventies vintage and made of good-quality silk in a basket-weave pattern of emerald and cobalt. It was generously cut and would hang a little loosely on Romeo's frame, which was fine. He could wear it with the tight jeans he had on now.

"I guess we'll take it," Romeo said.

They ended up spending thirty-two dollars, so technically Teddy lost the bet. But since that total included the sweater Marie had saved for Teddy, the overage didn't really count.

For lunch they finished off the pork chops and cornbread, and then Romeo put on his new clothes. "Wow," he said to the mirror.

"You like it?"

"I'd never in a million years have chosen it for myself, but yeah. I love it. Wearing it makes me feel…interesting."

"You're fascinating, in fact."

That conversation led very rapidly to Romeo removing the shirt in question, along with the rest of his clothes, and Teddy followed suit. The apartment was having one of its arctic days, but that hardly mattered because the two of them worked up a respectable sweat and then lolled in bed under piles of blankets.

"I like your place a lot," Romeo announced. His arm

was around Teddy's shoulders, and Teddy was pressed up tight against all that wonderful naked man.

"It's tiny."

"But you've chosen every aspect of it with such care. You should see my room. My decorating style is Stuff Mama Bought on Clearance When I Was Fifteen."

"I bet you have a lot of games and books, though. And at least three generations of outdated electronic gadgets."

Laughing, Romeo held him even closer. "You got me."

And that was the truth of it, wasn't it? Teddy got Romeo, and Romeo got Teddy, and that was the most perfect equation Teddy could think of. He was about to say so, and to assess whether they had the energy for a second round, when his phone buzzed.

He glanced at the screen. "It's Gram."

"Want me to give you some privacy?"

"How? Are you gonna stand on the fire escape naked in twenty degree temps?" Teddy kissed the tip of Romeo's nose before taking the call. "Hi, Gram! Back from New York already?"

"No, we have two more days here. We're seeing *The Book of Mormon* tonight. I hear it's very good."

Imagining his grandmother's reaction to some of the song lyrics, Teddy stifled a laugh. "It's great, Gram. You'll love it. Are you having a good trip?"

"I am. We've been seeing shows and eating up a storm. The only problem is that everyone on this tour is so old." She sniffed disdainfully, and Teddy decided not to point out that the trip was organized by her senior center and that she herself was eighty.

"Maybe sometime you and I could go together," he offered. It was sort of an empty promise, considering his income was about to evaporate, but his heart was in it.

"I'd like that. And what have you been up to, dear? Still working those long hours?"

"Yeah. Just got back from an impromptu business trip to Seattle, in fact."

She clucked her tongue. "You need to take it a little easy. You're young! You should be out painting the town red."

Romeo, whose head was close enough to hear both sides of the conversation, seemed fascinated and a little amused. Teddy realized that this was the closest Romeo might get to meeting any of his family, at least for the foreseeable future.

"Hey, Gram? I have some news. It's maybe not as big a deal as Jennifer Murray having a second kid, but it's important to me." He paused for dramatic effect.

"Out with it, Teddy! I'm not getting any younger."

Romeo had to muffle his laugh with a pillow.

Teddy took a deep breath. This wasn't an announcement he'd imagined himself making, at least not for many years. "I've found someone." Wait. That sounded as if he'd discovered Romeo lurking in his closet—which would be impossible, given Romeo's size and the closet's fullness.

Teddy tried again. "I have a boyfriend, Gram. He's someone special."

Romeo's eyes got that big, shiny manga look, and his lips curled into the sweetest, most beautiful smile ever. God, how had Teddy managed to strike it so lucky? He'd never done anything remarkable in his entire life, and yet here he was with this priceless man in his bed. In his heart.

"Tell me all about him!" Gram exclaimed.

"Well, his name is Romeo Blue—"

"Is he a celebrity? That sounds like a celebrity's name."

Teddy snorted. "Right? Or a spy. But he's a software developer."

"That's much more practical."

"True. And I want to give you all the deets, Gram, but the truth is, he's right here right now, and I—"

"You'd rather spend time with your new boyfriend than gabbing with an old lady." Before Teddy could protest, she continued. "And that's what you should do. Carpe diem. Or, what are those letters? Ah! YOLO. You can spill the tea later."

Romeo was laughing into the pillow again.

"Thanks, Gram. I'll dish on him soon."

"Good. Before I let you go, listen to my advice. That's a benefit of being old—you get to force your nuggets of wisdom onto young people. Teddy, love is a real thing and very precious. In the end, it's really all that matters. Your grandfather and I never had much money, and we went through some tough periods. Sometimes we argued like cats and dogs. But we loved each other very much. Even now, after he's been gone for so many years,

I hang on to knowing that. It makes even the difficult memories feel sweeter."

Teddy had always thought of his grandmother as a levelheaded sort, affectionate but never mushy. Now it turned out that she was a closet romantic. "Thanks, Gram."

"Have fun, honey. I can't wait to meet him."

They said their goodbyes and Teddy set the phone aside. He looked at Romeo. "That felt good."

"Getting relationship advice from your grandma?"

"Telling her you're my boyfriend." He shivered—not so much from cold as from happiness—and snuggled close to Romeo again. "Those are good words to say. Good words to *feel*."

In fact, the more times he said them, the bigger they became, until they filled him entirely. They made him feel bouncy and buoyant, a hot air balloon barely tethered to the ground. But that was the problem, wasn't it? It was like *The Wizard of Oz*. The balloon could take you somewhere magical and amazing, like the Emerald City or Romeo's embrace. But if you weren't careful, it could just as easily float away again, dragging you back to Omaha. Alone. Without even a pair of sparkly red shoes.

Maybe Teddy should tell Romeo straight up how he felt. Admit he was harboring something huge inside him. But God, Romeo had never even seriously dated anyone before. What if he freaked out? Teddy could hardly blame him. He was nearly freaking out himself, even though the feelings were his own.

It was too fast. Acknowledging these growing emotions would only jinx things.

So Teddy simply leaned his head against Romeo's shoulder and closed his eyes, inhaling the scent of his soap on his boyfriend's skin. Knowing that sooner or later, the thing inside him would become too big to hide.

Chapter Twenty-Three

"Teddy, we're going to be late."

"But I can't decide." Teddy stood in front of his open closet. His clothing collection seemed suddenly intimidatingly huge yet impossibly small. There was no way he could choose an appropriate outfit. "I'm just going back to bed."

Romeo, who looked perfect in Friday's clothes since he looked perfect in everything, grabbed Teddy's arm before he could escape. "You are coming home with me even if I have to carry you there in your corgi pajamas."

"How you got in my corgi pajamas, I'll never know." Teddy ducked to avoid Romeo's answering tickle. "Seriously. This is a crisis. I have no idea what I'm supposed to wear to meet my new boyfriend's entire family."

Like a man with a heavy burden, Romeo emitted a long sigh. "It doesn't matter. It's not a fashion show or a job interview. It's my family, and let me tell you, none of us are known for being especially stylish. Wait until you see the school photos Mama hung in the living room. You'll see me in all my eighth-grade glory, and then you'll see what I mean."

Okay, that prospect almost made the ongoing terror seem worth it. Teddy settled on a pair of beige pleated chinos and a long-sleeve knitted polo with an L-shaped pattern in shades of blue. He would have preferred penny loafers to finish off the casual fifties look, but the slushy sidewalks demanded boots.

"You look perfect," Romeo said as Teddy fussed over his hair in front of the bathroom mirror. "Let's go."

Teddy nodded and maybe would have come along peacefully, but then a thought struck him. "Oh, shit!"

"What?" Romeo seemed undecided between impatience and panic.

"I don't have anything to bring. No flowers, no wine, no— Jesus, I don't even know what you're supposed to bring to a meeting-boyfriend's-family lunch."

"You bring yourself."

"But...your nieces! Let's reschedule. And next time I can buy them toys or cute clothes or—"

"They're spoiled enough already. Let's *go*, Teddy."

Teddy put on his coat and scarf and followed Romeo down the corridor and into the elevator. They took a Lyft for the short journey to the station and then had to run to catch their train. "Next one's not for two hours,"

Romeo said through panting as the train pulled away. "Mama would have murdered me."

"In a pinch, we could have taken Lyft."

"Do you have piles of cash stashed away somewhere? Because I don't, and we're about to be unemployed."

Teddy glared at him, mostly because Romeo was right. Anyway, squabbling was better than having an anxiety attack on the Metra, so Teddy leaned away from him. "I should be bringing *something*," he mumbled.

"You're bringing plenty of unnecessary stress."

"It's not—" Teddy stopped himself so abruptly he almost bit his tongue. "Sorry."

Romeo banged his shoulder against Teddy's. "You want me to distract you with stories about this jerk of a flight attendant I used to date?"

"You used to— Oh. You knew I was trying to distract you, huh?" Teddy remembered how nervous Romeo had been about flying, and how he'd gradually calmed while Teddy blathered on.

"I knew. And I appreciated it. It's the first time I realized that you…"

"What?"

"That you weren't the noisy, opinionated, um…"

Teddy chuckled. "Asshole?"

"Well, I was going to say *jerk*, but… Anyway, instead of making me feel like an idiot, you were nice to me, and I appreciated it."

Tingly warmth spread through Teddy at the praise. "I was pretty much a jerk before. I made some wrong assumptions about you and—"

"And it's all good now," Romeo said firmly. "So, how about if I share the debacle that was my senior prom?"

Teddy was wiping away tears of laughter by the time they reached Evanston.

Romeo's house was about a mile from the train station. He explained that when the weather was truly miserable, he caught a ride from his mother or sister. Today, though, he and Teddy decided they were up for the walk. That turned out to be a good decision, because it meant Teddy could duck into a little grocery store and buy some daffodils in a cheery red pot.

It was nice to stroll along together, Romeo mentioning a few landmarks as he went.

"That's Mama's church," he said, pointing. "And don't look so panicked. She's nowhere near fire-and-brimstone, and the rest of us were never much into it. She didn't push. But I think she found support and fellowship there, especially after Dad passed."

"I don't think my family is any religion," Teddy said. "It never came up when I was a kid. We did Easter baskets and a Christmas tree, but they were, you know... secular versions of the holidays."

"Gotcha. C'mon. We're almost there."

The house was a neat brick bungalow with a small front yard currently gone to winter grays and browns. A heart-shaped wreath graced the front door. "It's past Valentine's Day, but Mama says she's not ready to take it down."

"It looks nice." Teddy meant it. The greenery and red

ribbons added a nice pop of color to the facade. "The entire house is cute."

"It's not fancy. And it's never really been big enough for everyone. But it's way better than where we lived before," Romeo seemed genuinely worried, as if Teddy might march off in a huff because it wasn't as fancy as Joyce Alexander's mansion.

Teddy put his hand on Romeo's arm. "It's your home, and it's full of the people you care about. Of course I'm going to love it."

Okay. If he got rewarded with smiles like that, it was worth letting his inner romantic out of the closet permanently.

They started up the walkway hand in hand, but Romeo tugged him to a halt before they reached the porch stairs. "I've never done this before. Brought someone home to meet the family. But, um, I've seen it when my sisters did, and I need to warn you. Brace yourself." With the cryptic caveat, Romeo stepped up onto the tiny front porch, and the door opened at once. Romeo pulled Teddy in, and a Blue wave crashed over them.

To the extent he'd considered it at all, Teddy had assumed that Romeo's relatives would be like Romeo: reserved at first, quiet. Maybe even a little awkward around others.

Wrong.

Right there in the living room, barely inside the door, a thousand people hugged him and clapped his back and shook his hand. Not just Romeo's mother and sisters, but also spouses and an array of children from toddlers through teens. Each gave their name—resulting in a dizzying array he was never going to get right—and told him how thrilled they were to meet him. It would have been somewhat terrifying, except every one of them radiated warmth and welcome.

Finally Romeo's mother—who'd insisted Teddy call her Wanda—placed herself between Teddy and everyone else. "Ya'll need to move back so this boy can breathe. Let him get his coat off at least."

Laughing, the crowd obeyed. Wanda exclaimed over the daffodils, took Teddy's outerwear, and handed it to a gawky preteen boy, who spirited it away. Smiling, she looked Teddy up and down. "Romeo told us you're a sharp dresser, and he was right. I've seen the outfits you helped him pick out too." She shook her head. "I sure wish I had your talent."

"But you look beautiful." This was honest. Like Romeo, Wanda was tall and attractive. It was easy to see the family resemblance; it was clear in Romeo's sisters, nieces, and nephews, too. Wanda's steel-gray hair was as closely shorn as her son's, a style that suited her well, and her aqua-hued maxi dress worked perfectly with her ample figure.

She waved away the compliment but looked pleased. "You don't have to flatter me."

"I promise, I never give false compliments."

"Oh, I'm gonna like you!" She threaded her arm through his and announced, "I'm giving Teddy the grand tour. Romeo and Portia, you go in the kitchen and keep an eye on things. Food should be almost ready."

Romeo gave a little salute and exited with his sister, the rest of the crowd dispersed, and Wanda became his guide. After dropping off the flowers on a table near the stairs, they peeked at the upstairs bathroom and the bedrooms occupied by Portia and her daughters. Then Wanda showed him around the main floor: her bedroom, another bathroom, and the kitchen, living room, and dining room. Finally they descended to the basement, part of which had been converted to Romeo's bedroom. There was also a bathroom, laundry room, and a utility area with the furnace, water heater, and a bunch of boxes.

"When we first moved here, his sisters complained because they had to share rooms and he got his own," Wanda explained. "He sure liked it down here, though. We called it his cave. I think it was good he had a place to escape from us now and then."

"He needs quiet to do his work."

Wanda smiled broadly. "He does! You already know him well."

"He's...really special."

She gave him a half hug and kissed his cheek.

Teddy would have liked to spend more time in Romeo's space, poking around his stacks of books and reading the framed certificates on the walls, but it was time to rejoin everyone else. Besides, Teddy wasn't nosy enough to look around without permission. Not *quite*.

"The house is a little underwhelming," Wanda said when they reached the kitchen and, presumably, the end of the tour. "Nothing like those fancy magazines."

The walls in the Blue house were covered in family

photos, and the fridge was almost hidden behind children's drawings affixed by magnets. Some of the furniture was mismatched, the floors a little scuffed, the shelves packed with books and knickknacks and school trophies. It was hard to walk anywhere without colliding with someone or getting run over by a darting child. Romeo stood at the stove, stirring something in a huge pot and teasing Portia, who was trying to reach around him to get something from the cupboard.

Teddy wanted to hug himself for the undiluted happiness that permeated the entire building. "I'd take your home over anything in a fancy magazine," he told Wanda. "Any day of the week."

She nodded. "Good. Romeo found himself a smart boy. Someone who knows what's important. One thing I always told him—Romeo Valentine! *What* are you doing to my rolls?" Wanda rushed over to intervene in the bread crisis.

The meal meant all the adults and a couple of the oldest kids crowded around a dining room table, while younger children sat at card tables in the living room. Wanda had prepared enough food for all of Cook County: bean soup, ham, greens, rolls, buttered carrots, and a host of other side dishes. Teddy sat between Romeo and Reagan and learned that dentists had more adventures than he'd imagined. Everyone talked a lot, gently making fun of one another and bringing up old family in-jokes without making Teddy feel excluded. They asked him questions too—nothing intrusive, but they really seemed to want to know the answers. Things like what movies and music he favored. Titania and her husband loved musical theater, so they had a good conversation with Teddy about that, and one of the nephews wanted to know more about marketing as a career choice.

As Romeo had predicted, his family also had questions about fashion, so by the time Portia and Reagan distributed slices of hummingbird cake, Teddy was happily giving wardrobe upgrade consultations. Two sisters, a brother-in-law, and a niece all made him promise to go shopping with them.

And throughout it all, Romeo sat at Teddy's side, joining in the repartee and beaming as bright as a lighthouse. Teddy felt that light inside himself, warm and comfortable. A little bittersweet, maybe, because this friendly chaos was something he'd been missing his entire life. But as Wanda said to a niece who was disappointed over a recent exam grade but vowed to try harder next time: a little salt makes things taste sweeter. And you appreciated a thing more if you knew what it felt like to go without.

Teddy helped clear the table but wasn't allowed to wash or dry. Apparently there was a complex system of rules in place about household chores. Romeo, who was also off the hook for the time being, took the opportunity to bring Teddy downstairs to his bedroom. "You holding up all right?" he asked.

Teddy was doing wonderfully. Being around the Blues made him feel energized and optimistic. "I love your family."

"They're not too much?"

Teddy pulled Romeo flush against him. "They're perfect."

"I've witnessed some of my sisters' prospective boyfriends run screaming out the door, never to be seen again."

"Well, then they weren't worth dating, were they? Seriously, Romeo. If you and I weren't a thing, I'd ask your family to adopt me."

Romeo wrapped his arms around Teddy and bent down so their noses touched. "But we are a thing, aren't we?"

"A really good thing."

Teddy ducked out from Romeo's embrace and walked the width of the bedroom, which wasn't far. A particleboard bookcase, its sides plastered with old stickers, was crammed with well-worn books. Including, if Teddy wasn't mistaken, the one about deserts. He stroked the spine with one finger but didn't pull it out.

When Teddy turned around, Romeo was waiting patiently. That was something else to cherish about Romeo—the way he gave Teddy time and space to think when he needed them.

"Can I say something?" Romeo had the same expression he'd worn when boarding a plane: terror mixed with a dose of determination.

Time for Teddy to draw on some of his own courage. "Go ahead."

"You don't have to look at me like that. It's nothing awful."

"Just scary?"

Romeo gave a tiny grin. "Yeah. So here goes. Um… so now you've seen our humble abode."

"I like your home."

"Good." Romeo's smile widened. "Because the thing is, there's always room here for more people. Sometimes we have to squish together a little, but squishing's not always so bad." He patted his mattress.

"Are you proposing we have sex right now? Because I think your family—"

"Teddy. Listen."

"Okay." And Teddy kept his mouth zipped while Romeo appeared to marshal his thoughts.

"I'm offering something here. Promising something. Teddy, we're going to land on our feet no matter what. I can feel it. But if you end up needing a place to stay—a place to live—we have room for you here. *I* have room for you." He pressed his palm to his chest, right over his heart.

Teddy's knees went weak. Not metaphorically, but real, true wobbliness so strong he had to brace himself against the wall. "You're offering to let me move in with you?"

"Yes."

"But your family just met me. Maybe they can't stand me."

Romeo snorted. "I've seen what happens when they disapprove of a boyfriend, and it ain't what's happening here today. I'm actually a little worried Mama and at least one of my sisters are going to kidnap you and keep you here in chains." His expression turned stubborn. "And anyway, what matters is how I feel about you. And the only thing I can't stand about you is the idea of…of not being with you."

Little cogs and gears turned frantically inside Teddy's brain, but his mouth simply hung open. In fact, he remained silent so long that Romeo shrank a bit.

"I know," Romeo said. "You don't believe in insta-love. Sounds like a sugary breakfast cereal, doesn't it?"

And then it happened. That balloon thing inside of Teddy expanded so much that his body and soul could no longer contain it. The entire state of Illinois could no longer contain it.

It was time to let it out.

Teddy lifted his chin. "I've revised my theories this past week due to the acquisition of new data. You ought to appreciate that, Mr. Scientist."

"What are your modified theories?"

"Not just modified, but improved. More accurate. First, True Love is not a simple marketing concept invented by jewelry manufacturers. It exists. And second, True Love can happen very fast. It's like putting together a good outfit. Sometimes I'm at a thrift store and I find a pair of vintage trousers…oh, something with a really bold plaid, maybe. And I think I'm never going to find anything perfect to pair with them. Then I stumble onto this amazing patterned bowling shirt. I think, *oh no, that's going to clash horribly*. But I try them on and bam! Perfect. Like they were made for each other. It doesn't take me months to see that—it's obvious right away."

Romeo listened to Teddy's extended metaphor with a fond smile. "I'm a bowling shirt?"

"You can be the trousers if you'd rather."

"What else can I be, Teddy Spenser?" Romeo stood and crossed the room, stopping only inches away from Teddy.

Teddy looked up at him and knew what he had to say. The universe had aligned itself so that no other words would do.

"You can be the man I love, Romeo Blue. You *are* the man I love."

Nothing in the whole world was better than how he felt saying that. No, not true, because that look of wonder in Romeo's shiny eyes, that soft smile on Romeo's lips? Those were better still. And when Romeo folded him into a tight embrace, well, that was the best of all.

Until Romeo whispered four little words that topped it all: "I love you too."

Chapter Twenty-Four

They remained exactly like that, leaning into each other and humming with joy, until a young niece bellowed from the top of the basement stairs. "Romeoooo! Grandma wants to know if you guys want more cake."

Laughing, Romeo disentangled himself. "You can have our extra pieces," he called back. He was answered with a muffled cheer.

With very little discussion, Teddy and Romeo agreed that Romeo would stay overnight at Teddy's again. And again and again and again, because sleeping apart was simply no longer a viable option for either of them.

Then they tromped upstairs to tell Wanda their immediate plans. "It'll be more convenient, because we have an early morning meeting," Romeo explained.

Based on her expression, she clearly saw through his excuse. God, they were both probably glowing like a pair of halogen bulbs. But she packed up leftovers for them and insisted on driving them to the Metra station. "I could take you all the way downtown," she said after they'd piled into her car. "Traffic's light on Sunday."

"The train is fine, Mama. And you've got a houseful of people."

"Did it ever occur to you that maybe sometimes I need a break from that mob?" She was laughing as said it, though, and she drove them only into central Evanston.

"Thanks for everything," Teddy said before he got out of the car. "I'm so glad I met you."

"You better be planning on coming every Sunday now that we have a place for you at the table."

"I wouldn't miss it for the world."

With his belly full, his heart fuller, and Romeo warm in the seat beside him, Teddy dozed lightly all the way home.

The two of them didn't do much for the rest of the day. Mostly they lolled on the couch under a stack of blankets, reading or watching Netflix. Making out a little now and then. And the whole time, Teddy kept thinking, *This is it. I could do this permanently. I* need *to do this permanently.* He was fairly certain Romeo did too.

They had leftovers for dinner and went to bed early. As they settled under the covers, Teddy pushed away his worries about what would happen tomorrow. Tonight he had more important things to think about. Tonight he and Romeo were in love.

"You probably know this," Teddy said as he scrunched more tightly against Romeo. "But in Shakespeare's play, Friar Lawrence warns Romeo and Juliet to love moderately."

"Yep. And they ignored him 'cause they were teenagers, and we all know how that turned out."

"I don't think I can love you moderately. Not if our opening scenes are any indication of what's to come."

Romeo kissed the top of Teddy's head, a gesture that was quickly becoming one of Teddy's favorite things. "No problem, babe, 'cause we're not a tragedy. I think we might be a romantic comedy instead."

"Can we be a *musical* rom-com?"

"Of course."

Good. Because that meant they'd get a happy ending, right?

Although Reddyflora's building in general was as busy as any Monday morning, the outer office of their suite was a ghost town. No sign of Imani, Skyler, or anyone else. "Creepy," Teddy whispered. Way more like a horror movie than a musical, even though he knew Lauren had probably told everyone to come in late so they could talk privately.

Romeo took Teddy's hand.

Lauren and Joyce waited in Lauren's office, tea in two plain white cups steaming on the desk. While Lauren sat in her usual spot, a new chair had materialized for Joyce. Its straight-back, carved wooden frame made it look almost like a throne, and Teddy entertained the notion that Joyce had brought it with her from Seattle. Crazy idea, yes; but not impossible.

Joyce wore a mauve wool pantsuit and plum-colored blouse with a lot of frothy lace near the high neckline. Simple diamond hoops hung from her ears, and her nails had a lustrous pearl-tone manicure. "Darlings," she said when Teddy and Romeo entered the room. A weird thing to call two guys you'd had fired.

But Teddy and Romeo smiled and shook her hand before taking their seats in Lauren's usual uncomfortable chairs.

"That shirt is perfect for you," Joyce informed Romeo, who was wearing the emerald-and-cobalt basket weave.

"Thank you. Teddy picked it out."

"I should have known. Teddy, I knew as soon as I walked into this suite which space was yours. You have such a clever eye."

It would be nice if they could skip the empty compliments and head straight to the sacking, but apparently they had to detour through small talk first. They had an extensive chat about the weather and Joyce's flight and then about a restaurant a celebrity acquaintance of hers was opening in Fulton Market. Teddy remained on his best behavior even though he wanted to scream.

No, what he wanted to do was grab Romeo and hustle back to his cozy little apartment. They could make more pork chops.

Finally—*finally*—Joyce turned to Teddy and Romeo with a serious expression. "Lauren tells me you boys have given her an ultimatum."

"That sounds more ominous than the reality," Teddy said. Romeo nodded his agreement. "We're not mobsters."

Lauren snorted quietly and Joyce took a sip of her tea. "All right, then. In your own words. What's your position?"

After getting Romeo's nod of encouragement to play spokesman, Teddy cleared his throat. "We want Lauren to accept your backing offer because we want the project—and Reddyflora—to succeed. We are grateful for the exciting job opportunity that Lauren provided. And we like our fellow employees too."

"And you understand my offer was contingent on one of you leaving?"

Time to be brave, Teddy Spenser. As if sensing Teddy's thoughts, Romeo gave his arm a supportive pat.

"We understand," said Teddy. "It's because you think we're a disaster together. But you're wrong about that. We might have failed your tests, but we're perfect together. And we *are* together. We're in love."

"I see." Joyce's expression hid whatever she was thinking. Lauren, on the other hand, covered her mouth with her palm as if to stifle her comments.

Teddy soldiered on. "Our jobs are really important to us, Joyce. But neither of us is willing to keep our own job at the other's expense. I'm sure Lauren will find someone to replace us so the project can be completed." He let out a heavy breath. "So I guess we'll go clean out our desks now."

He started to stand, but Joyce waved him down. "Wait, please. I need to explain something. I realize my methodology is unconventional at best, but it always has been. That's what has brought me success. And I'm old and attached to my ways."

"We're not arguing with you. I mean, you're wrong about us, but…" Teddy shrugged. "It's your money."

"But you didn't let me finish my explanation. I told you there were three tests for the three characteristics I believe are important for success in this endeavor. But darling, I lied."

Teddy and Romeo exchanged confused glances and then looked at Lauren for guidance, but she appeared to be as much in the dark as they were. "You lied?" she said, wide-eyed.

"There were actually four characteristics. Fortitude, intelligence, creativity…and loyalty. The results were somewhat mixed with respect to the first three, although honestly not so very awful given the oddness of the tasks. But when it comes to the final trait, you've both shone so very brightly! You're loyal not only to each other— understandable if you're in love—but also to Lauren and your other colleagues. Well done!"

Teddy hung tenuously between astonishment and anger. Perhaps luckily, he was too busy gaping to get any words out, and Romeo spoke first, his voice even.

"Please explain what you mean."

"I mean that I am prepared to offer my financial support, as promised. And that I'd be most pleased if *both* of you remain with Reddyflora."

Teddy spent several seconds blinking owlishly. When he finally glanced around, Romeo appeared equally gobsmacked and Lauren had her hand over her mouth. He tried to say something, then realized he didn't know what to say, didn't know what he thought. He had no idea what to do next.

Romeo saved him by jumping to his feet and hauling Teddy up too. "We need a few minutes to talk," he announced. Without waiting for either woman to respond, he pulled Teddy out of the office and closed the door behind him. They went to Romeo's office; he closed that door as well.

"Can they hear us in here?" Teddy asked. Yay, he'd managed words!

"Only if we shout."

That made sense. The bathroom and a storage closet separated the two offices. And Teddy had no intention of shouting. In fact, he was feeling kind of hollowed out, and he suddenly collapsed into Romeo's guest chair with a sigh. "She played us."

Instead of taking his own seat, Romeo moved behind Teddy, setting hands on his shoulders and pulling Teddy against him. "News flash. That's what rich people do."

"I guess."

"I don't think Lauren was in on it, do you?"

Teddy shook his head. Lauren had her faults, but she was generally straightforward, and she treated her employees fairly. Besides, she'd looked as surprised as Teddy and Romeo.

Romeo was now giving Teddy a scalp massage—another talent discovered. It was going to mess up Teddy's hair, but since it felt like heaven, he just closed his eyes and enjoyed. God, he loved Romeo's hands.

"What do you want to do?" Teddy finally said.

"Dunno."

"'Cause I think we need to reach a mutual decision. I'm not doing anything that makes you unhappy."

"Ditto." Romeo paused his movements, but when Teddy elbowed him gently, he huffed a laugh and continued. "Let's talk this through. Use logic."

"Okay, Mr. Spock."

"What Joyce did to us was crappy. I don't think she meant it to be, but I guess…some people reach a point where they sorta forget they're dealing with people and not cogs in a machine."

Teddy could see that. Getting so wrapped up in your own affairs and so certain of your convictions that you can't see past your own blinders. He'd been there himself less than two weeks earlier, although he hadn't manipulated others in that state. He'd only manipulated himself—and badly misjudged Romeo. "Okay. Crappy but not evil."

"And when you think of it, she did us a favor. If she hadn't dragged us out to Seattle and made us do her dumb tests, would we have ever gotten to really know each other?"

"No," Teddy replied softly, shuddering at the thought. He'd come so close to missing out on Romeo. So close to never finding True Love.

Romeo gave him a soothing pat. "Her methodology

and our personal outcomes aside, what do we want out of this? We can walk away on principle. Or we can stay."

"Stay at a job we both want. And need."

Now Romeo came around in front and pulled Teddy into an embrace. So good. In Shakespeare, Juliet was the sun, but in real life Teddy knew better. His Romeo was the sun, bright…and hot. The blazing star in the firmament of Teddy's life. The one who cast light that chased away the darkness.

"I'll walk away with you, babe. And we'll both be fine. We'll find other jobs—good ones—and someday we'll have enough money for you to open that store. Or stay, and I'll stay with you. Either way our future is bright. I can feel it."

Teddy could feel it too.

They kissed for a few moments, more tenderly than passionately. When they left Romeo's office, Teddy led them to his cubicle and opened the upper right-hand drawer.

Romeo patted Teddy's butt and whispered in his ear. "If you're reaching for your scissors, let me remind you that stabbing rich ladies is frowned upon."

"No stabbing." Teddy reached in and retrieved the little aqua-colored velvet box. He handed it to Romeo. "Open it."

A grin played at the corner of Romeo's mouth, but he didn't ask tedious questions. He just obeyed instructions—and then smiled widely when he read the tiny charm inside. "Love."

"Yep. Put it in your pocket, will you? Keep it."

"Always."

Another soft kiss. When they pulled apart, they gazed into each other's eyes before nodding. Yes. They knew what they wanted.

If Joyce looked somewhat tense when Romeo and Teddy reentered the room, Teddy wasn't sorry. God knew she'd caused him and Romeo plenty of anxiety. But he wasn't cruel—and anyway, he was eager to get this whole thing over with. He was done with mystery and drama for today. Time for the porn and romance to resume! So he remained standing with Romeo at his side and with his chin held high.

"We're staying. Both of us."

Lauren slumped and rested her forehead in her palm. "Thank God," she whispered. Which was a nice boost to the ego right there.

Better, though, was when Joyce stood and beamed at them. "I'm so very glad. And I'm very sorry that I've put you through the wringer. I truly am. I hope, when you're able to take a break from work, you'll accept a gift from me as my apology. A vacation somewhere warm, perhaps? I have a lovely little villa in Ibiza that I rarely use nowadays. If you'll allow it, I'd like to send you there for a week or two."

Ibiza. Teddy had his pride. But, well, *Ibiza*.

And then Romeo held out his palm to show Teddy the little charm. "Ibiza would make a pretty good choice for a honeymoon, don't you think?" His eyes were sparkling.

Honeymoon.

Because when that shirt coordinated with the trousers so perfectly, you'd be stupid not to wear them.

"Yes!" Teddy cried as he threw himself into Romeo's arms, not caring that Lauren and Joyce Alexander were watching. "Yes," he repeated, this time a trifle tearfully, sniffing against Romeo's pretty silk shirt.

Romeo whispered it back, sounding sort of weepy himself. "Yes."

Teddy Spenser wasn't looking for love. But he'd finally and most permanently found it.

Epilogue

Two years later

It was time to intervene.

Usually Teddy greeted customers near the door and then left them alone unless they asked for help. But this guy had been in the store for five minutes, floating hesitantly between the clothing racks and the mannequin displays. Fiftyish and heavyset, he was now examining the display of Reddyflora vases, but not with any indication of truly wanting one.

Teddy stopped folding sweaters and approached him. "Can I help you find something?"

The man gave an uncomfortable twitch. "I bought my girlfriend one of these vase things for Valentine's Day last year. I thought with all the hype, they'd be just a stupid fad, but she still loves it."

"Did you want to buy another? A different size, maybe?"

"Nah." The man shifted from one foot to another.

"You know, Reddyflora has a new product coming out soon. It's a multicooker with a Bluetooth interface so you can download recipes directly to the pot, and it'll tell you what to do, step-by-step." Teddy smiled to himself. Although he was no longer with the company, his kitchen bunglings had been the inspiration behind the new product. "You'll also be able to change up the exterior design to match your décor or the season."

The man nodded. "Sounds good."

"Yeah, but I bet it's not why you're here today. What can I help you with?"

"I wanted… You probably don't have anything." The guy eyed the front door but didn't quite make a move toward it. Instead he sighed. "I was kinda hoping to update my wardrobe a little. Be less boring. But you— you're probably geared for people who are younger, skinnier, and hipper than me. Like that man over there." He dropped his voice to a whisper. "Is he a model or actor or something?"

Teddy cast a quick look at Romeo, who was sitting in one of the leather armchairs near the back of the store, peering at his phone. "Nope," Teddy said. "He's a software engineer. And my husband. He got off work early and he's waiting until we go out to dinner. Valentine's Day, you know."

"Right. Um, that, uh, shirt he's wearing…"

Romeo looked scrumptious in skinny charcoal-colored jeans, a form-fitting red camisole in lace-covered satin, and a dark Armani blazer in a traditional men's cut. He must have sensed them staring at him because he glanced up, gave an amused wave, and turned his attention back to the phone.

"Not something most men would wear, huh? But doesn't it look great on him?" Teddy loved how some of the more traditionally feminine fabrics and cuts flattered Romeo's physique. And Romeo enjoyed having some of these items in his wardrobe. He said he liked the way he felt when he wore them.

The customer sighed again. "I couldn't pull off a look like that."

Teddy grinned—it was time for The Speech. He always jumped at the chance to share the philosophy behind his store. "That's not the point, though. Maybe Romeo's style isn't yours because you're two different people. What I want to do is help you find the clothes that best suit you. Not what you think other people will like, but the things that are going to make *you* feel fabulous. And you know what? As long as you feel comfortable and confident, as long as you feel like your outfit is a positive reflection of your personality, you can pull *any* look off."

The guy was pinching his chin thoughtfully. He wasn't quite convinced, but he wasn't running for the door either. "My personality. Well, I'm a lawyer for Conagra."

"That's what you do for a living, not who you are. Are you looking for work clothes?"

"Nah. Stuff for when Amber and I go out. Not super fancy or anything." He shrugged. "Dinner, a show. In a couple of weeks we're going to Vegas for her birthday."

"Got it. Smart casual."

"You got a section for that?" The man glanced around.

"Not a section, but I have plenty of items that'll work. Let's think about your overall look, though."

"That's where I'm lost."

Teddy inspected him carefully. The man wore a Burberry trench coat and a suit that had probably set him back five or six hundred bucks, but the only statement it made was Corporate Dress Code. His shirt was plain white and his tie was black with little white splotches. Ah, but that tie… Teddy leaned in for a closer inspection and saw that the white splotches were actually tiny skulls.

"Nice tie," he said.

The man lifted the end of it. "A present from Amber."

"Uh-huh. What do you like to do in your free time?"

"Don't have much of that. I play golf when the weather's good. I'm a big Bears fan."

Not much help there, Teddy thought. No way was he going to dress this man in a polo shirt or football jersey. Hmm. But there was something about that tie. "What music do you listen to?"

The guy seemed a little embarrassed. "Old stuff. I wouldn't recognize anyone on the charts nowadays. Now, back in the day I was into the Ramones, Television, the Clash. I even played guitar in a garage band in high school. We sucked." He laughed.

Bingo.

The man ended up with a sizable dent in his credit card and several bulging bags to show for it. Teddy had set him up with a leather moto jacket, an evening jacket with black satin lapels, some vintage jeans, a red tartan scarf, a skinny black tie, and several other items. All he needed to complete a vacation's worth of punk-inspired outfits was a pair of Chucks or combat boots. Most importantly, though, by the time he'd modeled the third or fourth outfit Teddy chose for him, the guy was strutting across the shop floor, his daytime-corporate-attorney persona forgotten. He was humming "Anarchy in the UK" as he left the store.

Teddy checked the time and locked the door.

Romeo, who'd given up on his phone some time ago to watch Teddy at work, stood up and stretched, making Teddy's mouth water. All that wonderful man—and he was Teddy's.

"You're good," Romeo said, grinning.

"You're just now figuring that out?"

Romeo took Teddy into his arms and nibbled lightly on an earlobe, reminding Teddy of all the beautifully wicked things that mouth could do. "You're very good," Romeo purred.

"Dinner reservations?" Teddy reminded him, although honestly he wouldn't mind a very different sort of meal.

Somewhat disappointingly, Romeo decided to be responsible. He dropped a kiss on Teddy's head and pulled away. "Yeah, don't wanna be late."

"Well then, we'd better head home and change into our fancy pants."

Darkness had fallen and the outdoor temperatures were plummeting, but it would only be a short walk to their apartment. Now that the store was making a decent profit, Teddy and Romeo had been talking about a bigger place. One with enough space for the nieces to have occasional overnight visits and for Romeo's entire family to join them for some Sunday dinners. Not that Mama's dinners weren't wonderful, but the poor woman worked really hard and deserved a weekend break now and then. Teddy would miss the little studio apartment, even though he looked forward to having a whole new space to decorate.

With Romeo standing close and blocking some of the wind, Teddy locked the shop door. "All good and ready to go?" Romeo asked.

Teddy peered at the window display, which he would need to change in the morning. It currently had a Valentine's Day theme, with red and pink clothing on the mannequins and giant reproductions of the type of cards that schoolchildren used to exchange fifty years ago, complete with corny puns. Then he glanced up at the store sign, unlit but still visible in the glow of the streetlamp. Spenser's Love it read, with a heart in place of the O.

He smiled. "All good and ready to go."

Gloved hand in gloved hand, Teddy and Romeo headed for home.

★ ★ ★ ★ ★

Reviews are an invaluable tool when it comes to spreading the word about great reads. Please consider leaving an honest review for this or any of Carina Press's other titles that you've read on your favorite retailer or review site.

To purchase and read more books by Kim Fielding please visit Kim's website at http://kfieldingwrites.com.

Acknowledgments

Special thanks to Brian, who supplied me with a few important Chicago details when I needed them; to Quinn, who helped me brainstorm about smart vases; and to Karen, whose guidance and friendship mean so much to me.

Also available from Kim Fielding
The Little Library

Copyright ©2018 by Kim Fielding

Elliott Thompson was once a historian with a promising academic future, but his involvement in a scandal meant a lost job, public shame, and a ruined love life. He took shelter in his rural California hometown, where he teaches online classes, hoards books, and despairs of his future.

Simon Odisho has lost a job as well—to a bullet that sidelined his career in law enforcement. While his shattered knee recovers, he rethinks his job prospects and searches for the courage to come out to his close-knit but conservative extended family.

In an attempt to manage his overflowing book collection, Elliott builds a miniature neighborhood library in his front yard. The project puts him in touch with his neighbors—for better and worse—and introduces him to handsome, charming Simon. While romance blooms quickly between them, Elliott's not willing to live in the closet, and his best career prospects might take him far away. His books have plenty to tell him about history, but they give him no clues about a future with Simon.

To purchase and read this and other books by
Kim Fielding, please visit Kim's website at
http://kfieldingwrites.com.

Discover another great contemporary romance from Carina Adores

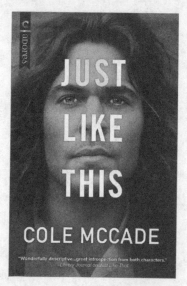

Rian's life as the art teacher to a gaggle of displaced boys at Albin Academy should be smooth sailing—until the stubborn, grouchy football coach comes into his world like a lightning strike and ignites a heated conflict that would leave them sworn enemies if not for a common goal.

A student in peril. A troubling secret. And two men who are polar opposites but must work together to protect their charges.

They shouldn't want each other. They shouldn't even like each other.

Yet as they fight to save a young man from the edge, they discover more than they thought possible about each other—and about themselves.

Available now!

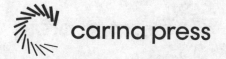

CarinaPress.com

CARCMJLT0121TR

Discover another great contemporary romance from Carina Adores

For single mom Adah Campbell, the executive chef job at a posh restaurant in quaint South Bay, Maine, is a dream come true—and the perfect opportunity to start over. But fitting in has never been easy, and between a new town, a new boss and the unexpectedly attractive owner of a rival café, things get off to a rocky start.

Never did free-spirited Beth Summers think she'd still be in Maine, stepping in to run her family's small-town café. However, once Beth commits to something, that's it. Soon, The Yellow House is the hottest spot in town, but Beth's out of energy—and out of ideas for moving forward.

Until Adah Campbell walks into her life. As sparks fly, both chefs have to decide if they are willing to make sacrifices…or if it's too many cooks in the kitchen.

Available now!

carina press

CarinaPress.com

CARKDFTSI1220TR

IF YOU ENJOYED THIS BOOK
WE THINK YOU WILL ALSO LOVE

Carina Adores is home to highly romantic contemporary love stories where LGBTQ+ characters find their happily-ever-afters.

ONE NEW BOOK AVAILABLE EVERY MONTH!

CARADORES1020TR